The
Patron Saints
of
Grocery

A NOVEL

Adam Jonathan Kaat

Inspired Forever Books
Dallas, Texas

The Patron Saints of Grocery: A Novel
Copyright © 2023 Adam Jonathan Kaat

Inspired Forever Books™
"Words with Lasting Impact"
Dallas, Texas
(888) 403-2727
https://inspiredforeverbooks.com

Library of Congress Control Number: 2023909520
Paperback ISBN 13: 978-1-948903-68-4
Printed in the United States of America

Disclaimer: This work is a work of fiction based on true and actual events. Names, characters, businesses, places, events, locales, and any identifying details from incidents have been changed. Any resemblance to actual persons, living or dead, or actual events is purely coincidental.

Denver, CO
adamkaat@gmail.com
Adamkaat.com

To Lindas everywhere. Not the good ones.
You know who you are.

Table of Contents

The First Ninety Days

I

I peeled the collar of an unfamiliar jacket away from my face, and the flat white light of the break room rushed into my eyes. I quickly retreated into the fabric shelter to admire the floral pattern on the inside of the coat while I listened to typical break-room chatter and decided my next move. The room was alive with conversation ranging from silly to serious, subdued to emotionally distraught. It reminded me of those church gatherings I had gone to as a kid where men and women, girls and boys would come together and gossip, grieve their failings, celebrate their wins, and share in the commonalities of misery and destiny. In the break room, laughter peppered the serious talk, and fact blurred with fiction, all glued together by fleeting fifteen-minute breaks or thirty-minute lunches. In the retail world, the earth rotates faster during these brief gaps between work. Time is always rushing to get somewhere. It never stops and always changes. But as I sat there, cocooned in my own embarrassed state, for a moment, I imagined the universe slowing down instead of speeding up while I enjoyed the rhythm at the heart of Dream Grocers.

My amusement was short lived as a slow-burning headache bubbled to the surface, followed by confusion and despair. I didn't know if I was in denial or paralyzed by the weight of the moment, but a burst of intuition told me the first victim would definitely be my reputation. I was sure the whole goddamn store had caught wind of the sordid affair—my coworkers were most likely passing judgment. And they should. I smelled like a moldy gym sock. A bird's nest of damp hair covered the lower part of my face and neck. From the type of fabric against my skin, I knew I was wearing a different shirt, possibly Hawaiian. *Who changed my clothes? Did anyone see my soft, shameful physique?* A fresh sense of anxiety lit the dumpster fire of a situation. But another, more pertinent question loomed over my predicament: *How . . . how did I end up on the couch in the break room?*

I tuned out all the other distractions to hear Neal explaining to Mary that love was a fool's errand. She disagreed, obviously, and reminded him that he was engaged to be married in the fall. Her retort was met with a doubling down, in which he responded that his relationship was the exception to the rule but that love was most definitely a very silly thing. They both laughed at the blatant absurdity of their conversation. I longed to join them, but I was ashamed to reveal that I was awake just yet, so I listened intently—hushed and uncomfortable while everyone continued about their business.

My smartphone sat on my chest under one hand like my blankie had when I was a child. I looked at the display to find ten missed calls and twenty or so unread text messages. I checked the day and time and begged God to relieve me from this nightmare—hoping I would wake up at home on my couch after a long night of whiskey drinking and pandemic-related conversation with my neighbors. Unfortunately, it had been only a few hours since my incident. There was no denying that it *had* happened. I needed to make a decision soon since I was sure everyone in the room was well aware of my transitory circumstance—and they would have questions. I ran through my options, but there really weren't many available.

It wasn't as if I had the choice to pretend I was asleep until everyone left—the place was busy all hours of the day, and I wasn't about to remain on the couch until the store closed. I just desperately wanted and needed to go home. The break room was an unexpectedly cozy nexus filled with chaotic and tranquil tendencies existing simultaneously. People scanned Twitter on their phones or played internet games. Multiple languages crackled and bounced off the otherwise drab walls covered in corporate propaganda like a chaotic marketplace in a much more interesting city than Denver.

My leg, which dangled off the couch, began to go numb as I sat there listening to that tiny place expand outward in every direction, so I tried to rotate slightly, but a sharp, throbbing pain shot through my neck. I chirped just a bit and stopped my movement, but dead silence came over the room—they were all looking at me. They had seen my adjustment. The gig was up, and I was now the center of attention. Rumors were about to be shared, and I would have to answer for my condition.

My soul screamed for me to stop moving, but my brain knew what I needed to do. I swung my other leg down, and I took the jacket off my head to find Mary, Neal, and a few other coworkers I didn't know staring at me.

But within my next panicked breath, the crowd went back to their food or phones or conversations—everyone except Neal and Mary. I could tell both were concerned.

With a mouthful of meatball sandwich, Neal said, "Dude, you were snoring pretty hard there for a second. I would've stopped you, but we agreed it added to the ambience."

I chuckled. "Thanks, I guess." I sat up and glanced at my phone again out of habit, as if more time had passed, but I concluded, as was customary with the laws of the break room, that time was an illusion.

"No problem. You were mumbling toward the end of your nap. Then you just laid there for I don't know how long like a weirdo."

"You knew I was awake?"

Mary rolled her eyes. "Of course we knew. Your body language and breathing changed completely a while ago."

"Damn. I thought I was being discreet. I promise it wasn't anything personal."

"Oh, we didn't think anything of the sort. We knew you might be embarrassed, so we just kept talking about random things."

My cheeks warmed with embarrassment.

Neal chimed in, "Dream about anything fun?"

"Sort of. I was stepping up one of those staircases on a runway toward some private jet."

"Sounds like it might have gotten interesting if you'd stayed asleep," Mary suggested.

"Yeah. Probably," I responded.

"What color was the plane?" Neal asked.

"What does that matter?"

"Just curious. I wanna live vicariously through you. Do you know where you were headed in the dream?"

"Somewhere out west."

"Were you covered with snow?" Neal asked.

I had been wondering when someone was going to say something.

"No. I wasn't covered in snow. I was naked."

"Walking onto a plane? Was it scary? Like, were you nervous?"

"Oddly enough, no. I was completely at peace."

"Anything else you can remember?" Mary asked.

"Well, the flight attendant was naked too. Everyone was."

"Maybe that's why you weren't nervous."

"Good point. But I do remember feeling like this wasn't normal. Like we were the exception to the rule. Then I woke up not really knowing where I was for a moment. But I figured it out pretty damn fast."

Neal's smile disappeared, and he asked, "But was it actually a good dream? It sure didn't sound like it while you muttered away in your sleep. You sounded pissed. Bitter, even."

"Well—"

"You don't have to answer that, homie. I think you have the right to be bitter. It's part of the allure of working at Dream Grocers. It's what bonds us together. You see—"

"What happened out there?!" Mary interrupted.

"Well, I guess that's one way to bring it up," Neal responded and then fell silent and waited for my reply.

"Honestly, I don't know," I said. "It's dim. My memory is going in and out." They looked at me like I was lying, but I was telling the truth.

"Dude. You just sat out in the freezing-cold sleet and snow and probably could have died," Neal said while still eating his sandwich. "We were worried about you. Hell, you're the talk of the store."

"Oh, great. That's just what I need."

Neal laughed, and some bread spilled out.

Mary punched Neal in the shoulder and said, "It's not funny, Neal. Look . . . Daniel, you know the company has resources if you need to talk to someone."

"I'm not suicidal, Mary. I promise. I just don't have a good answer for you. I think the pressure just got to me, ya know?"

Neal nodded in agreement. "Mm-hmm . . . he ain't lyin'."

"Everyone is feeling the strain of the pandemic," Mary said, "but most of us don't sit down in a snowstorm and refuse to move until our cheeks go blue and force people to carry us inside. Poor Billy was in a state of disarray. He is the one who brought you in."

"Shit. I need to talk to him. Is he still here?"

"I think he's gone for the day."

"Damn. Alright. So my cheeks turned blue, like, for real?" I asked.

"Yeah, dude. You almost got hypothermia," Neal replied with a smile.

I

I glanced down at the neon-pink-hibiscus array on my newly attained bright-green Hawaiian shirt, then looked back at Neal as if to ask, *Why?*

Neal shrugged. "It's the only shirt I had in my locker, and I didn't want you to be soaking wet."

"It's so small, though."

"Well, you're an enormous person, and we didn't have any better options."

I couldn't help but sigh and chuckle.

Mary was having none of the jovial conversation. "Forget the goddamn shirt, Daniel. This isn't funny. We were all terrified. We don't need such recklessness with a virus run amok, riots in the streets, and war about to break out at any moment."

"Funny, I think now's the perfect time to be reckless," I responded.

Neal looked at me and shrugged. "He has a point, you know? It's like that old saying . . . have some fun while the city burns. Or something like that. Just look at the man. He is in complete shambles. But that shirt is goddamn spectacular, if I do say so myself."

"Neal! Stop it! Daniel, that's terrible," Mary said.

"I am not saying that anyone should live in a heedless manner," I argued. "It just seems like the right time to let go of your past and be a little looser with those lines we normally stay between. I wonder if that's part of why I sat in the snow. Perhaps I was only trying to lay my burdens at the feet of chance."

Neal intervened. "He is still coming down off the adrenaline, Mary. Don't listen to what he's saying. I heard it's a hell of a high. Daniel is a fiend, a junkie."

"So this begs the question, Why did I wake up on a couch in a tiny vacation shirt instead of in a hospital?"

I said, realizing it was fucked up that they had left me in the break room with only a jacket covering me.

With burgundy cheeks, Mary said, "Todd told us to wait and see if you would just shake it off and there was no need to bring attention to the situation."

A chunk of meatball flew out of Neal's mouth from laughter.

"Yeah, that's the Todd-Monster for you," Neal said after he swallowed the food.

Mary's eyes were beginning to water. "I'm so sorry, Daniel. I wasn't thinking clearly. I just followed the rules and let you down. No one knew what to do. Guess we looked to the wrong person for answers. I am so sorry."

"It's not your fault. It can't be. I'm not entirely sure if Todd has any blame here either. The weight of the situation just got to me. I wasn't ready to be *made* a hero. I'm still not."

Neal's sandwich was finally gone. That classic smile on Neal's face crumbled to an authoritative stare that made me uneasy with its certainty. "I gotta say, if you *were* looking to be a 'hero,' then something is wrong with you. That's what sociopaths do on the internet. That might just be the biggest problem of our age—people searching for unearned love, affection, and fame. No decent person is *looking* to be a hero. They are forced by time, place, and accident to become an agent of salvation."

I was only half listening, lost in thought. "But wait, Todd definitely was in charge, and he told y'all not to take me to the hospital when I might have died?"

"He also mentioned something about attempted suicide and that you wouldn't want to go to a psych ward for the night," Neal responded.

"But I wasn't trying to kill myself," I said.

"We didn't know that, Daniel. But as you know, the store resembles a war zone right now, and no one noticed you until a Linda came in and said that a cashier refused to help her and was sitting on a bench staring off into the clouds. Billy basically had to carry you since you were covered in snow like a man carrying all the troubles of our time. Christian helped Billy bring you up to the break room."

"Jesus, really? A Linda saved me?"

"Yeah. Hell, it might have been the *one* that lost her shit on you earlier," Neal said, and we all began to laugh.

"Damn. I don't know what to do with myself now." I checked my phone, again—so many messages to get to—but my endless and potentially deadly shift had finally come to an end a little while back.

"Oh, shit. That reminds me. Todd said that you should stop by his office if you woke up while we were in here," Neal said.

"How long have I been here?"

"Hours, bro. You were here during my lunch. This is my final break."

"You mean second lunch. I saw the way you scarfed down that sammie," I replied.

"I'm a hungry boy, Daniel. But let's not get distracted with my waistline here. You have been here for ages."

"Shit. Alright, I'll stop by his office before I go home."

"Home? With Todd at the helm? Good luck, homie," Neal said.

"Yeah, you know how he is," Mary replied.

"Is he going to make me work even after something so traumatic?"

The hum of the centralized heating clicked off, and they said in unison, "Isn't that life on the grocery line?" I cringed. I'd heard that phrase so much during my time at Dream Grocers that I wanted to puke. I wasn't even sure what it meant anymore. Or maybe I knew too much and I hated what I had accepted about my life.

I stood up to leave. My feet were soaked. How could there not be a protocol for situations like mine? I should've been wrapped in blankets and given hot cocoa or something, anything. Good god. The fucking lack of compassion and situational awareness was astounding.

I looked over at Mary and Neal. "Thanks, guys."

"Thanks for what?" Neal responded but then paused for a moment. "Ahh, okay. Yeah, no problem, man."

"We are just glad you're alive, Daniel," Mary said as she stood up. "Pandemic be damned." She gave me a big hug.

I leaned back. "I needed that."

"Happy to be the one to give it to you, then."

I'll say it once again: these were my people.

* * *

I walked down toward the manager's office with dread in my heart and a wobble in my step. My first impression of Todd had been that he was discernably arrogant in speech and mannerisms. When I had sat down with him after being hired on, I had thought he was a robot masquerading as a human—with some glitches in the AI. He was jovial to the point where it rang false. And he paired that with glossed-over eyes and an imitation smile. He couldn't sit still and would continually switch which stubby leg he wanted crossed over while he clicked his pen and asked if I was comfortable. He had been sizing me up with every sentence that had stumbled from his mouth.

I knocked on the open doorframe.

Todd looked up from his desk. "Hey, Daniel! Come on in. Take a load off."

Behind him in the corner was our HR manager, Terry, who finished what he was doing and turned around. No smile. Just beady eyes behind wire-rim frames and a budding double chin.

"Hey, Todd. Hey, Terry. The crew in the break room said that you wanted to see me?"

"Yes, yes. We just wanted to check in on you. See how you were doing. You gave us all a mighty scare this afternoon."

"Not enough apparently," I mumbled under my breath.

"What's that?" Terry asked.

"Nothing. I'm just exhausted and ready to go home."

Todd leaned forward, put a hand on his knee, and looked into my eyes with faux integrity. "I totally understand, Daniel. We all have rough days. Hell, this pandemic has taken a toll on all of us. Terry and I just need to go over a few things with you. Then we will see about you getting out of here. How's that sound?"

"Yeah, that's fine."

Todd stood up and shut the door. Terry rolled his chair over and flipped open a spiral notepad. "So, Daniel, what exactly happened?"

"Like when I went outside, or do you want me to start from the beginning of the week?"

"From the beginning," Terry said.

"Okay. Well, it's just been rough, man. I mean, this is my *first* week, after all."

"Really? I swear you've been here a few months."

"Sure as hell feels like it."

"Daniel, if you could refrain from swearing. It's not how we want to present ourselves here at Dream Grocers. But please continue with your story."

I told them everything to the best of my recollection, with a stunning headache in full swing—I was dehydrated and unable to focus. I wasn't sure if I was making sense as my word vomit spilled out onto the floor, but Todd and Terry mopped it up and peppered me with additional questions.

They wanted more detail than I could give them, but I sensed that this was a make-or-break situation where I would be judged, mostly in silence—where my future with the company was not on the line, per se, but whether I could handle the job would be brought into question. I began to feel badgered and abused, and my patience was wearing thin. "Why are you asking so many questions?" I asked. "It really wasn't that big of a deal."

"Well, Daniel," Todd said, "that might be how you see it, but Terry and I are very concerned, and Dream Grocers also has a vested interest in what happened. Many of us were worried about your mental health. Some thought you were suicidal?"

"You thought I wanted to kill myself over some lady yelling at me and being overwhelmed with work?" *Are you even paying attention to what's going on in the store?* "I'm glad you think that I'm so weak that I would kill myself from such petty bullshit. Good god."

"Language! It's not just the one incident. We did some investigating, and it seems your very short time at Dream Grocers has been difficult. There were bouts of drinking and self-loathing. At least that's the word from the people we talked to."

"Who told you these things? How would you investigate something like that and in such a short time?"

"It's nothing personal, Daniel. We are just trying to find the truth. We need it now more than ever. And in order to facilitate transparency, we *have* to follow the rules and make sure you're okay. We must make sure the company is secure in this matter. Do you see what I am saying?"

His tone was sterile—surgical, even—but I understood the rules of "the company." No matter what form it took or what products were sold, once a business reached a certain size, they swallowed nuance like a smuggler swallowed evidence: stem and all, then shit it out, probably in a field somewhere. The proper thing to say in that moment flowed from my mouth. "I get it. You're just doing your job. You don't have to worry. I don't want anything out of the incident. But I'd like to go home, if I could. I'm beyond exhausted."

Todd looked at Terry. They nodded at each other; then Todd turned back around. "Okay. I'll let you go home," Todd replied, "but we can only put you down for a half day because you weren't working the entire time."

"What?! Are you serious?" I responded as I grew enraged.

"Yeah, I'm sorry, Daniel. That's Dream Grocers policy," Todd replied.

Terry nodded in agreement like a bobblehead doll.

"Really? Is it company policy not to call an ambulance when an employee might have a medical emergency?"

Todd's face tightened up. "Now, Daniel. We did what we thought was in your best interest. Billy brought you inside, and you were covered in snow and so gone that you kept rambling on about your life on the grocery line. I have never seen someone so broken, but I didn't think it was a medical emergency. And yes, it was my call to make. I thought it was best that you didn't end up in a loony bin for the night."

"If I can be really honest with you right now, that is fu—"

Todd put his hand up. "Let's refrain. I suggest that we *all* be prudent in the tone we take here. Emotions are running high. Plus, you are still on your ninety-day probation, and we did nothing wrong."

Terry scribbled on his pad furiously.

That short exchange told me everything I needed to know. A wide view of my importance to Todd and to Dream Grocers rang clear. I was being put on notice. The shit thing was that I didn't have any other options at the moment. Hiring freezes had spread across the country during the pandemic. I was right back to when I had left college in 2010. Trapped, controlled, lost, and patently overly dramatic.

I made up my mind right then that I needed to settle into this new game, learn the rules, and see where it went. There was no need to panic or posture—I should just accept my fate. I closed my eyes and said, "Alright. I'm sorry. I didn't mean anything by it. I'm so fried right now." I took a deep breath and asked, "Am I free to go?"

"Yes, that's fine," Todd responded. "And I have you scheduled for tomorrow morning at seven a.m. to make up for the lost hours today. I will see you bright and early."

"See you then."

* * *

The break room was empty. I put on my jacket and backpack, clocked out, and headed down toward the back stairs to avoid more awkward moments with any more coworkers. As I moved down the hallway, Lila popped her soul-igniting green eyes over the top stairs—I hadn't known she was here, and I was sure she had been informed about my mess, my breakdown, my "near-death experience."

Her auburn hair and energy bore truth like the sun peeking over the curvature of the earth—perfect breasts that jettisoned out from the front view of her body to cover part of her tattooed arms. Her hips worked in magnificent diagonal lines inward and outward from a tiny waist that was so, so thin. I'd thought on many occasions that her body was proof of a god, a reason to go on, an hourglass of evolution—a touch of heaven. Once the buzz wore off from her physical beauty, I remembered why I really thought she was so goddamn captivating: her mind. It was sharp and curious. She could swing from geopolitical discussions to freakish knowledge of modernism in early twentieth-century French paintings to a love for dark humor and obscure films. Men my age should not be intimidated by younger women. I was.

And for just a moment, I forgot my worldly troubles when our eyes reconvened in the middle. I could see she was smiling under her mask. I was immediately greeted by brilliant, fatalistic anxiety. My feigned confidence disappeared into her angelic glow. She appeared to carry herself with profound self-possession and a punk rock swagger. Most of my energy was zapped from the day's events, but my gaze was locked until we came to a stop in the middle of the hallway.

"Hi, Lila," I said sheepishly.

"Hi, Daniel. How are you?"

"I'm doing okay. I suppose you heard about what happened with me earlier?"

She laughed. "Heard about it? I was the one who called the management office once I saw you."

"Really? I'm sorry. I didn't mean to make a scene."

She giggled again. "No worries."

"What's your shift today?" I asked.

"I'm on my last break. I close tonight. Are you leaving?"

"Yeah, I think it's best I go home and sleep."

"I agree. I need you to be healthy and happy when you use that phone number I gave you."

She was always reenforcing positivity and avoiding negativity.

"Oh, yeah! I do need to use that, don't I?"

"You really do. There is something special about you, Daniel." She reached out and put her hand on my chest. "I like it when you stand over me too. Those embers inside here are ready to start a fire. It's fucking hot—sexy, even."

18

I

A warm rush of blood filled my face and my pants. My embarrassment magnified my reaction, and my face began to warm. A sudden need to move came in like a wave. She was unbroken by my insecurities. Her flirting was direct and honest and fun.

"Do you know what we are going to do when we hang out, Daniel?"

"Whaa—what's that?" I stammered.

"Get naked."

"Um . . ."

She broke out in laughter. I couldn't tell if she was serious or if this was the best way to deflect the awkwardness of my shell-shocked body language in a sexy, playful way.

"So. Daniel. Let's fucking hang out. Okay?"

"Yeah. Let's."

She touched my arm. "Get some rest, honey. We don't need you dying on the job. Text me."

"Okay. I will," I said and watched her like a teenager staring at a public-pool lifeguard as she walked away.

I didn't know how to quantify my feelings in that moment, even with my years stretching into my midthirties and a myriad of relationships and life experiences coloring my understanding, I was at a loss. One part of me was grateful for a distraction from the turmoil happening all around, if only for a moment. The other gave me pause because of our age differences—and I was a coward. I wanted to take her hand and run for the hills. She gave me the feeling of Pop Rocks going off in my soul, but I was cautious of my emotional endeavors. I had been in love before. It was a dangerous game. What Lila and I had at the beginning was fresh and interesting. Our "relationship" was akin to an AC/DC converter, as it turned me, by force, into something usable. Hell, that whole goddamn place, Dream Grocers, was changing me, probably forever. I was desperate to get laid, too, and part of me wanted it to be only lust, but I didn't think it was that either. I couldn't help but feel like I had tumbled into a confused and enchanted Venus flytrap. I was only a week in—was it really only a week?—and she had already put a fucking spell on me. But I needed to calm down. There was no need to overanalyze. *Just go with the flow,* I told myself. Goddamn hippies—they got me every time. Oh, and I desperately needed rest, as delirium was beginning to set in, and I couldn't tell up from down.

II

The next morning, when I stepped outside with my coffee, the air was cold and damp, which was unusual for Denver. Singular dollops of snow dropped from the sky, here and there, creating a soggy and brisk start to the spring day. I set down my cup on the railing of my three-story walk-up and stretched my arms out to the sky. I was sore from the booze and depleted, hollowed out from Adderall.

The neighbors and I had been drinking and smoking and carrying on every night. It was nice to feel a spark of life in that old apartment complex that I hadn't felt since I'd first moved in long ago. We were getting together for dinner on a regular basis and talking with fervor about all the current issues. Late nights with good people kept my world moving and hopeful.

I took a sip and decided to walk to work that morning and avoid the feeling of being whipped raw by wind and frozen to the bone by the time I arrived. Even if it was cold outside—hell, even if it was snowing—a slow roll through Capitol Hill in Denver, on the way to work, was relaxing and meditative. It gave me an opportunity to listen to good music, smoke a joint, and take in a wide view of my little world. I believed there was an art to waking up slowly, and the city was beautiful during the lockdown, as it was free of rumbling SUVs and angry drivers and that idea that we all *had* to be somewhere. Whether the closing of businesses, shuttering of schools, and stripping of civil liberties was wise or even necessary for this unprecedented blip in world history would be something for historians to debate for the next century, but one thing that wasn't up for discussion was that I enjoyed a nice chance to slow down for a while. It drove some folks mad. Friends of mine had lost lovers and family members to isolation and loneliness. The only thing to do was worry and face our lives head on. I should've been able to make that shift in my life, on my own, but changes like that were hard to come by and took an act of god or government to get most people to stop what they were doing at once, myself included. And I might have been giving credit where it wasn't due. I was captivated by having my giant concrete playground all to myself.

* * *

When I arrived at work, I was greeted by shivering, desperate customers in a parade that wrapped around the side of Dream Grocers like breadlines during the Great Depression. Their eyes followed my movements and burned through any sense of comfort I might have had as I walked past. It was as if I was made to feel like an outsider about my ability to get in the store right away. If only they knew what it was like on the other side of the register. When I reached the front of the line, a Linda and a Dave stared at me with the coolness of sociopaths. I looked off into the distance, as if I didn't notice them, and nodded at the cart attendant watching the front door, then took a deep breath.

"You alright?" he asked.

"Sure," I replied and walked through the doors.

Inside the store, I went through the normal COVID-19 protocol and got my temperature checked. My reading was way low because of the temperature outside. They made me wait for a while before rechecking, which was a daily occurrence. My temperature never got to 98.6 degrees after five minutes of standing and waiting. They let me in anyway. The readings were never consistent or accurate. No one cared. Everyone knew it was just for show. It felt like something people were supposed to do in order to combat the uncertainty, and every day we had more go-nowhere mandates, rules, checklists, and protocols, protocols, protocols, protocols.

Heaters hung from the roof and beamed down rays on my thinning hair and back as the blood came to life inside my fingers and toes, and I marched up the stairs toward the time clock. At the top of the steps, I looked back down on the temperature-check station. With the right eyes, you could almost see bars on the windows and guards standing around the prison yard. Everything had the austerity of wrought iron and cold concrete. Small pleasantries such as heat lamps overhead, the smell of hot coffee, and the enormous selection of products for our consumption were all to trick us into feeling like we were in a free society.

Walking through the rigmarole went beyond annoying formality. It piled on to the anxiety seeping into everything. What made it worse was that we all knew it wasn't helping. When you know something isn't working, it doesn't *actually* improve the situation. It only causes fear and annoyance and division. There aren't many choices in those circumstances, so one must pretend it's better, and that was what I did. I closed my eyes and envisioned the 1990s: the dot-com boom, riding bicycles, Blink-182 on the radio, the Sears catalog bra section in one hand while the other hand was occupied with feeding me all the sodium and sugar one could want. It was beautiful. The masquerade of American life beset upon me, and I swam the comfortable channels again. When I opened my eyes, the temperature-check station, the bars on the walls, and the cold steel barrel of a cocked pistol pressed to my head were gone. And I intended to keep it that way.

The time clock read 7:03 a.m. I was late but not enough to have my attendance dinged. After five minutes, you were considered *tardy*. If you were late enough, it added up to a strike, and strikes combined into reprimands, and reprimands led to meetings, and meetings to conferences, and finally you might get fired if you didn't shape up. Of course, that wasn't the only way you might lose your job. During my brief time at Dream Grocers, I'd already felt like I was on the edge of getting fired. Occasionally, they threw out the verbal chastising just to keep you on your toes and remind you of your place in the food chain.

Downstairs, Todd was waiting for me at the front-end manager's station. His impish legs were crossed as he leaned against the desk and tapped his fingers, observing the early-morning crowd of patrons.

He adjusted his thick-rimmed glasses and said, "Good morning, Daniel. How are you feeling today?"

"Like it's my bar mitzvah," I said.

"Are you Jewish?" he replied.

"No," I responded.

"Then how would you know how that feels?"

"I was trying to joke around. Swing and a missss."

"Oh . . . I see. Well, why don't you clock in, and I'll meet you down here."

"Way ahead of you, boss. I'm ready to go."

"Great. Punctuality is key to success here. I'm not going to have you on the front end today. I want to see if we can find something less stressful for you."

"Sounds good to this Smurf."

"What?"

"Never mind," I said, not sure why he didn't understand. Then I remembered that I was high and I should be more careful with my words. I may have hit the pinner joint one too many times walking through the park, but it had been so pleasant out. Every great walk deserves a couple of hefty drags of good weed on a chilly spring day.

His smug, early-morning energy summoned a demon in me, subdued only by coffee and marijuana. "Hey, boss . . ."

"Yes, Daniel."

"Can I grab a quick cup of joe before we do whatever it is that we are going to do?"

"Yes, but please hurry."

I lumbered toward the coffee stand on the other side of the registers, and I looked out at the expanse of linoleum tile and high-end packaged goods bathed in track lighting. Most mornings called for stimulants, and this day was no exception.

"Billy!" I yelled a bit too loud, considering the hour of the day. He looked at me and smiled like he had in our final interaction yesterday. I carried on. "My savior. My knight in shining armor. How are you? I didn't know you worked at the coffee bar. I thought you were just carts and cashiering."

"I'm a jack of all trades, so they say. Or as I like to call it . . . I'm wherever they want me . . . the whipping boy."

"Hey, it's good to be *something*, anything, ya know."

"I guess. I mean that's what I thought at first. But now, eh, I'm thinking it's not really worth the extra fifty cents an hour to be jerked around all the time."

"Damn, dude. So I'm a little short on rent this month. Think you could help me out with that extra coin you have been storing away?"

He laughed. "Fuck off."

The banter put me at ease. "Well, shit. I'm still happy to see you, dude."

"Happy to see you too, man. Especially after yesterday."

"Yeah. I'm so sorry about that. I was having a rough go of it after that one lady flipped out on me. Thank you for helping get me inside. You're a good dude."

"I know you would've done the same for me. I was just worried you might freeze to death or some shit."

II

"That's what Neal and Mary said yesterday. I had no idea how long I was sitting there. It was just supposed to be a fifteen-minute break."

Billy laughed. "Nah, man. It was way longer than that. Anyway, I'm glad you are okay. What can I get for you?"

"Thanks, man. I'll take a mocha."

"Oh, really? I didn't take you for a 'basic bitch drink' kind of guy," he said as he began to pour and steam the milk.

"Shit . . . I'm as basic as they come."

Without breaking from his task, Billy leaned in and squinted. "Well, now that I take a closer look, I see what you are saying."

The click-clacking and *sssst* of steam muffled his words, so I had to talk over the noise. "Glad we are on the same page now, asshole."

We both laughed. He continued his work. I had a moment to watch him work. I wanted to cry. I didn't deserve such nice people in my life.

After a short while, he handed me the finished product and said, "Have a good shift."

I walked back in a better mood. Banter and coffee made the world a more tolerable game of red rover.

When I returned, I saw that Todd wasn't happy. He had been made to wait, and that absolutely would not fly.

He leaned in close to my face and asked, "What does the mask you're wearing say?"

"Mask? What—oh, yeah . . . I almost forgot about it. I designed it myself. It says, 'Life on the Grocery Line.'"

"What is it supposed to mean? Wait . . . that's the gibberish you were saying when we brought you upstairs

27

yesterday. I think that's bad luck to bring back into the store."

"I thought it was a clever way to show solidarity with grocery-store workers. You know, like, we are putting our lives on the line during this pandemic."

"I don't think you're in any additional danger."

"You don't? I mean, I don't either, really, but are you supposed to say that as a manager?"

"Well, I guess not. We will . . . let's just pretend I never said it."

"Sure thing, boss," I said with a nearly audible eye roll.

"But you know that you can't have print masks on in the store. No slogans of any kind."

"Oh, sorry. I had no idea. When did that start?"

"When the protests and riots began," Todd responded.

"When did *they* start?" I replied.

"Who knows. Enough small talk here. Please just take this one." Todd handed me a light-blue medical-looking mask. "It was issued by Dream Grocers and won't cause any problems."

I kept my mind open during this third interaction with Todd to see if anything would change, but he was a company man through and through, like a caricature out of a goddamn fifties' TV show. Shined shoes. Pressed slacks. Polo shirt tucked in. He walked about like he owned the store. I had been told that if you blasphemed against the company, there would be hell to pay. I didn't fault him for taking pride in his work, but our short interactions and his demeanor combined made me feel like I was being led from behind by a red-hot blade—it wasn't inspiration; it was pressure, and not the kind one might use to succeed, such as putting responsibilities on me and expecting me to rise to the occasion. No. It was more of an "I'm coming for you," conspiratorial attitude that made me unsure if he was friend or foe. It made me want to go home and crawl back into bed.

Much of my adult life, I believed there was something repulsive about people who sold their entire identity to a corporation that was fundamentally indifferent to their existence. Even the thought of my path taking a turn toward that vacant reality made me long to find a shotgun and a quiet meadow to end it all. The sadness and weight, unbearable. And when I encountered those people, I thought our species was doomed. I appreciated the go-getter mentality, but those people should go start a company, not wallow in the shadows of an unknowable giant.

"Alright. Are you ready?" Todd asked.

"Yes sir."

He paused to look at me for a moment, likely to get a read on the sarcasm, but moved on quickly. "Okay. Let's go."

* * *

As I followed Todd, I quickly realized he was a junkie for power; the confidence with which he carried himself—company man or not—was admirable. He was more peacock than human, with his sense of accomplishment spread bright and proud as he strolled through the store. He was the king of his own castle as he asked a woman if she needed help with anything. She responded that she was looking for the Dominican radishes. He put his hand on his chin as if he was thinking, then waved down the first employee in the produce section. A young hippie with cutoff jeans, midback-length hair, and a gold tooth on his left incisor came over with a big smile.

A commander in the trenches of his own personal Vietnam, Todd announced, "We'll work with Jake here to find your product." Todd spoke with the overassured tone of a man who clearly had just learned Jake's name. "Did we get that shipment of Dominican radishes in yet?"

Jake's face scrunched with confusion. "Dominican radishes? I've never heard of them, but the regular radishes and rutabagas are over here."

The woman was aghast as she looked at Todd, then at me, then back at Todd again. "Those are all trash. Look, I'm trying to support the third world, and all you have is local bullshit. Dream Grocers has really let me and the people of Dominica down."

I stared a moment in shock and thought, *This must be parody, right? She's kidding.* But no. I was not mistaken. This was not a drill or a prank. We were letting the people of "Dominica" down.

"I'm sorry; I have never heard of them," Jake responded.

"I definitely bought them in the past," the woman fired back.

"I have too," Todd agreed.

Jake became flustered. "Umm. Well, maybe it's a newer product or something? I mean, I have worked here for five years, but I guess I can look in the back or something."

"Thanks, Jake. Let's make sure we take care of this wonderful woman. What was your name again?"

"Linda," she responded.

"Jake, let's make sure you take care of Linda. Okay? Thanks."

"Sure. I'll check in the back and talk to our department manager," Jake replied.

"Please hurry. I have other things to do, and I don't want to be here all day," Linda said.

"Of course. I'll be back."

Jake, Todd, and I walked toward the back room. When the doors closed. Jake said, "Sir. I know we don't have that type of radish. Dominica isn't even a goddamn cou—"

"Jake. You know what we say about scenarios that feel overwhelming," Todd scolded.

A giant, pulsating vein emerged from the side of Jake's head, and his hands started to tremble. "Yeah. I do."

"What do we say?"

"Pressure is privilege. But we really don't have that product."

"I'm going to leave you to make the best decision here. I need you to step up as a leader."

"Okaaay?"

"Awesome. Let me know how it turns out."

Jake walked away, and Todd turned to me. "Daniel, I hope you learned a valuable lesson from what just happened with me and Jake."

"Umm . . . I might have missed it. Can you tell me?"

"That's disappointing. There was much wisdom to be gained in that moment. If you want to get anywhere in this company, then you will need to learn to pay attention to details. I'm not going to tell you what to take from that. You will have to think about it yourself, and I hope you come up with something of value."

"Sure. I'll think about it," I said with apathy on bright display.

"That's all I ask. Now, have you ever done a cardboard bale?"

"Not in a long, long time."

"Sounds great. The wire is behind the baler. I'll be back in a bit, and then we can move on to the next task."

Todd walked away.

I stared at a massive metal box with a giant hydraulic cylinder for compressing cardboard inside. I looked down two separate hallways and peeked in the meat cooler and seafood area to see if anyone was available to guide me on this adventure, but not a soul was found near that tiny receiving dock. Pallets stacked with different nonperishables had been shoved into every corner of the room. I wondered how they could get all that shit through those doors. Three dock bays for semi-truck trailers lined one side of the room, and a janky desk covered in papers was placed at the other end. Two electric pallet jacks sat in the corner, ready to move this world around like hands in a giant chess game. One gate was occupied with a truck for what looked like extra storage. Cooler and freezer doors faced the dock. I looked back at the compactor, still baffled and annoyed that I had been left to figure it out by myself.

I made a couple of laps around the compactor, then decided I needed a wide view of the scene. My memories of another stint in retail were coming back to me. A voice that resembled the starting of a Plymouth Barracuda from the seventies crawled out of the silence from behind me and said, "Need a hand?"

He startled me, but I turned around slowly to show I was in control. I wanted to hug him, as I was so relieved someone was here and willing to help. Before me stood a man with a medium build covered in biker tattoos. He had amber eyes, chestnut skin, and shocks of gray running through his black hair. Under one eye a small tattoo said, "Let there be light."

"Well, Todd just saddled me with a task that seems relatively dangerous and that I haven't done in years."

"Yeah. He does that. Did he tell you that 'pressure is privilege' bullshit too?"

"Yeah. He laid it on thick."

He rolled his eyes. "Yeah, man. Todd is a monster. But that's what makes him good at this . . . this corporate-climbing shit. But he also makes people miserable around him."

"Is this your department?" I asked.

"Yup. I run the dock here. I receive the load every morning."

I stared for a moment, then said, "Sounds aggressive."

"It is, my brother, but someone's gotta do it."

"You ain't lyin'," I responded with a smile.

"What's your name? I'm Ozzy, but you can call me Oz."

"I'm Daniel. Nice to meet you, man. But, hey, I have a question for you . . ."

"Go for it."

"How old is Todd?"

"Not sure. Maybe early forties. Why?"

"Well, is he really that good at this corporate-climbing shit if he is middle management in his forties?"

Ozzy laughed. "Well, it seems like there is plenty of upside for him. There are regional managers and other folks higher up the chain. And he knows how to suck up to the man. Forty-something is still pretty young when you think about it. Hell, I'm a young buck at forty-four."

Regret swallowed me whole, and I remembered that I was nearing the big four zero myself in a couple of years. "Point goes to Oz. I'm an asshole." I started backtracking. "I wasn't implying that you were old or anything like that."

"Nah, dude. You aren't wrong, but you *are* an asshole. Both things can be true at once." He tilted his head forward and smiled as if to double-check I knew he wasn't serious. "I feel old as fuck working in receiving at a grocery store. But I've been doing this for so long that I might as well keep going and show new assholes how things work around here. Someone has to show them the way. And it keeps me in shape. Keeps me moving. I need to stay mobile, limber, and strong so I can do what I love."

"And what's that?" I asked.

"I'm a professional wrestler."

"No shit?!"

"Yes sir. I'm in a duo, and it's a goddamn blast."

"Can I see you perform sometime?"

"Of course, but the pandemic has all but shut it down for now, though."

"Ah, I keep forgetting about that thing—that pandemic thing . . . how about when it's all said and done? After we bring out the dead? Can I come watch the wrestling then?"

He smiled. "I like the dark humor too. I expect to see you there."

Every conversation I found myself in with other Dream Grocer employees was funny, casual, silly, dirty, or interesting, and maybe that helped shelter us from the woes of life outside. I loved that. I longed to feel normal again. And maybe I needed to embrace the absurd existence we were living through during the time of COVID-19. Everyone was on the same level, suffering with a smile, and I was beyond comfortable. I was finally at home. I had been there for only a short time, but it seemed right.

"You ready to get this thing done?" Ozzy asked.

"Yup."

"Word. Now, grab the baling wire on the back side of the box."

"Great."

"Alright, now grab the blue pallet over there, and lay it in front of the compactor."

"Like this?"

"Yes. Now, since it's already compacted down, we can just open the door." He opened the door on the compactor to reveal the mangled cardboard guts inside. "Push those wires through the bottom of the pack."

"Done."

"Good. Now go to the back, and pull the wire up, and push it to the front."

"Alrighty."

While I was behind the machine, a female voice chimed in, "Whatcha doing, Ozzzz?"

"Teaching the new guy how to do my job so I don't have to."

"Smart man. Hi, new guy!"

"Hi, Lila!" I replied.

"New guy? That's Daniel. He isn't new, Oz?"

"He is new to me." Ozzy shrugged.

"That's fair."

I walked out from behind the machine to greet her, and I was met with a hug.

"Hey, buddy!" she said.

My hands rested on the small of her back for just a second, but I must have looked like the happiest man on earth because when I glanced at Ozzy, he was laughing like a man who had known that twitterpated madness older men feel when they have escaped their fading shadow for just a moment. "She does that to all of us, man."

"Not to *all* of you, Oz. Daniel's special."

"Oh, is he?"

"Yes. Yes, very."

"Good. He seems *special*."

"Asshole," I fired back.

"Give him a break," Lila insisted. "He went through quite an ordeal yesterday."

Ozzy looked intrigued. "What happened . . . oh shit! Wait! Are you the guy who tried to kill himself with snow in front of the Lindas?"

"I wasn't trying to commit suicide," I replied, annoyed that I kept getting the same responses, but I understood why everyone said the same thing.

"Shit, why not? I mean, I would if I was a cashier right now. You're taking it right on the chin from all those Lindas and Daves. God bless you. I'm so glad I can hide back here in the shadows and receive the loads."

"Wait, so you don't have to deal with the hordes of people? Lucky bastard."

"Well, I help out because we are short staffed all the time. So I still get my fill of nightmare Lindas and dumbass Daves. I just can come back here and zone out for a bit. It's nice," he said as he leaned against the tall desk.

"Sounds like a dream. How do I get back here?"

"There are openings from time to time, man. You just gotta make good connections. I'll keep you in mind for the next gig."

"Thanks. Say . . . do you all practice wrestling moves back here? Pile drivers? Choke slams?"

"No, Daniel. I don't fuck around with that stuff. It's very serious."

"Shit. I'm sorry, man. I didn't mean to step—"

Ozzy put his hand on my shoulder, looked off into a distant corner, and said, "If I could, I would, brother . . . now, back to the cardboard bale."

"Oh, yeah. What do I do next?"

"Now that the wires have been pushed through, you match up the lines with the loop and tie them together."

Lila helped. "Okay. Done," I said.

"Alright. Everyone, back away. I have to release the package."

Ozzy pressed a button, and the hydraulic shaft began to move up. The wires tightened as they dug into the compacted cardboard. Underneath, the deck raised and tilted the giant mass forward, then slammed it down onto the pallet with a thunderous crash.

"There ya go, my man," Ozzy said. "That's it. I'll grab the pallet jack and move this thing over to the corner. Thanks for the help."

"No, thank *you* for the help."

"Anytime."

"But I have one more question for you."

"What's that?"

"What is your wrestling name?"

A light found only in the hottest of suns beamed from his eyes. "Well, that's a long story—"

Todd's meatball-shaped head popped in from the side door, and he pointed to the cardboard bale. "Oh, well, lookee there! Great job. I knew you could do it."

"Well, Oz and Lila helped me."

His mood changed instantly. "Disappointed Todd" emerged. I imagined the Todd-Monster had many sides and no love in his life. Poor Todd.

"Okay. Well, I'm sure there will be other opportunities."

"Thank god," I said.

Everyone laughed except Todd, who pretended not to hear my remark.

I think we should keep you back here for a while. Oz, are you okay with that?"

"Umm . . . I mean . . . yeah. He seems cool."

"Thanks. We don't want him to have another *incident*."

"Ahh. That's true. Do you need a break, Daniel?" Ozzy asked.

I shrugged. "I just got here, but sure."

"Good," Ozzy said, "because I gotta go take a shit."

"Thanks for letting everyone know that, Oz," Todd said.

"Todd, you told us to be honest with each other here at Dream Grocers."

"Just go, Oz."

II

Ozzy walked down the hallway toward his transcendence.

Todd looked at Lila and me for a short moment, then said, "I'll be up in my office if you need anything." He left without waiting for any reply.

I was left all alone with the lovely Miss Lila. My heart started to pound loud enough to drown out the hum of the industrial-size cooling fans they used to help circulate the air on the dock. I waited for her to speak.

"Guess it's just you and me now, huh?" she asked.

Before I had a chance to reply, she pulled down our masks and came for a wet, sexy kiss that soldered our forms together. I leaned in for as long as I could. I perched my hands on her perfect hips. A static blanket pulled up all the hair on my body—I felt young and half-terrified, poking through my jeans.

When she finally pulled away, I asked, "Where did that come from?"

"Ha. I have been wanting to do that to you since the moment we met."

"Really?"

"Really."

"Can I ask you something, Lila?"

"Of course."

"What magical chemicals in the universe concocted such a wonderful and interesting goddess?"

"Daniel, you're silly. How long have you been waiting to say that goofball poetry?"

"How long have I worked here again? That long."

"I'm just a normal woman in my midtwenties who loves current events and slightly outrageous sexual encounters with balding men of a certain age."

"Am I wrong to assume that I fall into this category?" I asked.

"You're not wrong."

"Are you sex crazed?" I asked. Trying to joke with her.

"Kinda. Sure. Why?"

"I just get that vibe. I'm not complaining or anything," I said and put my hands up.

"Am I sensing judgment coming from you?" she asked.

"Oh, god, no! I'm sorry. I tend not to think before I speak when I'm around women I find attractive. I think you're fantastic, and I would never disparage your sexual proclivities."

"You might once I break out the handcuffs."

"Oh my."

"Am I being too forward?"

"No. I mean, with the right-colored glasses, yes, and it's a good thing—I need a woman that's up front with me. One who is honest and open. I like how optimistic you are. You ooze affection and prowess. Why *are* you so optimistic?"

"More flattery, Daniel. Oh, please. Just stop." She touched my arm. "Now, is there any reason not to look at the bright side in this weird and fascinating world around us?" she responded.

"Well, I don't know if you noticed we are in the middle of a pandemic."

"Right. And that didn't stop us from kissing."

"I guess you have a point there."

Lila laughed. "How am I the youngest one here? I feel like you are stuck as a teenager."

"Daaamn! Low blow. But you're right. I never really had to grow up. That's the story of my generation."

"Don't fool yourself. It's the story of mine too."

Ozzy walked up with a blissful look on his face. "What are you two doing? I thought you were going to break, homie?"

"Sorry. We got caught up talking."

"All good, man. I couldn't give a shit what you do in between when we need to work. Just go take your break. Sit down. Eat some pizza. Just make sure to *always* take your goddamn fifteens."

"I will."

"What should *you* be doing right now?" I asked Lila as we walked up the concrete stairs toward the break room.

"I should probably be out on the floor," she said with a giggle. "But I don't really know how to take this job seriously. It's weird. Something about the 'pressure is privilege' bullshit they try to push that makes me want to get high on lunch."

"So you don't think there is anything to that, huh?"

"Yes and no. It's true that diamonds are made by pressure and heat, but in the world of employment, more elements are needed—and one big thing is missing from this job that could turn it into a diamond."

"What's that?"

"Carbon in the form of currency, skrilla, money, money, moonaaay. Whatever you call it, they don't give us enough to live on. The powers that be need to inject a decent paycheck into this pressure situation, and shit might be taken more seriously."

"I don't know. It seems like marginally hard work—I mean, besides the pandemic stuff going on. That made everything worse, but I'm not sure that deserves a huge paycheck."

"You might be right, but you'll get 'marginal' effort from everyone, then."

"So wise and fair. How do you do it, Lila?"

"It's hippie magic . . . alright, I gotta go check the floor. Enjoy your break."

Lila leaned in, then pulled away and fluttered her eyes as she turned to go.

III

I cradled my phone without purpose. I stared into the abyss it provided while an envelope of doom, how-to videos, and performative outrage formed around me and time drifted past. I felt rudderless, like a man who didn't know what to do with his hands in a family photograph, as I sat in the break room that had sprawled out into the hallway for social distancing. There I was, in the depths of a fool's errand, a last will and testament to letting it all go in your thirties. I started to think about the book I was *always* supposed to be writing. The one I started years ago that I perceived as fuzzy, distant, useless, and tragic, like moths burning in a lampshade. It was the same one I had talked about with my friends and family for so long that the words had lost all meaning. My heart told me to open the notes app on my "smart" device and write something, anything. Maybe I should write a tragic tale of love and consequence. My mind drifted to the chaos of a world wrapped up in a pandemic. I glanced at my social media to check on Frankie. He was fine—which helped ease my troubles. But the Twitter world was abuzz about a potential vaccine. Words like *disinformation* and *misinformation* were being thrown around with frightening recklessness, and it was nearly impossible to decipher fact from fiction. I headed back to the notes on my phone that would lead to the next Great American Novel, but my break time was up.

I decided it would be best to see what Todd wanted me to do next. I walked down the hallway to see if he was in his office. His door was open. I stepped inside to find him staring at a security camera feed on his computer screen. He was undeterred by my presence. "These little shits," he mumbled.

"Hey, Todd, do you want me to stay at the dock and help Oz, or do you want me to head back up front?"

"Just do whatever," he responded.

"Umm . . . can I go home?"

"What? Of course not, unless it's time for you to go." He was hooked on whatever he was watching on the screen.

"I guess I'll just check with Oz and Alejandro to see who needs my help."

"Alejandro quit," Todd responded.

"Wait . . . what? He quit?" I said in a rushed exhale of sadness and surprise.

"Yeah. He put in his two weeks about two weeks ago. Today should be his last day." Todd hadn't looked at me yet.

"Damn. Alright. I guess I'll just figure it out."

"Sorry to be the bearer of bad news. People quit all the time here."

"Not surprised," I said without thinking.

My comment got his attention, and he looked up. "What are you saying?"

"I . . . I . . . I didn't mean anything by it. This job is an in-between job for most, right?"

"Sure. I could see that, but it's all about perspective. I never looked at it that way. I found this avenue, and I climbed to the top."

"Are you really at the top, though?"

With a huff, he said, "The top is relative."

"I guess so," I replied.

Todd turned back to the security footage on his computer and said, "Alright, go figure out your situation, and I'll check in with you later. I have to see what is going on here."

I'd rather not endure the waves of rabid Lindas and Daves at the front, but I felt I had an obligation to Alejandro to go up and see if they needed help.

I looked down the hallway lined with announcements on corkboards—some reminded me that I needed to purchase work shoes from dreamgrocers.com. Others told me all forms of harassment would not be tolerated and should be reported to HR immediately. Near the end of the corridor hung frames with faded paper inside, reminiscent of a bygone era in the store when they would celebrate the hard work of one employee a month. I examined the tattered pages encased in plastic. Alejandro and his enormous smile were the last on the wall.

Around the corner I witnessed a slow-burning fire drill with lines backed up into the middle of the store. It was a crowd that never ended, full of every cross section of affluent life. There were Lindas, Daves, and Normans at every turn. I walked down to the floor. As I passed where the temperature-check station used to be, I smiled at Neal and Christian, who ignored the long lines as they laughed at something ridiculous on one of their phones.

"What up, dude," Neal said. Christian nodded. I gave a peace sign and wove through the carnival-ride lines.

The faces of people were scrunched and miserable, with their masks burning their humanity to ashes with anonymity. I saw only partial expressions—most of which conveyed a deep lack of satisfaction with their state of affairs. Some people elected to wear cloth masks or bandannas, which we'd learned quickly were worthless and offered no protection; others wore N95s or gas masks. Every person had a different reaction, and I understood them just a little from that small decision. I knew my face usually looked the same when I moved in public spaces. I also carried a scowl everywhere I went. Breathing was difficult, and we all had a feeling about the masks' efficacy. Not seeing the smiles and frowns on our fellow human beings hurt in a way I couldn't have imagined before all the madness had gone down.

Even in the early days of the pandemic, I could see that some people would never take them off. They would never be free. Maybe they never wanted to be in the first place, and it was their way of getting the loneliness they desired. The pandemic gave license for shitty people to be outright assholes to others at their leisure. Those desperate and empty souls felt they had the right to tell people what to do with their bodies. It went the same for those who thought the pandemic was a planned-out attack on the populace—an exercise in control and manipulation. I tended to lean toward the latter strain of thought more every day, like you might expect when

III

everyone, from politicians to wild-eyed Lindas, was taking advantage of an unseen circumstance. We were in a
clusterfuck of a situation, and I didn't see the end. The
worst in people festered like a wound open to the world.

While I worked in the store, I got the sense that I
didn't need to fall into either category of people. I could
think critically and logically and still keep my dignity.
Hold my own opinions and encourage others to do the
same. Suffering was a choice. There wasn't a necessity
to acknowledge the masks in my world. And ignoring
their presence didn't give credence to pro- or antimask
people. But a decision to dissolve the face coverings and
look past the isolation would keep me sane. I needed to
plug back into smiles and laughing and thriving.

I stepped in between lines and scanned the crowd,
where I found a fit gentleman with salt-and-pepper hair
wearing a Patagonia fleece and Nike running shorts
and shoes. He was standing next to a woman with
short brown hair pulled up in a ponytail, and quite
literally their outfits were matching—except her fleece
and shorts were pink. She remained still as he bounced
slightly, and they chatted away with each other like any
good couple should. In their hands were postrunning
snacks like Bobo's bars and electrolyte water. I leered for
a moment—concentrating on their faces. If they saw me,
I would look like a kind of creep, but that was the price
I was willing to pay.

In the grocery world, everyone was Linda and Dave
first until proven innocent. I wasn't proud that I ste-
reotyped people, but it was part of the deal when the
majority of your customers were either indifferent or
profoundly upset at your existence. But that was on me.

Not them. There was a rule of law in this country, and you should be innocent until proven guilty.

With that in mind, I couldn't say those people were rude or full of malfeasance. They just wanted a snack after a nice 5K. Maybe they would go home, make love, and then volunteer at a local homeless shelter. All I knew was that I couldn't see their faces. I wanted to see their goddamn smiles or scowls. I *needed* to see them. I closed my eyes and took a deep breath. Then another. Then one more. I must've looked so strange just standing there with my eyes closed as I meditated on the moment.

I opened my eyes and looked over at the couple, who, by now, had put their food on the conveyor belt of a register. To my pleasant surprise, my momentary vision board found absolution, and their masks were gone—at least the ones that were mandated by the store. If they hid their true selves from the world, I couldn't have known. *Did they take them off?* They didn't look like rule breakers. I scanned the area. Now, there wasn't a soul wearing a mask. I glanced at the reflection of a cooler full of organic energy drinks—mine was gone too. I put my fingers to my mouth and still felt the fabric against my hand but not against my face. I swung back to the reflection. It was nowhere to be found. How the hell . . .

The couple was standing at the register, smiling, laughing. They looked normal. Like the *old* "normal."

"Excuse me. I need to get past," an elderly woman said to me as she stood with her cart next to my left side.

"Oh, sorry, ma'am."

"Please move," she said again.

"Oh, okay." I looked around. She had plenty of room to maneuver anywhere she pleased. I was in no way blocking her path, but nonetheless I stepped over, and she strolled past. I smiled as I imagined her stretching her tongue up and out like she was trying to lick peanut butter off the tip of her nose. That satisfied me, and I headed toward the head cashier's desk.

* * *

Alejandro and Mike talked casually at the corner office that doubled as a register.

I leaned over and asked, "Does anyone here care about the lines at the front?"

"Oh, we care, Daniel," Alejandro said with a mischievous smile.

I waved him away with my hand. "Psssh . . . I know it doesn't matter to you, dude. You are out of here."

"Exactly. I hope one day that you know this feeling. The feeling of complete and utter relief."

"Jesus. I didn't think it was that bad."

"Really?"

"No, I totally get it. I'm just gonna miss you."

"You're a good guy, Daniel. Just don't let this place take your soul."

"Well, before it takes my soul, I gotta ask—do you need me to do anything up here?"

"Of course we could use you."

"Okay. I'm game. But I warn you—I may not be long for this world."

"Daniel, don't do it. We love you. We *need* you."

"Oh no, I'll be here. I might move departments. I'm making a name for myself everywhere I go."

Alejandro grabbed each of my cheeks with a pinch. "It's because of this adorable face."

"Ouch. That hurts, asshole."

"Sorry. It's just so pinchable."

When he let go, I rubbed my sore face and smiled. "Jerk."

"It's only a defense mechanism, I promise. This place brings out the sass in me."

"Me too," Mike said as he counted money. "Shit! I forgot the number because I was listening to you two fools."

"It was definitely four hundred and thirty-four. Trust me," I said.

Mike didn't respond and began counting again.

Alejandro stepped closer to Mike. "Six, eight, twenty-two . . . wait, five, four, thirty-three—"

"Goddamnit! Stop! I need to get this done."

"You never *need* to get anything done. This is all make believe, Mike," said Alejandro.

"Says the guy who is done working here," I responded.

"Excuse me." I looked over, and it was the Linda from my earlier encounter. "I have been standing here for a while now, and none of you even bothered to ask me if I could use some help."

Alejandro immediately walked off and whispered, "She just walked up, dude," as he passed. Mike was still counting money.

"I can help you, ma'am," I said.

"Oh, not you! You were so rude earlier."

I looked at her for a moment. "I'm sorry, ma'am. I didn't mean to be ru—"

"Well, you were."

"And I am sorry for that. Can I point you in the right direction for what you need?"

"I guess. Just tell me where the canned sardines are."

"Of course. They are on aisle sixteen."

She said nothing and walked away.

Mike stared at me. "Those aren't on sixteen."

I smiled.

He shrugged. "Hey, buddy, what do you say to jumping on a register?"

"Whatever you need, boss."

"I'm gonna send you to give a break to Christian."

"Damn. I don't get to work with him?"

"I'll put him on express after he gets back from break too. That okay?"

"You're the sweetest."

"I know. But, hey, are you feeling alright? Yesterday got pretty weird after the crazy lady."

"Yeah, dude. I'm fine. I just drink to get through the hard times."

"Like right now? Like, you are drunk right now?!" Mike replied, startled.

"Nah. Not now," I said with a wink.

The lines were unrelenting and stretched deep into the store. But I was ready for whatever may come.

* * *

"So you didn't kill yourself?" Christian asked.

"Not sure if we should joke about suicide, homie."

"Maybe, but I am a fan of dark humor. Besides, how else are we supposed to deal with this bullshit?"

"That's fair. But to answer your question: no, I didn't. I was just having a tough day."

"A rough go of it is getting snippy with a customer. Letting go of this earthly life in the middle of a shift is a different story."

"It must not have been that bad. Todd told them not to call for an ambulance."

"Todd's an asshole."

"I won't argue with you about that. I'm here to give you a break," I said as I raised my hand and waved the next customer over.

"Sweet. I'll be back," replied Christian.

* * *

My first customer was a small child. Maybe seven years old. He handed me a half-eaten all-natural fruit bar with a wrapper that was sticky to the touch. The remnants of his plunder were smeared across his jovial face. I peeled back the end of the wrapper and scanned it.

"Alright, little man. That'll be two dollars and fifty cents."

"Grandma!" he screamed out into the ether.

"Yes, honey. Hold on."

I looked toward the voice. It was that old woman from my previous two interactions. Her medium-length Armani black dress made her look like she had just attended a funeral. She was incredibly slow to move, and she winced in pain with the smallest of adjustments.

III

I examined her closely, and now that I had a chance to give her my full attention, I realized her eyes carried a thousand disappointments with the occasional joy that was easily forgotten. Her slumped, candle-like posture told a story of osteoporosis or a couple of decades of wine and benzos—or maybe she had flown too close to the sun as she'd tried to reach that pedestal she had been promised from previous generations. It was hard to say, because all the cracks caused by the annoyance of our previous run-ins were filled with pity.

"Oh, hello, ma'am. Did you find the sardines alright?"

"In fact, I did not! You sent me on a wild-goose chase. That was the bread aisle."

Some may have judged me or called me cruel, but at the sound of her plight, my soul began to smile. "I'm so sorry. I'm pretty new here and still getting the lay of the store."

"It was the bread aisle. And you didn't have them."

"Again, very sorry."

She began to unload her cartful of groceries. I looked at the sign that said "Fifteen or fewer items" but ignored the rules. I had probably put this woman through enough. Her hands were full of liver spots, and a catheter flowed up her arm. She seemed to be struggling. "Ma'am, did you need help?"

"Oh, so now you want to help me?"

I didn't respond but pointed at the basket.

"Yes, I could use your help," she relented.

I started to unload her groceries when I heard "Thank you," followed by a squeeze of my arm. She said, "I *was* a bit of an asshole this whole time. Wasn't I?"

"Hey, I know how it is. Life . . . ya know?"

"It's rough sometimes. Thanks again."

"Glad to help," I replied to a woman who suddenly resembled a grandma more than a Linda. My loathing waned.

The boy ate his snack, and his grandma remained uncomfortably but patiently behind.

"So besides a trip to the grocery store, do you two have anything fun planned for today?" I asked.

"There isn't much to do these days with the pandemic, so we will probably just head home."

"That's fair. At least there is the internet to keep everyone entertained."

"Yeah, that only goes so far with this little one. He has so much energy."

"I was the same way when I was a kid. We lived in Maine, and I would make forts with friends and play make believe for entire days. Not sure how I would handle something like a pandemic."

"Hopefully, doing those exact things," she said.

"That's a good point."

"A child accepts the here and now much better than us jaded adults. I worry about how they put those masks on two-year-olds, though. But that's a different conversation for another day. I've held up your line long enough."

I smiled, half-hoping she'd stay awhile, then asked, "Would you like your receipt with you or in the bag?"

"In the bag."

"Alright. Have a great day."

"You too."

* * *

A few more customers rolled through my line—hurried, worried, and uneventful. Christian returned. And the banter resumed. "Did you miss me, Daniel?"

"No."

"Lies," Christian replied. He looked at Sunshine and slapped my shoulder. "He wept like a baby, huh?"

Sunshine was a sweet and unassuming girl with thick-framed glasses and medium-length brown hair. Her name wasn't Sunshine, but that was how she had been introduced to me, and I didn't see the need to know her Christian name. We talked from time to time, and she was very nice, but if I didn't say anything to her, then we would probably only be ships passing in the night.

She nodded. "Yeah, he cried like a little bitch."

"Oh, shit! Did you hear that, Daniel? Sunshine called you a wee widdle beotch!"

"Sunshine!" I protested. "I thought we were friends."

"We are, but I have to be honest." Sunshine shrugged.

"Man, I can't win here."

"No. No, you can't, Daniel," Christian agreed. "Accept your fate, and tell me you missed me."

"If it will stop harassment, I'll tell you anything you would like."

"Oh, in that case, tell me that my dreadlocks look fantastic. I just cleaned them up."

"They look fantastic, Christian. But I have been meaning to ask you about that. Do you think that you are culturally appropriating those since you are a white dude rockin' a predominantly Jamaican hairstyle?"

"Oh, dude. Did you just go there?"

I laughed and smiled. Really, everyone was half paying attention to their lines and mostly focused on Christian's answer.

"The origins of dreadlocks come out of Greece and
the Middle East. They don't belong to a specific culture.
Culture isn't something that can be appropriated. It's a
collection of ideas and traditions. It can be appreciated
or desiccated but not appropriated. They're purely aes-
thetic for me. And like you just said, I look great."

"I said that to end the harassment."

"Were you lying?"

"Ask Sunshine."

"No. He wasn't lying. You look great," Sunshine
fired back.

"My god, she's quick. I'm not trying to be vain here,
you know. Just being silly," Christian replied.

"Of course we know," I responded.

"Okay. Glad we could clear the air."

"I'm so confused."

"Good. That's how I like it. Next!"

Since the capacity constraints had been relaxed, people came through my line at breakneck speed—customer
after customer after customer. I found that I missed
the days of the extreme limits to the number of people allowed inside. The lowered volume was a nugget of
relief from the tendrils of panic being wrapped around
our throats. Things were changing. Unemployment was
steadily increasing. People were opting out. Plexiglass
still divided the plebs from the patrons, and everything was muffled and muzzled, but people had started
to slip back into the routine, an erratic normalcy that
tricked us into a strange comfort—all the while leaving
neglected tension hanging in the air like shitty elevator
music slowly driving us insane.

Every conversation I had with my customers felt like being at a family gathering after a big fight. We were obligated to be there.

Little did I know that this would be my last memorable interaction on the front end at Dream Grocers. I stood there for a couple more blurry, redundant hours, and in between customers, I took a panoramic view of the rat race before me—full of parents telling children to take items back and otherwise normal people getting flustered at the register for no reason, as if they had never been in public before. Over time, I would attempt to remove the stereotypes of Linda and Dave from my vocabulary. My path would split time and time again, and I would have to pick whichever felt right.

* * *

On the way home, I usually strolled through one of the oldest and wealthiest neighborhoods in Denver, and I thought to myself that those were castles, not homes, with their sprawling stone exterior fencing and immaculate yards that resembled golf course greens. In that area, they didn't have sidewalks, so people just walked in the street, sometimes four abreast. Traffic was almost nonexistent. It had been designed in a bygone era with seclusion and prestige in mind.

Two giant Tibetan mastiffs—one black and one burnt orange—wandered along the wrought iron rails that linked the stone pillars of a fence. The sun peeked through trees, revealing a guesthouse or servants' quarters on a couple of acres stretching back behind the property.

An older woman with a shock of gray running through her hair, draped in a tan cashmere cardigan coat, was standing at her stone mailbox. She adjusted her thick-rimmed glasses to see who had sent the letter she held. She smiled at me as I walked by, and I said, "Hi."

She replied back, "Hello. Beautiful day out."

"Sure is." Truthfully it was a bleh spring day, but I wanted to be nice. I was trying to avoid bitterness, at least in that moment. Maybe she would invite me in, and we could chat about my desires to write a novel and change the world. She would share a story from her life, then tell me about how I reminded her of her son who had died last year of leukemia. I would meet her husband, a retired, middle-level executive, and we would drink scotch and smoke cigars like old pals. We'd carry on and on—our new little family—for years and years. Eventually, after much discussion with the rest of the Tindendales, I'd be added into their will. Uncle Kevin would be upset, and he would never get over it. He would call me the Grocery Store Whore, and we'd fight over everything after Evelyn and Jerry passed away. But in the end, it would be inevitable that I would be cast out into the streets because I had no claim to the throne. Kevin would claim that E and Jay (as I like to call them) were turning senile when I met them. The pedestal of mediocrity was all Uncle Kevin ever wanted, and what power I had would die in the fading light of unrealized dreams.

I stopped for a moment, as if to begin such a conversation, but it was only a fantasy, and it was cold outside. "Have a good day," I said.

III

"You too," she replied and shuffled back through an iron-and-stone archway, and I walked on.

IV

A couple of weeks later, the rising sun gave an orange hue to a pyramid of spaghetti squash placed in a Las Vegas skyline of raspberry and blueberry crates, boxes of peaches and pears, and a hundred different types of potatoes and tomatoes organized in patterns that made them enticing to the eye. The sugar inside, the aroma of fresh produce—the entire process was addictive, and like a casino they hooked you in and made it so hard to fucking leave. Chilled mist hit the back of my neck and shoulders as it dissipated onto the cucumbers and exotic roots. From my vantage point, I observed a tie-dyed landscape of edible wonderment. The process by which it all got there was complex to the point of confusion. To bring such a diverse supply of food from the farms of the world to our tables was quite simply astonishing. I knew enough to be in awe of the process. But not enough to be invested. "You interested in working in produce, bro?" a voice said from behind me. It was Jake.

"Not sure yet, man."

"We always need good people."

"Honestly, I get the feeling Todd has a plan for me."

"Todd has a plan for us all, Daniel."

"All hail Todd!"

"He is the one true Todd. He is omniscient and omnipotent."

"Toddamnit!"

"Hey, Daniel, let's refrain from blasphemy, because, you know, Todd is listening."

We both burst out laughing. "I like you, man," Jake said. "I've watched you working in different areas at the store for a while. I hope you find a good home here and stay away from the front end."

"I'm kind of in a career limbo—in more ways than one—at the moment. I think I might end up in prepared foods."

"Shit. Really?"

"Yeah. Is there anything wrong with that?"

"I mean, not really. It's tough, though. It's a restaurant within a grocery store. Shit gets weird over there, and they are constantly short staffed. But I'm sure you'll crush it, and it's the best area to test yourself. To see what you are made of."

"Damn, dude. You aren't really selling me on it."

"I know. We need you over here. Like, for example: I need your help with people-watching and fighting back the crazies. Do you see the thin fella with high-water skinny jeans, Birkenstocks, and thick-framed glasses over yonder? He has been squeezing the avocados for a fuckin' half hour."

"Jesus Christ. That's insane."

IV

"Yeah, dude. It happens all the time. I see him in here like three times a week. People can't seem to make their fruit selections. It's a difficult task, apparently. I'm not sure what they're doing exactly. Are they just avoiding their families, their lives? Are they haunted by emotional pains that cause them to fixate on the quality of their fruit? What are they doing with their short time on this earth? Because to me, it seems silly to focus on getting the right veggies when there is a great big world out there to absorb and see. Am I missing something, Daniel?"

"You only have one life, so maybe it's not such a bad thing to only consume the foods that make you happy and healthy," I suggested.

"That was a very thoughtful answer to what was clearly a tirade—sorry, I am in a shitty mood, and I see where you're coming from on the issue, but all this crap we sell is unnatural anyway."

"It's unnatural?"

He grabbed an orange. "Yeah. You see how it says GMO-free on this thing?"

"Yeah."

"Well, oranges don't look like this naturally. Humans genetically modified the original plant to get this tasty, magical sphere of goodness."

"Ah, I see what you are saying. So these things are natural but in an altered state."

"Exactly, brother. Exactly. And speaking of creatures in their habitat, I think you will be most at home here with me, watching these weirdos navigate the difficulties of finding the right type of flaxseed for their salad. It's a wild time."

"I'll keep it in mind. I've only heard of part-time work in your department, and Abby in prepared foods has already approached me about a supervisor role. I need the money."

"Greedy fucks."

"Sorry."

He laughed. "Not you, man. I am talking about the company."

"Oh, yeah. That's just the name of the game, I guess."

He turned his side to me, as if he was hiding something. "Sure, man. But I think we should unionize," he said.

"I gotta be honest, Jake, I think it is far too early in the morning for discussions about the finer parts of collective bargaining. I need coffee before we get into that."

"It's never too early for revolution!" he said as he lifted his fist in the air.

I couldn't tell if he was completely serious at first, but I understood his true fervor the moment I looked at his face—the whites of his eyes stretched to the edges of his skull. Jake's passion was unquenchable, and there was no break in his revolutionary stance on workplace politics or judgments on a given shopper for even a few moments. People were starting to stare. A nervousness grew over me about the topic. Plans to overthrow the system should not be made in open air. That was talk for the underground. And being new to the store was not the time to shake things up. I needed the job, so I asked, "Are we allowed to talk about that?"

"Goddamn right we are! Freedom of speech."

I decided to take him at his word, but without my morning coffee, the heightened activity struck me as obnoxious for some reason. I couldn't handle Jake proclaiming the injustices of the corporate world. People were looking at us with grimacing faces. A nasty scene was beginning to assemble like a storm front coming in over the mountains. But something inside me wanted to egg it on.

"What do you think a union will do for us?" I asked, knowing this would probably set him off.

"Get us a pay raise. And all this coronavirus shit is scary. We need to be protected."

"Do you *actually* think they could protect us from an airborne respiratory virus?"

"Goddamnit, Daniel. You're asking the hard questions, and I am trying to start a revolution."

I looked away, amused by his response, and smiled to no one in particular. But when I turned back around, Jake was becoming increasingly animated. His voice was elevated, and his hands were speaking as much as his words. People were looking. One Linda watched us and leaned over to another Linda. I couldn't hear what they were saying, but I knew it wasn't good. I didn't want the all-seeing, all-knowing Todd to get wind of our riotous behavior.

"Dude, we might want to go in the back," I suggested.

"Fuck that! And fuck the man."

I grabbed at his arm and began to pull him toward the receiving area. I started laughing. "Bro, let's go in the back."

"They can't fucking do this, man."

"Dude, yes they can. And this isn't worth it right now."

"Ugh. Whatever. Okay, let's go in the back. I have to grab some fucking kumquats anyway."

I couldn't help but laugh.

"They'll understand."

"Did I tell you I love you today, Jake?"

"Love you too, bro. But seriously, we deserve better."

"I agree. Now, let's go to the back. You can grab those kumquats, and I have to clock in for the day."

When we reached the receiving dock, he was shaking with rage. I put my hands on his shoulders and asked, "Are you really that upset? You know this isn't the end for you, right?"

"I get that, man. I'm just getting so sick of dealing with the same shit day in, day out."

"But we weren't dealing with any person. We were just chatting away. Frankly, I was a little lost with the conversation."

"Oh, we were dealing with people. That Birkenstock asshole needs to just make a decision and stick with it."

"That's what got you so upset? Ah, dude. I wouldn't worry about it. I'm sure he found what he wanted."

"You're right. I shouldn't get so pissed. I just see these people, and I think about all the problems of the world, and I start to lose my mind. Forming a union might help us."

"Do you think we can help our *own* situation?"

"Of course."

"Then why rely on others to change our circumstances for us?" I asked.

"We are stronger as a group," he replied.

"A chain is only as strong as its weakest link. And the larger the group, the more likely people would choose to just remain weak," I responded.

"It's not that easy to change."

"I agree—"

"How are you boys doing today?" Ozzy chimed in as he walked around the corner.

"Jake isn't doing so well. He's all fired up," I said.

"About what?" Ozzy asked.

"That we should unionize. Daniel doesn't think so," Jake replied.

Ozzy's eyes got wild. "What?!"

"I didn't say that. I just don't think it magically solves anything," I responded.

"Shit, Daniel, we need to talk more."

"I'm down. But can I go clock in before you hand out pamphlets about the revolution?" I said.

"Of course. We can always talk about viva la revolution!"

I laughed. "Good Lord. I'll talk to you all in a bit. I need to clock in and grab a beverage."

"Don't be late now!" Ozzy said with a southern accent as I rounded the corner.

* * *

6:42 a.m. displayed prominently on the time clock. I was about twelve minutes late, which could be a big deal, given I was on my ninety-day probationary period. But we were allowed some discretionary mistakes. I wasn't automatically screwed just by being a few minutes past.

"Hey, Todd. How are you today?" I asked.

"I'm fine, Daniel. How are you?"

"Doing great, boss."

"Aren't you late?" he asked.

I wondered how he could know such a thing unless he was monitoring my every move. "Yes, I got caught up helping this old lady with her groceries. Sorry about that. I just figured it is the Dream Grocers way to help our customers."

"That was very nice of you, but clock in first next time, okay?"

"Sure thing."

"We don't want you to be late too many times so early in your career. We can use you around here."

"I don't want that either. I need this job."

This morning, the lines on Todd's face were soft with empathy—he was more like a grandfather looking at his grandchild and future heir to his kingdom. "Daniel, have I ever explained to you the vision of Dream Grocers? Hell, have I ever explained to you my vision on what *I'm* trying to do here with this store?"

"I went through the video training at the beginning. Does that sum it up?"

"No, I don't think it does. At least by my standards."

I looked at my phone and wondered how much work I could avoid. "Lay it on me."

"The force of our will is enough to change the course of history."

I looked at him a bit cross-eyed.

"Bear with me. I know this fact because it *has to*. It's the only way we can truly believe in what we do. It's how we choose our path to prosperity. Think of George Washington Carver or Henry Ford and all that they accomplished. They changed the course of history because they put their mind toward a goal. I believe we can do that at Dream Grocers."

"How would a grocery store change the world?" I asked, as if to pour gas on another revolution.

"I'm not sure yet. I am still working on that. I just know that you can do it. We can revolutionize how people interact in a grocery store. Imagine, if you will, a store that is not only the place people shop for food—but it is also the place where they spend other spare time. Restaurants, movie theaters, miniature golf, and go-karts. We can set up a metaverse for the stores so that people can spend digital time here. Imagine a world that centers around the grocery store."

"I kinda feel like that's already happening since it's pretty much the only thing open at the moment."

"Nonsense. There isn't a virtual platform for shopping, and that's really the key to the whole thing working."

"You want people to wear goggles and shop for digital food at home? Like they are in a dream?"

"Yes, yes, yes. Precisely. It will be great."

"How will they get the actual food to eat?"

He paused for a moment. "We can fly it in via drone or have the gig drivers deliver it."

I remained silent. I had nothing to add, and I just wanted to watch him squirm. And that he did. We sat in the quiet of a moment.

"Sir, were you going to tell me more about 'the vision'?"

"Yes, I was thinking about what you just said, and I may need to work a few things out."

"Sorry. I didn't mean to make you second-guess yourself."

"You didn't. But I do need to work on some aspects of *my* own personal vision. I never second-guess myself.

That is part of knowing that I will, one day, revolutionize the world through the grocery virtual platform."

Internal. Eye. Roll. But I had to give him credit for
trying. Who knew what the future might bring? I'd never
envisioned living through a transformational event like
a pandemic. I'd watched the rise of the internet and
decentralization of information within my lifetime, and
those same institutions that tried to control the changing tides were crumbling under the weight of history as I
pondered this, and they sure as hell were choking down
their own medicine as I talked to Todd about his vision.
And at that point I had seen far too much real shit go
down on the front end of the store to second-guess the
idea that anything was possible. The world was full of
people on the edge. It was baked into a bold new version of modernity. I saw people go through my checkout
line with looks of raw, coagulated desperation on their
faces. The grocery store was their saving grace. It was a
lifeline. I wasn't sure if taking away the act of going to
the grocery store would help anyone, but I was willing
to keep an open mind.

"That's quite innovative, Todd."

He smiled.

I continued, "But weren't you going tell me your
story also? How long have you worked here? What's
your deal?" I asked with the hope that we wouldn't have
to work.

His body language relaxed even more. "You know,
Daniel, you are the first new employee to ask me that
in years. The last guy who did is now a general manager at a store in Colorado Springs. Anyway, I started
as a bag boy in the summer of 2001 at store number
three in Rancherito, California. Back in those days we

had baggers, cashiers, and cart shaggers at the checkout lines, if you can imagine. The front end was even more crowded than it is today with the self-checkouts and all. Dream Grocers was started in Taborville, California, about a hundred miles north. Near the California and Oregon state line. It was a simple time in the store's history. The founder, Jack Benson, would go to every store during the week and meet with the employees. He would even shoot the shit with the youngsters like myself. He told me early on that I was going to go somewhere in the company. Although, between you and me, I think he said that shit to everyone. But I think he meant it. He was a man that came from nothing. Bottom to the top, so they say."

"Sorry to interrupt, but is he alive today?"

"Oh, no problem at all. I'm just glad you are showing interest. Sadly, he stepped away from the company maybe ten years back. No one really knows what happened. He left a note on his secretary's desk that explained he was leaving the company and his wishes going forward. A week later, his lawyer informed the board that Jack wished to sell all of his stock in the company. Every. Last. One. A board member asked if Jack had a reason for the liquidation, but the lawyer ended the meeting, and it was all left to our imaginations. If he's alive, he doesn't return phone calls or talk to anyone associated with the company. He never had children or a wife. Dream Grocers was everything to him as far as I could see. Wish we knew what happened."

"What a shame," I said.

"Indeed. Well, back to my story. So I was out there in Rancherito. The energy was bona fide for all of us front-end folks. Like we knew that something big was happening at Dream Grocers. Everyone wanted to be general managers and turn the world upside down with this little grocery store. Boy howdy, we were competitive as all hell. We would fight over who could help someone out to the parking lot and who could pack out the bags the most organized and clean the fastest. It was a glorious time. It really was. One night I even got in a fistfight with a cashier named Timothy Johnson because he was going at a snail's pace on our line."

"You punched a guy because he was ringing up groceries too slow?"

"Yeah. I am not proud of it. I ended up with a nasty black eye. I learned my lesson. You have to be patient. Soon enough I moved up to cashier, and we'd race, and I'd time it. We would talk trash. I beat him every day. Then one evening after I'd embarrassed him so often, he quit his job and moved to Missouri."

"Wow. What's he doing these days?"

"At our national conference, another manager told me that Timmy was selling his own art somewhere in the Ozarks. What a shame. I was hoping that he would find his way. I worried about his work ethic, and I still do to this day."

"I see. Did that manager say that he seemed happy? It kinda sounds like he did find what he was supposed to do."

Todd ignored me and continued. "After I became a cashier, I climbed the ranks of Dream Grocers from head clerk, then into different departments like produce and grocery. Eventually, I was made assistant GM, where I remained for seventeen years. Jack's model was to take our time growing into the general manager role. And we also needed time to grow as a company. But during that twenty years, we grew to over two thousand stores. It's pretty amazing."

"You were an assistant GM for seventeen years before they gave you a general manager position? Didn't you say we have like two thousand stores?"

"What are you trying to say?"

"Oh, it's nothing personal. I guess I'm just amazed by how long they took to 'grow' you into the job you are doing now."

"Yeah, well, sacrifices have to be made sometimes, and I knew what I wanted out of life."

"Seems like you did, and you achieved it. I bet you are in line for that regional manager role any day now, huh? I mean, they have to see your work here for the last . . . what . . . five years?"

"Yup. My five-year anniversary is coming up at this store. But hopefully they see *me*. However, I don't let it bother me. We have this amazing store to work on right now."

"So then what is your plan for me? I need something to do."

"Good point. Here's the thing. To avoid another frozen-break incident, I think we are going to keep you bouncing around and helping different departments since you seem to be learning quickly. So that's what we'll do."

"Sounds good to me. Who should I report to?"

"Go talk to Ozzy again."

I walked out of Todd's office less at ease than ever. Todd's version *of* the Dream Grocer vision seemed cultist with underlying hostility. It was vain and ridiculous. Todd struck me as more complicated, manipulative, and sad than before. But I also found it inspirational for a reason I had yet to discover. I wondered if that was the grocery world I was stuck in for the foreseeable future. From the look of it, the beast could swallow you whole.

On the way down to the receiving dock, I stopped to buy a drink. I knew I would end up sweating and purging all the demons of this life and others.

An expansive selection revealed at least two hundred choices of bottled, canned, and jarred beverages, chilled, shiny, and ready for my consumption, lining a glowing wall that disappeared into the horizon. Did I want raw oat or almond milk, banana-cream-flavored seltzer, or kiwi kombucha? Maybe the best route was to stay safe with plain soda water. I walked down to the end. There were fifteen different options. I could see the clock on the wall in my mind. I was running out of time, and I was so damn thirsty. I closed my eyes and reached out to run my hands along the cold bottles, like a blind man reading braille or a teenager trying to undo a bra. Each bottle was unique in composition and shape—glass, plastic, aluminum, cylindrical, rectangular, all the shapes and sizes—all the options but none of the knowledge. Should I grab my phone and research each one? That was not appropriate, and I knew it. I promised myself that my decision would be final. No matter what. I would allow myself to let go—to let Jesus take the wheel. I'd do that Bukowski commitment and go all the way. I closed my hand. The sweat on my palm cooled rapidly, and a chill ran down my spine, telling me I'd chosen the right one. I picked the perfect bottle. The. One. I knew it. I opened my eyes.

"Fuck! It doesn't have bubbles," I said as I looked at the spring water in my hand. The price tag read seven dollars. "Oh, for Christ's sake!" I was disgusted by my choice.

"Sir, are you about done here?" a voice asked, startling me out of my zone. A frail woman with thin-rimmed glasses looked at me impatiently. "Seriously, are you done? I have been standing here for ten minutes."

"Yeah, I guess I'm done."

"Jesus. Finally," she said.

She opened her mouth to say something else, and I walked away.

We had nothing to talk about. There was nothing to say. I reached the register and looked back in longing at the wide array of seltzers that had gone unchosen. Why did I leave my choices up to the gods? Jesus took the wheel and drove me into a ditch, and I was destined to drink seven-dollar glorified tap water. "Fuck!" I said to no one in particular.

"What's wrong?" Mary said from a different register.

"Nothing, I just made a poor choice."

"Oh, well, is there any way I can help?"

"No. I think I need to go it alone."

"Alright. Come over here. I'll ring you up." She looked at the bottle. "That is some expensive water. Are you sure you want this?"

"I made my mess. I have to live with it."

"What? We can always give you a refund. You can choose something else."

"It's okay. Refunds are for quitters."

"You're ridiculous. Will you be unhappy?"

"Yeah, I'm not excited."

"Well, then hand that to me, and we can get you a different option."

"I think I need to make the best out of the situation."

"Were there cheaper options? Are you being financially responsible, Daniel?"

I laughed. "You are too sweet, Mary. Probably not, but something about it seems to be worth the risk."

"Suit yourself. Enjoy your seven-dollar tap water."

"It still hydrates me, right? Like survival is the most important thing. Or no?"

"You are wise beyond your years, Daniel. All good points."

"Really? I was going to say the same things about you. Plus, you don't even know how old I am."

"Another good point. Not sure how—dammit, a customer is coming. Let's talk later. Love the deep conversations."

* * *

Ozzy walked past me as I stood drinking my overpriced and dissatisfying water. "The truck's here, bud. I'm going to have you help the prepared-foods department today. They're short staffed and need someone to receive their shit. You down with that?"

I looked down at my phone. "Yeah, I'm down for whatever." I glanced at my phone once more and saw Frankie had twenty new followers. But it was that time again, so I followed Ozzy down one of the many stairways to the labyrinth inside that forlorn monument to 1970s' architecture that consisted of incredibly narrow, ravaged, and cluttered hallways and doorways painted over a dozen or more times. Every inch of empty space on all sides of the building housed extra shelving, spare racks for bread or produce, canopies for the summer sale, and other miscellaneous items that might be important but were never put in storage. But no spare rooms were to be found.

Every passageway was teeming with life as we moved in a choreographed dance through the underbelly of grocery life. I maneuvered by someone at their desk in the middle of the hall (due to lack of office space), then dodged a person holding up a huge wheel of cheese that blocked their vision as they almost sideswiped me into the wall.

"Jesus!" he said.

"Sorry, bro," I replied.

Down this strange dark and winding path, I made my way to the receiving docks. As I passed the meat department, Chase popped his head out. "You ready to throw the load, homie? Heard you are helping us today."

"I was born for this," I replied.

"You and me both, brother. I'll be out in just a minute. Gotta cut the meat nice and proper."

"Heard that," I replied.

Ozzy turned around to talk to me but kept walking backward. "Hey, man, I gotta help out on the floor. So you are on your own here. Others might be able to help."

"Damn. Alright, man."

"You'll be fine. Just take 'er easy, ya know?"

"Sure."

"Thanks," he said and walked away.

There were twenty-eight pallets stacked maybe eight feet high with any grocery item you could imagine, creating a maze of products representing all the sections of the store: produce, grocery, floral, prepared foods, bakery, and specialty were all accounted for in the Saran Wrapped columns that mockingly stared at me, telling me my place in this world. I was over six feet tall, but I shrunk to the stature of an ant.

Chase arrived to my rescue.

"Dude, what do I do here?" I asked.

"What do you mean?"

"This is too much shit."

He laughed. "Unfortunately, it's our lightest day of the week."

I was shell shocked, and I stared off into the madness of the scene.

Chase leaned into my view. "But what I would do is focus on time-sensitive products first: meats, cheeses, fish. Next, put away frozen. Finally, you can work on the nonperishables, like those giant cans of beans."

"Sage advice," I said, embarrassed I hadn't seen that logic originally.

"But don't worry, man. Ozzy is around here some-where. I can help too. Just take your time. This is one of the best jobs because you have zero customer inter-action during your time back here. And it's a workout. Just you and your thoughts. Maybe listen to a podcast. Or music. Whatever you want."

"Oz just left me." I shrugged.

"Shit, I would too. Have you looked in the mirror?"

"Asshole."

"Go, Oz, go. Go, Oz, go!" he chanted with his arm up.

Chase made me feel naturally at ease with this ridic-ulous show. He was kind and surfer-like with a slightly over-the-top personality. He carried a desire to make the

IV

people around him join in the party no matter what. Good people.

"But now you have to find the U-boats to put the shit away. And it's a goddamn battle some days."

"The U-boats? Like the German submarines from World War I?"

"Umm . . . if you want to think of them in that light, sure. I just think they are shaped like a *U*," he replied, then pointed to a cart. "These things," he said as he pulled a cart with tall railed ends attached to a narrow metal board with wheels fixed at the center to allow for sharp turns. "These are goddamn gold around hee-ah."

"I see what you did there," I said.

"What did I do?"

"You got all country with *here*."

"Why whateva do you mean, Daniel, my boy?" he said in a strong southern drawl.

I began to laugh uncontrollably. "Alright. You won. I'm relaxed."

"Good. Now just *receive* the *load* at your own pace. Be gentle. Take your time," he said with a big smile.

"Jesus. I am glad we are so serious around here."

"The only way to make it through this bullshit is to fuck around. Have you worked retail or customer service before, bro?"

"Most of my life."

"Then you know what it is, man. It's how we roll."

"How is that?" I replied.

"You know . . . the suffering."

"Suffering?"

"Yeah, I mean, life is pain. And the best you can do is suffer well and make the best of it."

79

"Looks like we have a Buddhist monk in the house."

"You tease, but you know it's true. Like, look at what we are doing. Does this look like the pinnacle of human flourishing?"

"I suppose not."

"But this is what we have. So make the best of it, and abide this life with a smile on the soul."

"Well, I like that."

"Right on, Daniel. Now, let me know if you need any help."

I reached out to him. "Quick question . . ."

"What's that?" he replied.

"Where do I bring this shit?"

"Good call. Take the freight elevator down, and you will see the prepared-foods cooler on the left."

Chase walked away, and I examined the cityscape of pallets. This job in receiving, I thought, couldn't be worse than what I'd endured working as a cashier with Lindas and Daves at the front of the store. In receiving, I could hide from the pandemic and the world. If anything, this was a golden opportunity for me to correct course and relax. The pallet in front of me had boxes of chicken piled high. I was surrounded. I got to work.

Each box of chicken weighed at least fifty pounds. I had thirty of them to clear off and put away in the cooler downstairs. Sweat poured down my face as I moved the stack, layer by layer, onto a U-boat. My muscles bubbled and burned with lactic acid, and I could feel tension in my back. I'd lost all momentum toward exercise in 2020. In my mind, I was a slob with padding around my midsection. I drank whiskey every night and sat around my apartment with my neighbors. I could feel the failure in my misshapen frame. Lila told me I looked great.

Friends with whom I shared my concerns reminded me everyone was gaining a little weight from this formidable year of our lives. I had good people in my life. But there was still something missing.

With the U-boat piled high, I pushed it toward the freight elevator at the back of the store. The giant metal gate opened to a concerned Jake with a U-boat loaded down with boxes of peaches. "What's up, buddy?" I asked.

"This place drives me crazy, man."

"Why so?"

"We are treated like animals," he replied.

"Well, aren't we?"

"Smart-ass. Yeah, of course we are, but we should be kind to each other."

"What happened that is making you feel this way?"

"Richard is all up my ass about something. It's really not a big deal. I shouldn't have brought it up."

"First off, who is Richard? Second, I am sorry he is up your ass. Hope he's gentle."

Jake showed a half smile and said, "Richard is the assistant manager . . . the evil one."

"How have I never met him?"

"He hides in the shadows and only comes out when it is most unnecessary to give comment on our performance. And I think he was on paternity leave or something. Frankly, it's disgusting that he's a father."

"Damn, dude. Don't hold back on my account."

"Thanks, man. You're one of the good ones."

A rail-thin man with light-blond hair and oversize work shoes emerged from the basement, and Jake disappeared into the produce-preparation area of the store.

"Hey, you . . . do you need something to do?" the blond man asked.

"No sir. I'm putting away the shipment." I looked at his name tag. It was Richard, assistant general manager. I wondered if he was stalking Jake. *Fucking weirdo.*

"I need your help at the moment, so that can wait."

"Uh, alright . . . whatcha need?"

"Let's clean up this area, eh? Like sweep and wash the baseboards, ya know?"

"You want me to leave out raw chicken to clean the receiving dock?"

Richard stopped for a moment. He was mumbling to himself, as if he was thinking out loud.

"On second thought, I think it can wait," he said. "You can clean after the shipment is put away."

"Sure. Anything else I can do for you?"

"What's your name . . . Daniel. Well, Daniel, it's not what you are doing for me. It's what you are doing for Dream Grocers. We are Dream Grocers."

"Sounds good, boss."

"I expect this area will be cleaned by tomorrow morning."

"I will do my best."

He laid out his best Scottish accent. "You will try your best? Losers try their *best*. Winners go home and fuck the prom queen."

I stared for a moment. "Are you suggesting I perform sexual acts at work, Richard?"

"Oh no, of course not. I was just quoting *The Rock* with Sean Connery. It's my favorite movie," he said with pride.

"I bet it is, Richard. I bet it is." He looked hurt, so I relented. "I'm just fucking with you, Richard." I moved toward the elevator with a fresh U-boat full of product.

"What is your name again? Oh, Daniel. That's right. Well, make sure you get this area tidied up by tomorrow." He was pointing in the general area of the dock, and I thought that the guy must have nothing to do. He was playing pretend manager because his mom hadn't paid attention to him as a child.

"Of course," I replied while pressing the button, and the elevator door closed. I knew full well that I would not be cleaning that area. I wouldn't have enough time, and if anyone made a stink out of it, I would report to Ozzy.

The giant metal doors opened slowly, revealing a flurry of people moving pallet jacks, filling carts, talking, cutting, and unwrapping and breaking down the product they had just received. The entrance to the elevator was crowded with people beginning to organize their departments. I focused on what Chase had told me and just went for what I knew. I made a beeline toward the cooler where the raw poultry went and began unstacking the chicken I had loaded not five minutes ago. My arms were weak and my back tight. I realized then that I was in for a very long morning.

I walked by the bakery area, where they prepared towering confetti cakes, brownies, cookies, and cinnamon rolls slathered in gooey frosting. They looked happy while they worked away and listened to early 2000s' rap. "Whaaat uuup, bakery ladies!" I said. They waved back. I didn't know their names, but I had always found it wise to be as friendly as possible at the beginning of any relationship, especially when they had fresh-baked chocolate chip cookies at their disposal.

Next to the bakery was a massive kitchen with six grills and four cutting tables. The smell of rotisserie chicken filled the room with a thick fog that immediately clashed with the robust produce-receiving area. In the far back, rows of carts were lined up for the online shoppers, who were newly part of the crew. The basement was the center of the hive. Worker bees everywhere. A mix of smell and sound and sight that most would never see. It burned bright like a coal fire deep in a mine. And it seemed oddly safe, buried and out of sight.

Trip after trip after trip, my legs turned to mush, and great rings of sweat hung beneath my armpits. I drank hearty, full gulps of electrolyte water. I looked as a tired fool might after trying to impress the powerful who were nowhere to be found. The rods of muscle that lined the small of my back sang old slave-plantation tunes as I sat down at the receiving desk.

"How's it going, man?" Ozzy asked.

"I feel tenderized and utterly destroyed."

With some concern, he asked, "You aren't hurt, are you?"

"I don't think so?"

"Good. I just worry about the health of our workers. That's why I am trying to get a union together."

"Here we go again," I said with an eye roll.

"Nah, man. Hear me out. They fired a dude last year because he threw out his back while working."

"That was the entire reason he got fired?" I asked, knowing full well that dude would sue and win if something like that happened.

"Well, that's the only reason I could see."

"So then there were other reasons. Look, I'm not doubting his or your or anyone's case. I just want to peel back the layers all the way before I go donating to a cause that may benefit me but will for sure benefit certain people in higher positions and make them very powerful. I don't intend to work here forever."

"I get it, dude. I do," Ozzy said. "It's just when I look at the group, I just wish we made more money and were treated with a little more goddamn respect. You should not fear for your job while working."

"Like you should have no fear at all? I think you should be held accountable—for your coworkers if nothing else."

"You're making some fair points, but we should support each other, no?"

"I can agree with you on that, for sure. Speaking of support, I feel like I haven't gotten anything done unloading this shipment."

"That's not entirely surprising. It takes some time to get used to the volume of work. How much do you have left?"

"About half."

"Good god. Well, I *would* stay and help crush it out, but I have a meeting. I know that Abby really appreciates your help. They are very short staffed. Maybe this could lead to something bigger in the company. If people see you bust your ass, they are more likely to hire you full time or move you into management. I think that's what you were hoping for, right?"

My gums hurt from the lactic acid. "Yeah. That's what I would like."

"Well, keep going, and you will probably get there."

"Speaking of which, I'd better get back to it."

* * *

If you have ever lifted hundreds of boxes, you will know what I am talking about when I tell you that the tips of my fingers were raw and crack-dry as I put the final box away. My lateral muscles were sore to the touch. Judging by the glances of employees who walked past, I knew I looked like a sad heap of neglected youth. The tragedy and triumph of aging was front and center for me as I cleaned up the wood pallets and threw them on the piles to be recycled. Exhaustion laid a heavy hand on me, but robust satisfaction of a twelve-hour workday was something I could carry going forward.

I left work at dusk, a man of revolution, or so I liked to think—I found out how much effort I really wanted to put in, and once I was removed from the situation, I realized that maybe sitting on that dock like a man melted down to the very basic minerals of existence was one of my favorite moments of my life.

The time had come to walk home. A breathless, full-tilt city awaited the senses. Denver's midsize sprawl provided a tunnel of life cheering me on, all the way home. Outlined by streetlamps and doorways, ramshackle apartment buildings stood next to elegant, refurbished old bungalows that comprised the dense blocks of the Cherry Creek and Capitol Hill neighborhoods. Soon enough the city would be a raging furnace for the entirety of 2020 into 2021. Riots near the capitol. Nights filled with fury and commotion. But on this particular evening, I could block out an asteroid heading toward the earth as I remained undeterred from the glory I felt with my delicate steps headed anywhere I pleased. Freedom to be one's self was a hell of a thing after a lifetime of going along with everyone else's idea of how it all should work.

That woman's house—the one where I'd stopped and said "Hi"—didn't bring the same bitter visions of a different life as I passed by the iron gate. No, my soul was peaceful this time around, like a feather caught in a gust of wind. It was not as if I'd lost my edge completely, but at least I knew some of my options. This go-around, things didn't feel as heavy as I moved on into the night.

V

Days melted into weeks and eventually months, and my ninety-day review was just around the corner. When I would look back on this time in my life, I would imagine that I worked tirelessly every moment to climb the corporate ladder, but many days I just went through the motions. That was all you needed to do. Just show up to work and do your job, and you could gain favor with the powers that were. It really was remarkable how little most people would do while still complaining about how they couldn't get anywhere.

I watched the wheat separate from the chaff in real time primarily from laziness or entitlement. I wasn't particularly skilled. I just showed up. And that garnered positive attention. People rotated in and out of employment at the store with such regularity that I didn't bother to learn names. One day we might have three new employees. The next day only one of them showed up. Every day several people called out and everyone else was left to pick up the slack. The work had to be done. The ants marched on.

On the most indiscriminate of days, after unloading the last of a shipment—which randomly had a micropallet of caviar and limoncello pastries—I found myself in a cramped hallway that connected to the dock, talking with Lucas from the grocery department. Our bodies were staggered a little distance apart, and we were definitely breaking the protocols involving distancing that were prevalent during the pandemic. Everywhere I went during that year and into the next, I would look down on the floor and see social-distancing stickers telling people to stay at least six feet away from each other. Those rules seemed so arbitrary given our circumstances. Being part of the grocery-store collective had tweaked my behavior. I was less risk averse than the general public. The information pipeline was congested with different voices speaking in tongues about serious things. We had our nose on the sweating forehead of a disaster; other people's unfounded problems became less important to me. Everyone made their own judgment calls. We weighed the risks. We were reminded of our constant peril through every media outlet or paranoid customer—but everything became filtered through an honest raw lens rather quickly.

"I am going away for a while," Lucas said.

"Are you in some kind of trouble? Did you kill someone?" I asked with a wink, then slurped my seltzer-juice fusion, trying to break the tension.

"No. My mom has cancer."

"Jesus. Is it bad?"

"Well, it's metastasized and in stage four, so I would say so. It's spread everywhere in her body."

My attempted levity flatlined in that moment as I looked over at this young person—younger than me by a good seven or eight years—about to lose his mother to her own body. Yet he was stoic and prepared and thoughtful. Then I thought about my parents passing away. My eyes began to water, and he noticed.

"Dude, it's okay. She has been sick for a long time."

"My god. Man, I'm so sorry."

"I just don't want her to suffer anymore."

I didn't know what to say. We had gone from silly to serious in one giant swing.

He sensed this and said, "But anyway, you were saying something about wanting to have sex with Lila?"

"What? No, I wasn't."

"I know, but you are depressing me. Life is already incredibly sad. Let's stick to the lighter things."

"I can do that," I responded.

Lucas was the kind of person it took a while to get to know. He was lanky and a bit on the taller side, with a rainbow flag on his work hat. He was quiet but not in a meek sort of way. It was more like he was waiting to deliver a thoughtful or smart-ass remark. Intellect in limbo, if you will. Would he go dark or light? What would he bring next? Thunder or lightning?

Chase walked around the corner and yelled, "What up, what up?"

"Lucas was just telling me about the meat," I responded.

"Dude, he doesn't know shit about *that meeeeat*. If you want to know about the meat, you need to look no further than myself."

"Ah, so you are the resident expert on meat?" Lucas asked.

"Well, I have a wide breadth of knowledge, you know?"

"Oh, how so?" Lucas asked.

With all the swagger available in any given moment, Chase said, "Well, as a man that swings both ways, I have seen much of what the world has to offer."

"What can you tell us about a porterhouse steak?"

"It's not the best cut, but it sure can take a pounding."

"Good god." Lucas held his hand to his mouth.

"I know, brother. I know," Chase said and put his hand on Lucas's shoulder.

The reflex was almost supernatural in how incredibly easy it was for my coworkers to switch off negativity. A conversation about tragedy was instantly buried under ridiculous sexual-harassment-level silliness. We were turning vinegar back into wine in those moments. Not a serious face among all who contributed. No one was being hurt—or if they were, they hid it well. On the contrary, maybe we were saving one another by giving each other shit. It was instinctive to tease comrades in our increasingly dark circumstances, given the world that was indifferent to ours. The conversation I found myself in was gender fluid, and no one was excluded, but it was clearly about men and what we did when we were left to our own devices.

From around the corner, Neal arrived with a big smile.

"What are you doing back here, bud?" I asked. "Aren't you supposed to be working the front end?"

"Shiiiit. I'm on my third walkabout this morning, which is a fancy term for an extended bathroom break where I tour the store and bullshit with as many people as possible."

"Fucking genius," Lucas said, and I couldn't have agreed more.

"Did y'all see that one in blue yoga pants snooping around seafood? Good god."

Chase responded with closed eyes and an audible "Mmm . . . I can only imagine."

"You don't have to imagine, dude. She is right out there strutting around in bright-blue, tight-fitting pants."

"I do like that meat," Chase said.

"I know. That's why I'm telling y'all about it, dude," Neal replied with a shake of his head.

"I guess we need to take a field trip," I said.

Jeanie, our short-haired, firebrand grocery manager with a southern accent and a penchant for telling it like it is, popped out from one of the coolers and said, "She's a regular. Boy howdy, it's worth the price of admission. She reminds me of a gorgeous brunette I dated in my last year of college."

Chase interjected. "You don't know, Jeanie! You don't know the meats like me!"

Jeanie immediately smacked him upside the head. "Shut up, boy. Like what the hell are you talking about? I've been chasing *bird* my whole life. *Bird* is made of meat just like you and me. You don't know shit about *bird*, Chase."

"Excuse me, Jeanie. I am an expert on *bird*."

I held up my hand and asked, "Just so I can follow this conversation properly . . . you two are talking about women, correct?"

Jeanie responded, "*Bird*. Can be anything, really: men, women, anything you can think of. I often use it in reference to things ejaculated from the body. Like, you boys probably been throwin' *bird* way too much recently, huh? Or you got some bird on your lip there, Chase." Chase laughed and turned a reddish hue. "Do what you please. Language shouldn't be used to control people. That's evil. It's supposed to liberate us."

"Ahh . . . I see. Okay. Well, please continue with your regularly scheduled discussion."

"Ah, yes . . . Chase, you scoundrel. I was wrist deep in the game before you were born. I was trying to sleep with ladies in the goddamn eighties."

"Uh, that's gross," Chase retorted.

"No, it ain't. It's natural, honey. And you don't know what I went through to talk openly with y'all about my sexual proclivities. I earned my right to objectify the ladies I love in an open manner without being banished from home by my father or society, and you can't take that away from me. Something tells me that y'all aren't ready for whatever gift the magic babe in blue would or wouldn't be willing to give you. Move along, son. Now . . . Daniel?"

"What can I do ya for, Jeanie?" I asked.

The roar of laughter washed away our sins for just a moment until Chase paused and, with a look of concern, said, "Honestly, despite your valiant explanation, I'm not sure if we should be objectifying women."

Jeanie took the role of teacher in that moment, and the crowd muted to listen. "Honey, I have been around a long goddamn time, and we are all objectifying everyone all day, every day: men, women, they and them . . . whatever spice you got in the marinade . . . we are a human object at first. Then you get to talk to them and know their nature, and shit changes. It transcends the physical into the spiritual and emotional. Doesn't mean you go around being a creepy cunt to every hot-bodied piece of ass you see. You should treat every person you meet like someone you will have to work with later, like a potential coworker. At first your interaction will be tenuous, but then soon enough you will know them and see what it's like when the wall comes down. Anyway, that's just my two cents. I hate to lecture y'all, but too often people wanna get upset about things when there's no need. It's as if everyone has been living in some internet hole and never struggled once in their whole goddamn life. That beautiful woman who was the subject of this conversation was at the seafood counter just a moment ago. There is something special about that one, so best not make a fool out of y'all. Be respectful. She wore those pants knowing someone was gonna take notice. Go take a gander before she wanders out onto the savanna."

Lucas and Neal went in search of Ol' Blue. Chase looked a bit confused about how he had been shot down so quickly by Jeanie. I patted him on the shoulder as he walked away and said, "Win the crowd, and you'll win your freedom."

"Huh?" Chase turned toward us.

"He's sayin' don't try and outshine me, bitch," Jeanie responded with a kissy face.

"Oh, I'll be back! Better than ever!" Chase called and walked through the saloon doors.

Only Jeanie and I remained.

"Something tells me that you took a sledgehammer to that wall a long time ago, Jeanie," I said.

"What? Oh, yeah. Sorry, things happen fast when shit-talking is at maximum velocity. Honestly, there never was one, but you learn how to navigate this life when you live long enough to become your own enemy."

"You look at yourself as your enemy?"

"I've fucked up so much in life that it's hard not to. Hell, I have worked at Dream Grocers for twenty-five years. That's one of my biggest fuckups."

"Why do you regret it?" I asked.

"Well, I guess I looked at this job as something that'll never change. I thought Dream Grocers was gonna be the same forever. I'm not sure why. I feel like an idiot saying it out loud. But then they were bought by some big alphabet corporation—ABC International, or whatever—and common workers became unimportant. After the buyout, everything turned into trainings and risk avoidance, and instead of prioritizing happy employees who know our customer and products, we became just a number—a goddamn automaton who puts bags of grapes in a fancy pyramid or fills another empty hole on a meaningless wall of products. The passion burned from my body a long time ago. Like, has Todd talked to you about that virtual-shopping bullshit?"

"Yeah, a little."

"That's what I am talking about. I mean, Todd is an idiot, and his idea is silly, but they still want to eliminate us. I dedicated myself to an industry that is actively trying to extract the human element. I'm their enemy."

"Sheesh. That seems pessimistic as all hell. Isn't change inevitable, though?"

"Christ, I sure as hell know it is. But I enjoy what I do. I don't want it to change. What the fuck am I gonna do after this? Am I the last grocer in the Grocery Cathedral?"

I put my hand up. "Hold that thought, Jeanie. I almost forgot about Ol' Blue. Do you think the location of that woman in blue yoga pants has changed yet?"

Jeanie looked deeper in thought now and said, "You have a limited time frame to see her in the wild. She could be gone already. I suggest you go out and see."

"Deal. I'll be right back." I rammed through the swinging doors out onto the floor. A rush of cluttered grocery-store ambience hit me, and I was suddenly aware that I might have to answer questions about artisan cheeses, rare pickled hen from Austria, and the lack of Wasabi roots this season. I quickly moved past the meat and grocery departments in hopes that I would see the lovely lady in blue.

I arrived in seafood, but she was nowhere to be found. I walked around the corner to produce, and she appeared out of the midst of a radish mountain. Her basket was casually hanging off her forearm as she strolled aimlessly in search of nutrition. Yoga pants were all my shallow mind needed to align my chakra after the conversation in the back. Jeanie had gone to a dark place. The pendulum was swinging hard that day. Ol' Blue turned my way, and we locked eyes for a moment. Her eyes were gentle and her body language easy. I smiled one of those boyish, hopeful smiles, but she pretended not to notice me. Maybe she was nervous, or maybe I was misreading the room. I pretended to fix a display and stared for a moment longer, then walked to the back.

* * *

When I returned to the hallway, the only person in view was Jake—with his mustache, windbreaker shorts, long thinning hair, and contagious disposition—looking at an extremely ripe pear under a magnifying glass.

"You see the woman in the blue out there?" I asked.

His head raised from the task to look at me, and he said, "Which one, homie? This is Dream Grocers, the land of unknowable women, and they're beautiful and found in abundance."

"You don't think I could ever get to know her?"

"I just mean there are too many to count, and *unknowable* is just a term I picked up in a philosophy class. It has many applications, but in this case, it just sounds cool."

"Fair enough," I replied with the thought that he might expand on the *unknowable* term. But he just went back to what he was doing.

"Whatcha looking at there, bud?" I asked.

"Well, this pear ripened faster than any of the others. I'd like to know why."

"Any answers so far? Is that knowable?"

"Ha. Yes, I believe I can 'know' what happened here. We don't have a lab or anything. So I'm just killing time trying to understand this pear. I fuckin' love plants and fruits. I used to grow weed."

"I gotta say I am not surprised."

"I know. My attire screams pothead. It's about more than getting high to me, though. Horticulture and the natural world fascinate me."

"Nerd, hippie, philosopher, union organizer. You're an interesting fella, Jake. Where is your kryptonite?" I asked.

"Honestly, I tend to go off the rails from time to time. I can't really explain it. But I am sure you will see eventually."

"Eh, I think the most interesting people in history have an edge."

"I also like making pottery."

"Ah, yes . . . the unknowable man emerges."

"Now you are starting to get it. But I think women like me for my mustache. This monster is a lighthouse in a hurricane." We both laughed.

"That's all there is to it, eh? I just need to grow a mustache, and I will find someone to fall in love with me?"

"Shit, it works for me, dude. Hey, but speaking of the ladies, I heard you are scoping out Lila. She is mighty fine. She's a good catch too."

"Oh yeah? Do you know her well?"

"Well enough. I mean, she's unknowable, remember?" He looked at me for a moment, as if to let me respond, but before I did, he continued, "Just fuckin' with you. She's great."

"Aren't all women, according to your philosophy?"

"I did say that earlier, didn't I?"

"Only a couple minutes ago."

"Sorry, dude. I'm stoned. I forget what I say from time to time."

"I knew it! That's the only reason you are staring at a moldy pear, huh?"

"Hey now! It's only part of the reason. I'm genuinely curious about many things. Drugs just enhance my experience sometimes."

"Understandable," I replied, knowing how life could be. Knowing drugs could seem like the only way out, for the common folk.

He slapped his cheeks lightly and shook his head side to side. "Also, I say go for it with Lila. She is straight-up hot magic."

"I think so too. I'm just taking it one day at a time. We chilled last night and watched a movie."

"Very nice. You get a little sexy time?"

"Not yet. Soon? Maybe?" My heart began to race at just the thought of it.

"Attaboy. I wish you smooth sailing and rough sex."

"Good god. Thanks, I guess?"

"Of course, man. And if you need any advice on how to navigate, let me know."

"Yeah, man, women are complicated, and sometimes you just need direction—you know, like a lighthouse," I said.

"Oh, I see what you did there," he replied.

"You like that? I'm thinking that I will only speak in ocean metaphors from here on out. It will be my calling card."

"I like it . . . hey, I know this is a big change of topic, but did I tell you I got these *fire* mushrooms?"

"No. I have been microdosing acid on and off since the start of the pandemic. Maybe I should switch it up. Can I ask you a question?"

"Sure."

"Does it feel like we are tripping right now?"

"Always, my man. Always."

"So I am not the only one?"

"Definitely not."

"Good."

"Are you interested in these magic mushrooms? They are super mellow. They will get you right where you need to be quick. Then you can run flush against the hot nerve at the end of the world."

"Um . . . sure. Whatever you say. Anyway, I'll take an eighth," I said as I laughed and typed twenty-five dollars into an app on my phone and pressed send. The ease of modern drug dealing occurred without nervousness or ridiculous hoops like when I was a kid. Those awkward nights searching for friends of friends who lived halfway across the city in an apartment that smelled like ramen and cat hair were a thing of the past. Denver had also decriminalized mushrooms, so there was that.

"Do you need anything else? I got some Special K and Molly."

"I think I'm good. This place doesn't pay me enough to have *all* the fun."

"Why do you think I sell drugs on the side, homie?" he said and pointed at himself. "This mothafucka is poor."

"Heard that," I responded.

"Look at your elder millennial ass using the Gen Z slang."

"Is that what that is? I thought I was just saying that I heard you."

"Definitely Gen Z. I'm not sure y'all should be using our language."

"I quit my corporate job, and now I work in a *grocery store*. I think I earned it. Plus, fuck you, language is for everyone."

He laid his hand on my shoulder, smirked, and said, "Hey, brother, don't disparage my job. I am one hundred and ten percent committed to this place."

"You're right. I'm sorry, dude. Should we go up to Tracy in HR and talk about it? I didn't mean to crush your dreams."

"I think we may have to, man. I mean . . . this is my career," he said with a huge smile.

"I knew you were a lifer."

"I dream of Dream Grocers. You don't even know."

"Oh, I *know*."

"That's why I like you, Daniel. You understand that it takes commitment."

I decided to break the sarcasm bubble. "Dude, if I had even a slightly better option, I would leave."

Jake laughed. "Shit. Most of us would. You have an out, though, right? It's not the same for you. You're a literary fella with a book on the way and a long history of working in corporate business roles."

"Well, the book part is only half-true. I might have something even better down the pike. But you're right. I guess I could look for different work."

Jake rubbed his hands together. "Dude. Whatcha got goin' on? Anything I can help with distribution on?"

"Well, you can help spread it on the internet, but there won't be need for much else."

I pulled out my phone to show him my social media for Frankie Bombay. "Check this out."

He looked at my follower numbers. "My god. Dude, if that keeps going up and it affords you the ability to get out, then leave this shit show."

"Here's the thing, man. I feel like I owe it to myself to give this place a try—to suffer enough to better understand it, to own it—to feel in control of my life. And I don't want to go back to *just* another desk job and have nothing to show for it. I might as well use this time

V

to write the book and grow a nation of followers for Frankie."

"That's fuckin' great, man. I'm excited for you," he replied.

"I want big things for my life. And grinding day in and day out at this goddamn place will all but ensure that I'll be ready, when the time comes, to embrace whatever the future holds. It will harden me and make me more durable."

"What comes next, then?"

"Honestly, I think I am going to try to rise in the ranks a bit."

"Heard that. Wait . . . what?!"

"Yeah, I can't afford my apartment on minimum wage, and I am going to be here for a while, so I might as well make the best of it."

"Shit, dude. We could use cool managers around here. I approve."

"Aww, thanks, Jake."

"Just don't drink the Kool-Aid, alright? Don't turn into Richard."

"I won't. I promise."

Jake's face was solemn. "That's what they all say."

"Listen . . . I'll be chill. It's only a chance to see what I am made of in this situation. I want to prove my grit."

"Brother, I'm sure you will do great."

"Thanks, Jake. That means a lot. Now, don't forget those mushrooms," I said.

"Heard that," he responded.

"You're right. I shouldn't use y'all's words," I said with a sigh.

"It's all good. You're not like the rest of them."

"Well, thank god for that." I looked at my phone. "Shit, I gotta go."

"Sounds good. What time are you off? I will swing by receiving before I leave."

"I close."

"Okay. I'll bring those boomers to your prepared foods, then."

* * *

The load was put away, and the leftovers of my body were piled up in a chair on the receiving dock. Free time was a rarity at Dream Grocers. Breaks and lunches were mandatory but rarely used. Usually, I was clearing the load for prepared foods, then doing the dock paperwork all the way to the end of my shift. I didn't have a department to call my own yet. Todd referred to me as a floater. The linings of my gums burned from lactic acid as I looked out at my space, my scene, thinking that I was lucky to be trapped there. At least I had this small man-made hovel to shelter me from the world. I had two hours left in my shift. *I deserve a break,* I thought. Ozzy had gone home a while ago, and I had been left to my own devices. I'd organized the pallets from the different departments. The only one that hadn't been cleared was seafood. I emptied Styrofoam boxes onto a U-boat and pushed it into their freezer.

Through the freezer-door window, I could view the long line of customers standing at the seafood case. They were animated with lust for oysters and scallops. One of the guys working in the department saw me watching the commotion and walked back to the freezer. He burst in. "Whatcha doin' back here!"

I smiled and showed him the stack of seafood product I had brought in on the U-boat.

"Thanks, man," he said. "It's a goddamn zoo out there today. I haven't had a moment to think about anything else."

"I gotchu, my friend."

"Thanks again," he said, then walked back out to the counter and began filling a bag with Prince Edward Island mussels for a woman in a beige Armani tracksuit with a paint roller's worth of makeup caked onto her face. He handed her the food. I watched her argue with her boyfriend for a moment. Her face looked like a rubber glove packed to the brim with silicone. His body was overly sculpted, tanned, and prematurely aged. I longed to hear their disagreement. Her face was stoic from Botox, and even his body language looked dumb. They were like a puppy and a toddler having a conversation. The fight was short lived; he conceded whatever point she had been trying to make, and they walked away. A man with thinning brown hair and a slightly disheveled gray suit walked up after her and ordered two whole king crabs and two one-pound salmon filets.

"Big event?" the employee asked.

"Event? No. Just having a couple friends over. We do this once, sometimes twice, a week."

What insane luxury, I thought, and I closed the freezer door and walked to the dock.

I scoured social media to kill time. Frankie was gaining traction, with tens of thousands of followers now. I made videos every night. It consumed me. I was living a fantasy. People were following, commenting, and connecting, and besides a few people at work, none of my friends had the slightest idea about my double life or knowledge of my sins. That was the way I liked it. I loved the anonymity.

The difference between quicksand and dry ground was indistinguishable during my time slaving away on the grocery line. The pandemic still raged on, and the enemy class on TV was still doing its best to scare us all. I was thankful that I had a job that involved interactions with real people in real life, because it kept me in the zone of normal humanness. I decided to move on as best I could. I felt deeply unsettled, but I had an anchor, a grocery-store home base.

I looked around the room at what I might be able to do for the last little bit of my shift. I wanted to find Lila and talk about whatever came to us for my remaining hours, but she was gone for the day, and she was slow to return my texts. I wondered about the friends I'd made at the front end: Christian, Mike, Neal, Mary, Sunshine, and Alejandro, who was gone—it seemed like forever since I had seen them. The back of the store was almost entirely separate from the front, and at a company this size, if your schedules didn't align, you would never see them unless you met up outside of work. Given the nature of those times, it was hard to get together.

My texts with Lila were sporadic. She would send me naughty little messages that made me nervous, if only because I liked her and wanted something more from the relationship, but I knew she was looking for sex and fun. I was out of my depth. She was ten years younger than me, and I had no idea how to behave. Something had broken in me during past relationships that had led me to this point. All the excuses were available to me, and I used them with regularity. I was turning into a sad old man who looked into the past for answers while my chance to live in the moment and embrace this strange time in life was goading me to hang out. *Fuck it. No more excuses*, I thought.

Me: Hey

Lila: Hey hey

Me: Let's hang out tonight.

Lila: I thought that was the plan.

Me: Well, yeah. I guess I'm just double checking.

Lila: Dork. 7 work?

Me: Yup

VI

The day seemed like a normal Wednesday afternoon. The summer was in labor with a heat wave, but I made it to work on time. I walked through the front doors, into the icy air of the front end, red faced and drenched in sweat.

Customers peppered the three open registers. There were no big commotions to speak of yet. Soon, the evening rush would be upon Dream Grocers, but for the time being, there was peace.

I stopped at Lila's register and said, "Hey, hey . . . how are you?"

"Just gravy, baby. How are you?"

"Just getting here. But I wanted to check in with you to make sure we are okay. I hope last night wasn't too awkward. We are new to each other, and I get anxious."

She paused for a moment, then said, "Oh, man. I didn't think anything of it, and I'm a bit surprised you brought it up, but yes, of course we are fine. I'm gonna empty your ball sack one of these nights, and you will never forget it."

"Jesus," I said while coughing with surprise.

An elderly man walked up to me. "Sir, do you know where I can find the homemade lobster bisque?"

"Are you talking about the hot soup that we make in-house or the soup called *homemade* that you actually heat up at home?"

"Young man, did I stutter?"

"Uh, no sir. I jus—"

"Ju, ju, juuu point me to the lobster," he demanded.

"Over in the seafood section, or on aisle thirteen, they have the canned stuff."

He fired back immediately, "Canned? Gah. What a bunch of bullshit." Then he stormed off.

I looked back at Lila and asked, "Well, where were we?"

"You are becoming a veteran at dealing with the Normans."

"What else is a boy to do in these strange times? It's a pandemic, after all."

"That it is. I forget sometimes."

"Me too. Now that I am in the back of the store, it's easier to escape."

She half smiled. "Another customer is coming. I'll see you later, okay?"

"Sounds good."

* * *

It was nearing the end of my shift, and the long day was bearing down as I wiped away hard-earned sweat from my brow and looked out at my accomplishments. The entire shipment had been put away and sewed up like a wound from surgery. In reflection, I suppose what I was feeling was a little thing called *pride*. And maybe for the first time in my life, I felt like I had earned my keep. The corporate world I'd left because of a Linda hadn't offered me anything like that in the same way. For all the status and large paychecks, I'd found myself miserable there. Here, I knew I was contributing—and I was appreciated, even if it was shown only in the smallest of gestures and compliments. The rigors of manual labor and tangible accomplishments freed my soul. I hadn't done consistent "hard work" since I was a teenager. And that might have been just the perception that work at fast-food restaurants was difficult, not the actuality. When I was in my early twenties, I'd worked in a warehouse full of every size of tire you could imagine: tractor to wheelbarrow and every kind in between. They had been stacked to the ceiling in an icebox masquerading as a warehouse. My back had been sore every day then also. Again, some people had a tenuous relationship with showing up to work and understanding they were meant to put in effort. But the exercise from lifting and clearing and pulling was enough to satisfy my primal needs. The receiving dock of Dream Grocers looked magnificent. I set down my receiving checklist with a sense of absolution and leaned into the chair at our desk.

Ozzy walked by and asked, "How ya doing, homie?"

"I feel like Andy Dufresne from *The Shawshank Redemption*."

"Aww, that's adorable. Just give it a few more months here, and you will have apathy oozing out of every pore."

"Every one?"

"Every goddamn one, dude. I'm telling you. There is something profound about this place that turns minnows into monsters."

"Jesus, Oz. Can I get a moment in the sun here? I am trying to stay positive. No one is hiring right now anyway."

"I'm sorry, man," Ozzy said and tensed up his whole body to the point where veins were sticking out. "I just wanna get ooouuut on the mat, ya know!"

"Alright. Settle down, Randy Savage."

"Hey! That dude changed my world, man. RIP, Randy!" Ozzy yelled to no one in particular and pounded his chest.

"RIP," I replied with genuine love for the legend, but then I remembered a previous conversation. "Hey, so, what is your wrestling name?"

"Oh, yeah, I forgot to tell you. Well, I'm in between names right now, but I think Savvy Johnson."

I burst out laughing. "You want to call yourself Savvy Johnson?"

"Yeah, dude. Like it's slightly sexual but has a double-oh-seven vibe."

"Honestly, I think it sounds rapey. But if you want to be Savvy Johnson who works in receiving, by all means, you do you."

"Dammit. That's a good point. I need to think of something else. Help me, Daniel."

"Okay. I'll help you, but I'll also call you Savvy Johnson forever and ever."

"Shit. Well, only until we figure out a new name."

"Sure," I said with a smile.

The phone rang, and Ozzy picked it up. He listened for a moment.

"Alright, Daniel, we are needed up front. Let's roll."

"We are?"

"Yup."

"What's the reason?"

He pointed to me and said, "We are going to see if this little birdie can fly!"

Todd was waiting for us when we arrived at the front of the store. He walked up and asked me, "How are you feeling?"

Ozzy paused at the question and waited for my response. "Umm . . . I am doing alright?" I responded with a hint of confusion.

"Good, good. Because we are now at your ninety-day review, and we have a tradition here at Dream Grocers."

"What's that?"

"We ask what your peers think of you."

"How come I hadn't heard of this until now?"

"New employees aren't allowed in on the process. It's more fun when it's a surprise."

"Jesus . . . really?"

"Yes sir. It's only a small formality. And I am sure you will pass with flying colors."

"What if I don't?"

"We kick you out into the cold, dark world."

"Isn't that pleasant."

"I am only kidding, Daniel. But if you do get a bad score, there may be some disciplinary measures taken."

"Sounds like one hell of a tradition."

"It's an unusually cruel one at that, but you got my vote, buddy," Ozzy said as he walked past me to go sit by Mike and Lila.

The employees were gathered around the ends of the registers—a high table from the coffee bar had been placed in between registers six and seven. "Please sit down, Daniel," Todd said. Todd had spoken the truth when he'd said they would put me on trial. My sins were to be put on display before god and man. People pulled up chairs or stood with arms crossed and legs spread to stabilize them. I knew some of those folks, but there were also many I was unfamiliar with who may have secretly hated me. Many on this jury fiddled with their cell phones or chatted with other workers. I realized quickly that my peers were about as interested in the ninety-day ceremony as a kid at a grandparent's cousin's funeral. Some looked exhausted and stared off into the distance. They were present only in the physical sense. But they stood, nonetheless, ready to crucify me or rectify my position there at Dream Grocers before the gods of produce and bakery.

Todd announced to the crowd, "I would like to thank you all for coming to Daniel's Day of Judgment. We all know this as a fine tradition here at Dream Grocers."

A voice chimed out from the crowd, "You never had one."

"Jim, as you well know, I was grandfathered—anyway, that is beside the point. Today we shall be legal, judicial, and punitive with our assessment of Daniel. Shall we begin?"

"String him up!" a voice screamed from the back. Everyone laughed.

"Let's hush down now. We have votes from everyone that has worked here over ninety days submitted, but we must voice any indiscretions also. You know there is a process to the Day of Judgment. First, we shall start with a weighing of his past discretions: How'd he do? Do we have to worry about any other meltdowns?"

Jake went first. "Nah, the guy is gang."

"What is that supposed to mean, Jake?"

"Means he's cool. We like him."

"Good." Todd turned toward Lila. "What do you think, young lady?"

"He's a good egg, Todd, sir. A tad skittish when it comes to getting frisky, but we will solve that soon enough," she said with a smile and lightly grazed my hand.

"Umm . . . wildly inappropriate. You over there. What do you think of this man?"

"Never met him. Seems like a good chap, though."

"And you over there? Please state your name, and let us know what you think."

"My name is Jeff, and I am aggrieved."

Todd smiled. "Please state your case."

"Once, Daniel didn't say hi to me in the hall. He walked right by. Sure, he looked busy and had his arms full of shit, but I deserved that hello. And I will never forget."

Todd turned to me. "What do you have to say to that?"

"I have no idea when that happened, but I am sorry, Jeff."

"It's alright, man. I was just making it up because this is a big goddamn waste of time and I needed entertainment."

Scattered laughter broke out.

"Jeff, we will talk after the meeting," Todd said. "If no one has anything else to say, I will make my appraisal; then we will read the vote total."

A woman's voice rang out from the crowd. "We'd like to say something."

"Yes, who is speaking?"

Christian and Sunshine stepped forward and said in unison, "We would like him to stay."

"Me too," Mike yelled from the back.

"He throws bird damn well, and he is mighty handy with the meat," Jeanie said from the staircase.

I held my laughter.

"Well now, I understand your sentiment, and I won't say he is not going to get the pass, but I need to say a few things first."

The farce. The sham. The prospect of this show being anything but a chance for Todd to show prowess publicly was downright silly.

"First off, I would like to say that we were all a little worried when Daniel sat outside until the point of hypothermia. It was unprecedented, but these are unprecedented times."

A voice rang out from the crowd. "You left him on the couch instead of calling 911."

"Who said that? I swear to god . . ."

Mumbles came from the crowd. They were becoming restless.

Todd, clearly flustered, carried on. "Buuut he worked through his issues and became a solid teammate."

A man with an English accent said, "He was a solid team member the whole time, mate."

Todd ignored the man. "So I think as long as he keeps his life in order, he will have a bright future ahead of him."

"I need to get back to work. I want to go home!" said another voice from the back.

"We will count the vote; then you can leave." He pulled out a piece of paper. "Drums, please, someone." Richard started to pound on a desk. A few people rolled their eyes. At the end of the noise, he announced, "Yes votes total one hundred sixty-five. Votes for *no* are . . . *zero*! Woo-hoo! Step one has been cleared."

"You doing alright there, Daniel?" Todd asked.

"Yeah, I'm good," I replied.

"Now for the in-person voting," Todd continued. "All in favor of Daniel being kept on the team, vote aye."

"Aye!" roared the crowd.

"And all in favor of not keeping him on, vote nay."

Not a sound came from the crowd. In fact, the people in the back were already walking away. A few of my closer friends stayed and said they knew I would make it. Once the dust had settled, Ozzy said, "Go home for the night. I'll finish up the paperwork. Welcome to the team."

The only people left were Todd and Richard. They conferred for several moments; then Todd leaned over and whispered, "Congratulations, Daniel."

"Thanks, Todd," I said with muted pride.

"Don't let me down, now," he responded and slapped my back.

"I won't, sir," I said, half believing and half kidding.

"That's good news. So now that I have you for a moment, let me ask you a question."

"Go for it."

"Have you ever thought about going into management?"

The Grocery Manager

VII

As I prepared for my management interview, I began asking employees to share their concerns and likes and dislikes about their jobs—what we, as management, could do better and what they thought I could do to help their situations.

"I don't know, man." Jamie scratched the side of his head. "I think shit is just fine here. I guess if management could listen to the employees more, that would be great."

"Thanks, dude. Let me know if you think of anything else," I replied, knowing that not only was Jamie stoned, but he also didn't care that much about the job. His canned answer was a version of all I could salvage from most folks around the department, and I didn't fault him for that. He would do whatever was needed, and he worked hard, based on what I had seen. In my mind, that's what mattered most as I went into the uncharted waters of middle management.

"Sounds good, man. Can I go on break?"

"Jamie, Jamie, Jamie, we talked about this . . . gingers are not allowed to have breaks. And technically, I can't tell you if you can go on break. I'm not a manager yet."

"Well, what purpose do you serve? And I heard that. We gingers have rights too! So you can fuck right off!"

I laughed. "Yeah, dude. I can't technically *tell* you to go on break, but you can go ask Achilles and tell him I'll keep an eye on the pizza station for you."

"Sweet. Just so you know, we gingers are *not* to be trifled with."

"You are barely a redhead. You're strawberry blond at most. Now those freckles are a bit out of control, but still, let's be realistic. They probably don't even let you in the meetings."

"I'm on the Committee for Redhead Injustice. We run shit," he said and pointed at me with a big smile on his face.

I burst out laughing. "I'm glad you've attained such incredible status among your people. Now, go to break, ya damn heathen."

"Sure thing, boss."

Next, I needed to talk to Pedro. He was standing by one of the grills with a rag in his hand, spraying a surface that had already been cleaned while a customer waited patiently for his help. I ran behind the counter, asked what they needed, and grabbed the item from behind the prepared-foods case. "Did you need anything else?" I asked.

"No. I'm good. But I was standing here for quite a while. Just an FYI."

"Thanks for letting me know. Have a good day." I turned to Pedro. "Hey, dude, how's it going?"

"It's alright, man. Been super busy up here."

I looked around and saw we were the only people standing in my visible range within the store.

"Is there anything I can do to help you right now?" I asked.

"Actually, I need to take my fifteen. Can you cover me?"

I looked at the time, and I was suddenly caught in a good-cop, bad-cop situation. He had been there for only a little while, and he was the only one up there. I could cover for him, but Jamie had just left. I also didn't want to seem weak and not follow the rules. What kind of potential Dream Grocers manager would I be if I broke the rules right away? I decided to play it safe. "When did you get here?" I asked.

"At eleven a.m."

"It's only eleven thirty. Sorry, dude. I think you'll have to wait." I suddenly realized I was in over my head again. I needed to weasel my way out of faux authority and explain my situation. "We can ask a supervisor, but I'm pretty sure you have to be here for at least an hour and a half before break."

"I thought you were a supervisor."

"Not yet. Well, I'm the only one who applied, but I have to interview for it, and there is a chance that I might not get the job."

"Nepotism at its finest," he replied.

"I don't think that's what *nepotism* means."

"Yes, it is."

I wanted to correct Pedro, but I thought better of it. And I didn't want to start off on the wrong foot since I would be working with him regularly. I changed the subject. "So do you think there are any areas we can improve around here?"

"It's a bunch of bullshit around here."

I took out my pad of paper. "Go on."

"Well, for one, I think breaks should be when the employee needs them. Not when the company says so."

"I understand, but aren't you the only one up here because Juanita is on her last break and the other closer is running late?"

"Yeah, I am. But I really need it."

"After we talk, I'll get with Achilles about getting you one."

"Thanks, man. I just really think the management here doesn't listen to the employees. I have been here for almost three weeks, and I make suggestions *all* of the time, and no one does anything about them."

"Well, what are some of your suggestions? That's what I'm here for."

"Like I said, I think the hardworking employees should be able to take breaks when they need to. Not just every two hours or every hour and a half or whatever."

"I see what you are saying, and I'll definitely bring it up in my interview. Is there anything else that you need?" As we talked, I noticed, again, that he was cleaning essentially spotless areas instead of any meaningful dirt or grime.

"Yeah, man. Can you help that customer while I clean?"

"Sure. But maybe we can tackle it together? There is a small line forming," I said as I turned around to three customers looking annoyed.

"Abby told me to clean right now. I better just stick to what she said."

I didn't have time to fight his reasoning. I had a job to do. That was probably the first time I swallowed my pride for the sake of that job. It burned like whiskey and smelled like the ocean.

Once I was finished helping the customers, I told Pedro, "Alright, dude. I gotta head to the back. Let me know if you think of anything else that we could *improve* on with the department."

"Hey, man, what about my break?" he replied.

"I'll ask Achilles and have him talk to you," I said as I walked through the swinging door into the back, where a classically handsome Achilles with well-groomed dark-brown hair was at the computer. "Hello, my love," he said while staring at the computer.

"Hey, puddin'. So Pedro wants his break. Do you think that is possible?"

"What time did he get here?"

"He said eleven a.m."

"Is Juanita back?"

"Not yet."

Achilles looked at the corner of the computer screen. "That motherfucker has only been here for thirty minutes. Hellll no, he can't have his break yet. Lazy piece of shit."

"Do you want me to tell him, or will you?"

"Shit, let him suffer in silence. He has been a pain since the moment he started working here. Always finding something to complain about. Like, Jesus, dude. You don't even know what you're doing yet. Shit, Daniel. I'm sorry. I don't mean to get all fired up. It's been a long life. And some of these employees are fucking worthless."

I laughed again and said, "I am getting that feeling, and I'm not even a supervisor yet."

"You will."

"I was told no one applied."

"Yup. You're the only one. But more than that . . . everyone likes you. You're affable. Oh, and those baby blues are to die for."

"I think I need to report you to HR, Achilles. These inappropriate comments will not stand," I said with a big smile.

"It's all in love, my Daniel. You work in a kitchen now. This is how we talk. So suck it up, buttercup."

"Pretty sure that's how every department at this store talks. Everyone communicates almost exclusively in sexual and mildly racist innuendos around here."

"True. It's all in good fun. No one is actually being serious."

"That's why I'm falling in love with it."

"My only question is . . . are you down to have dance-offs every once in a while?"

"I think I saw that in the orientation videos. I knew what I was getting into."

"What? Oh wait . . . yeah, it's standard practice."

"Where do I sign up?"

"No sign-up. Just a commitment to motion is all I ask. We will be working together all the time, and I need to know that I have a fellow manager that's down to get weird."

"I'm down."

"Good. Now, are you asking everyone in the department about the things that need to be changed?"

"Yes sir."

"Don't worry about that shit. Or at least don't take it too seriously. You will always get the same answers from people about how the management doesn't listen and blah-blah-blah. Nothing changes. Just work hard, and you'll be fine. I'll leave you with that, and I'm rethinking my previous statement—I think I'll go tell dum-dum out there that he needs to wait for a break. I want to see the dull rage on his face as he wipes down machines that were spotless to begin with."

"Can I watch? That sounds like quite the show."

"Nah, don't waste your time with it. I will probably tell him, look at the reaction, and walk away, and you need to go out in search of answers. Welcome to the team."

I wove in and out of the coolers and storage where one could find supplies for the prepared-foods department in search of employees, but I found myself alone and lost among the shelves filled with ingredients to make almost anything I could imagine. The culinary world was very foreign to me. My nights were comprised of frozen pizza, basic tacos, and eating Chinese food over the sink of my one-bedroom apartment. My lunches consisted of leftovers and vodka in my juice. For most of my life, food had served only as the base for the alcohol I consumed. For example: I didn't really eat breakfast without booze—I was part of the brunch generation. Millennials and mimosas collided on Saturdays at eleven o'clock. It was fun and grossly self-indulgent, and I learned with every passing day that the trend was fading out with my age. And I felt like my time was running out, quickly, like sand in an hourglass.

In those quiet and chilled rooms full of deliciousness, I came to feel embarrassed at my failings. I enjoyed a homemade meal. I respected the craft. My mother was an amazing cook. I had eaten at many fine-dining establishments. But with every glance at a shelf, as I went in search of coworkers, I saw a road not taken.

From what I could see, the prepared-foods department was a stripped-down version of the world Anthony Bourdain had written about in *Kitchen Confidential*—a book I loved from a person I admired. The opportunities seemed deep in breadth and scope. Maybe this could be a new direction for me, a true fresh start.

Downstairs, a fission engine of cooks churned out rotisserie chickens, fifty pounds' worth of Caesar and kale salads at a time, mass amounts of chicken cordon bleu, and anything else our department required. Everyone had a task. A mist of cooking oil hung in the air and coated my face as I walked through. I walked around for a little while, trying to take it all in, but hunger overwhelmed me. It was time to go on break.

* * *

Both Neal and Christian were upstairs by the time clock.

"What's up, fellas?" I asked.

"Oh, look who it is. Mr. Fancy-Pants Manager," Christian said and slapped the side of my arm.

"Good to see you too, friend," I responded.

"Well, Daniel, now we are on opposite sides of the fence. We can't just talk to you the same way anymore. You might report us to HR."

"I already did. They said you're done here."

Christian put his hand on his chest. "Not now! How will I feed my family?"

Neal leaned in. "Daniel, think of the children."

"The idea that either of you would have children horrifies me," I responded.

"Hey now," Christian protested. "I think Neal will be an excellent father. And I have a dog. He's my baby, and he is a very happy boy."

"Alright. You made your case. I think you both will be fantastic parents. I take it all back."

Neal looked me in the eyes. "Thank you. Now, how is it going in prepared foods? Are you liking it?"

"It's okay. Right now, it's essentially the same thing I was doing in receiving. Abby seems cool. I like the managers. Hopefully, I get the supervisor role."

"Ah, man . . . look at you, all grown up and taking this seriously. I'm happy for you."

"Well, I don't know how serious I am taking it, but—"

"Dude, just moving into management is taking it further than most people could ever imagine. You have ambition. Make some moves. Burn the whole thing down. Pillage and plunder. We need good people with the keys."

"I'll try my best."

Christian got wide eyed for a moment, then, with the ever-so-slight Scottish accent, said, "Your best? Losers always whine about their best. Winners go home and fuck the prom queen."

"You know, I remember when Richard said the same joke a long time ago."

Still in the Scottish accent, Christian replied, "Oh, fuck off. He did not."

"Swear to god. Dude, you're channeling Richard." Both Neal and I began to laugh.

"Jesus, I've brought shame upon my family."

Neal put his hand on Christian's shoulder and said, "It's all good, baby. Everyone has their demons."

"I say that quote all the time. Fuck," Christian said.

"You and Richard are as *one*," I replied.

Neal leaned against a doorframe and wheezed from laughing so hard.

"But I will say . . . that was pretty good. Sean Connery would be proud."

"Oh, fuck off," Christian replied.

Neal came up for air and said, "Daniel, you were supposed to say, 'Carla was the prom queen,' in your best Nicolas Cage impression."

"Damn it; I failed. Is there any way to get that back?" I asked.

"No, there isn't, and I don't think you even have a Carla in your life," Neal responded.

Christian's eyes lit up at the possibility of changing the conversation. "Wait. Yes, he does. He has Lila in his life."

"Oh, daaamn! Playa playa," Neal howled.

"How's that going, by the way?" Christian asked.

"Slow," I said.

"How slow?" Christian replied.

"I mean, we haven't fucked, if that's what you're asking."

"That's exactly what I'm asking. But why haven't you sealed the deal?"

"I don't know. She scares me a little."

Christian wound up like a batter ready to swing for the fences. "Daniel, I say this with love. Stop being a pussy. Have confidence. She obviously likes you, and you two have been carrying on for months. This type of behavior will not fly in management here at Dream Grocers."

"Goddamnit. Alright, I'll text her."

"Right now."

"Fine, fine." I pulled out my phone, and on the screen, it said I had missed texts from Lila. "Uhh."

"Uhh what?" Christian said and stared at me.

"She just sent me two texts a couple minutes ago."

"Well, get back to her, and then report back to us immediately. Do we have to do everything for you? Jesus, Daniel."

Neal was still cackling as I walked away.

* * *

Lila: Hey hey

Lila: How is the prep for the big management test going?

Daniel: Heyo! It's going alright. Not sure how I feel about some of the people that I will be supervising if I get it but overall it's going pretty well. How's your day?

Lila: I'm bored.

Daniel: I'm sorry.

Lila: Let's hang out tonight.

Lila: I know you don't have anything to do because no one does. Sooo…let's hang out.

Five minutes passed.

Lila: Daniel? Are you there?

Daniel: Yes. Sorry. I was looking at my notes for my test. I'm down to hang out tonight.

Lila: Good. Don't bail on me like last time. I feel like you've been worried about the past too much. Let's relax and have fun.

Daniel: I know I have. I won't bail. I promise.

Lila: If you do, I am going to cut off your balls.

Daniel: Jesus Christ.

Lila: I am mostly kidding but I seriously want us to connect and hate when people ghost me.

Daniel: Terrifying and understood.

Lila: Lol. OK. Good.

Lila: You have a place all to yourself, right?

Daniel: Yup. No roommates.

Lila: Good. How do you feel about cheap wine and a blowjob to take the pressure off?

Daniel: Uh I feel like that's a great idea.

Lila: Good. Me too. When are you off?

Daniel: 8pm. I walk home. So probably be around 9.

Lila: If you wait for me, I can give you a ride. I am off at 9. Can you wait for me?

Daniel: Of course.

Lila: Perfect. ✌️

* * *

The rest of my shift was absorbed by receiving the load for prepared foods and putting things away. I felt sufficiently ready for my management interview, which was scheduled for tomorrow, but I was plagued with uncertainty. I had talked to people. I had a plan. There was only so much one could do. Pedro would need what he needed . . . and he needed far more than I could offer him. It was time to enjoy myself.

At the bottom of the stairs, I waited on one of those mass-produced designer chairs that were uncomfortable and frequently seen in large coffee shop chains and fast-casual restaurants. My restless leg syndrome kicked in as my mind raced into the past and back out to the future. I normally didn't notice the wobble in my legs, but Lila seemed to be taking a long time, and I had nothing else to focus on—or maybe I was just excited. My legs squirmed and bounced, and I thought back to an ancient, wrinkled author I had met when I had been fiddling around with the idea of being a writer in my midtwenties.

He lived in a house that smelled of mothballs and cheesecake, where the light of the day would break through the dark shades, illuminating a house forgotten by fashion and time for at least three or more decades.

My father, affable and ever kindly, had discovered this old man when he had done some electrical work in his house a few months back. They had begun talking about life, and apparently, his lost artist of a son, who longed to write, had become a topic to pass the time while rewiring the kitchen.

I was obliged to visit this old man because I had nothing going on in my life. It was openly pathetic how I would tell people I wanted to be a writer but had nothing to show for it besides the occasional obscure quote I'd drop at a party to impress people and sound smart. Desperate to find a path, one that would lead to a nirvana of the written word, I sought out this old man's wisdom in hopes he would bestow upon me the thoughts I needed to transcribe my life in a meaningful way.

One afternoon, we sat in his living room and talked about the structure and pace of some hot garbage I had written a week prior. He looked over it for a little while. He was kind and said it needed work, and he pointed out some parts he found interesting. My voice on the page existed, but only for the sake of my tormented failure. It was a navel-gazing screed about my unhappiness with life. The "story" read like a fictional version of a diary—unorganized and ranty—with possibilities but no substance. I hated every sentence he read out loud. I cringed and fidgeted around. Here, my restless leg syndrome started to act up also, and my feet bounced and moved recklessly. He was judging my work, my soul. But more than that, I felt my inadequacies spill out in a room decorated with TV trays, stacks of old books, and the kind of vaguely phallic trinkets that old people collect. I had the thought that I shouldn't be there. He didn't really know me. I didn't really know him. The vulnerability of that moment was something I would never forget.

Suddenly, the old man stopped for a minute and looked down at my jiving legs to say, "Did you know that restless legs are a sign of sexual frustration?"

His words bounced around the room for a moment, then hit me right in the forehead. "Uh . . . no, I didn't know that," I responded and immediately wanted to wrap things up. I awkwardly asked, "Well, what do you think? Am I on to something? You know, with the writing shit."

"I hope that didn't make you uncomfortable, Daniel."

"Oh, what? Me? Nah, I'm fine."

"No, you're not. I'm sorry I made you uncomfortable."

"Everything about this exchange is uncomfortable. That was just the icing on the cake."

"Please forgive me, Daniel. I hope this didn't cause any harm. I'm so lonely, you see, and sometimes I just say things that I feel. I'm old, you know. The filter is gone."

"You're fine. No worries. We're good. I really do have to go, though."

"Oh, okay. Well, here, this box is full of books I think you would like. Will you take them, please?"

I didn't want to but responded, "Of course I will."

I grabbed my jacket, picked up the crate, and headed toward the door. He followed behind me with his cane. As I left, he said, "Please do visit again. I think your writing is excellent, and I know I can help you."

I looked back and said, "I'll come by again. How does next week sound?"

"That sounds lovely," he responded.

The drive home felt awkward and lonely. After being hit on by an old man, everything seemed abstract and intense. I thought maybe I was imagining things. Maybe he was just an isolated old man with a bagful of Viagra and some young hopeful writers to bring into the fold. I couldn't tell his intentions, but I was hesitant to go back.

At a stoplight, I looked in the box to see what books he had sent along with me. Inside, I found a Henry James novel, a few film-review collections, and, well, some erotic fan fiction called *The Quiet Sexual Test of Jesse James*. People began honking at me. The light had changed at some point. Uncontrolled mirth filled the car. They continued to beep their horns. I drove on into the day and never talked to the old man again. Later I wished I had gone back and listened to the wisdom he had been willing to share. My anxiety had gotten the best of me. It would've been easy enough to avoid giving foot massages to ancient feet. But I'd panicked about what I had perceived as his attempt to do whatever it was that he wanted to do. I had been ignorant. And with the car horns fading behind me, I determined that I would figure out my path with writing, no matter how uncertain.

***

Lila walked down the stairs like she was heading to a prom in a nineties' teen movie. Curves and shadows radiated in the soft glow of can lights. "You ready to go?" she asked.

"Lord knows."

"Good," she said, then leaned into me and pecked me on the cheek. "Sorry I took so long. I was talking to Mary. Did you hear about Jake?"

"Ha. I can only imagine. What did he do now? Talk to a customer about the evils of Dream Grocers?"

"You don't have to be like that."

"Like what?"

"You know. You don't have to mock him. He's passionate."

"Oh. I'm not mocking him. I fucking love Jake and his fiery nature. I'm just teasing."

"Oh, okay. Good. He's a great guy."

"I know."

"Well, anyway, he got his second strike. One more and he could be in serious trouble."

"How did that happen?"

"Mary said that he got COVID and couldn't come into work."

"Are you sure? I don't think it works like that."

"Works like what?"

"COVID. I don't think they can fire him for that. It would be a PR nightmare."

"I don't know. That's just what Mary told me."

"Well, if that's the case, that's some bullshit. Even if he was sick, why do we always deal with strikes? Incentives don't work like that. If you are sick, you're sick. Why are they always putting us in a pinch?" I lamented.

"It's the way they remind us of our place in the world. I know that sounds extreme, but it's the damn truth."

"Do you think that place in the world is fixed?"

"Nothing is fixed," she replied. "Now should we go get some food or what?"

"Yes, please. I'm starving."

Another summer day was falling slowly behind the Rocky Mountains as we walked toward her red Honda Accord. She turned to me and asked, "Why don't you have a car?"

"The world has enough of them," I responded.

"Well, aren't you a saint," she said with a smile.

"More like a sinner."

"Good. That's the way I like 'em. But seriously, why?"

"My car broke down, and I didn't feel like having a car payment."

"Ah. That makes sense."

"Plus, it seems unnecessary living in a major city. If I need to get around, I can take my bike or an Uber. When I first got rid of my car, I was struck with a fear that I would be stuck in time and place. I thought my life would become more difficult, but it's pretty damn pleasant. Aaand it seems to be working out well for me tonight since you're giving me a ride. In fact, I have been following some people on Instagram that live the 'van life,' and I'm intrigued, to say the least."

"Did I ever tell you I think hippies are sexy?" she replied.

"No, you didn't. But if I am honest here . . . I'm not surprised." We each smiled a rip-your-clothes-off kind of smile. "Do you think I am a hippie, Lila?"

"I don't think you know *what* you are, Daniel. But you have a free spirit, and that makes me want to jump your bones."

My cheeks warmed. Instantly, I was nervous.

"And I can see my charm is working on you."

"Everything you do works on me."

"Good. Let's get some red wine and pizza and go to the park."

"Sounds like a plan."

* * *

A box of wine sat on the ground in front of us as her soft, cool hand moved inside my shirt and to the top of my jeans. Streetlights were scattered across the park. We'd found a secluded bench shrouded in alleyway darkness. Occasionally, a shadow or two walked under a light, then headed off into the concrete maze that surrounded the public greenery. My nerves were heightened with strangers passing near us. Even with her hands taking me into a better place, I had anxiety looming large, ready to ruin our good time at any moment. But in the cooling air of a summer night, her energy melted my face as we kissed, and I was very happy.

It had been a long time since a woman had touched me. Along with the isolation of the pandemic, I'd been a good boy as I'd searched for the "one" or whatever such nonsense I had convinced myself of in my thirties. My hands were under her shirt as I tried to remember what that spark of vibrance felt like. And it didn't take more than a moment for all of it to come rushing back.

Lila stopped and pulled back from the kiss for a moment. She looked at me and asked, "When is the last time you fooled around with someone?"

"Um—"

"I just want to know before I make my next move."

"Is that a serious question?"

She moved her hand to my balls.

"Dead serious." She smiled, but before I could say anything, she laughed, put a finger to my lips, and then pulled my pants back to midthigh.

"What's wrong?" she asked.

"Nothing. That feels great."

"Are you sure?"

"Definitely. I guess I am just a little paranoid with people out and about. It's like I can see their goddamn eyes popping out from behind the trees, and they are judging us because we aren't wearing our masks."

"Would that turn you on if I did?" she asked.

"What? No. I am a simple man with simple tastes, Lila."

"Well, let's simply get you hard next time."

"Ouch. I mean, I'll try." Lila sat up, and I pulled my pants up and zipped the fly. "I'm sorry."

"Don't be, sweetie. I'm not worried about it. I just want to make sure you are having a good time."

I took a long drink of wine and said, "I'm having a great time," followed by another swig of the good stuff. "Like I said, I just get worried when fooling around in a public park."

"Daniel, people walking through Cheesman Park see way weirder things all the time. But maybe we are rushing things. Let's just get drunk and enjoy the night."

"I like that idea."

Her face scrunched as she looked at me with curiosity and longing. I grabbed the box of wine to fill my cup.

The night was jet black and stoic as it engulfed Lila and me. She slid her arm under mine and laid her head on my shoulder. "Do you think we are gonna make it, Daniel?"

"Like you and I or the royal *we*?"

"The humans. Do you think we are going to make it?"

"Honestly, no."

"I don't think so either. When do you think we'll go?"

"At the first opportunity . . . we try to destroy ourselves any chance we get. We've been trying since the beginning of time."

"But at least we have wine."

"You can say that again."

"At least we have this wonderful wine."

"And a beautiful woman on my arm."

"I am just a girl, Daniel."

"Huh? Aren't you, like, twenty-six?"

"I mean, I am just a girl in the grand cosmic vision of my life. We are all children in the big picture—little specks of immature, narcissistic stardust."

"Who has this grand cosmic vision you speak of?"

"God."

"You believe in God, Lila? I'm surprised," I remarked as I enjoyed her delicate touch on my leg and warmth against my arm.

"Not in a traditional sense. But yes, I believe in God."

"Okay. Where is he, then?"

"It's not a *he* or a *she*, Daniel. It's energy."

"I'm not following," I said before I licked the corners of my mouth free of red wine.

"There is a cosmic glue that holds this whole fucking thing together. I don't know how to explain it more than that."

"Can you try?" I asked.

"Yeah. I can try. Pour me more wine first."

I turned the nozzle and filled her cup up about half-way. I tapped the side of the box of wine. "Damn, I think we put quite a dent in this already."

She looked at me and smiled with sluggish, soothing eyes. I leaned down to give her a hasty kiss. She pulled my neck in at her own pace, and I put my hand at the base of her jawline. Our lips were just centimeters apart. She breathed out with a satisfied moan. Her hand was on my leg as she whispered, "That's it."

"That's God."

"Yup."

"But we haven't even kissed."

"Doesn't matter. That's God."

The entirety of my body tingled as I suddenly didn't care about people watching or vaccines or mandates or pain or fear. My hand traced down her braless back. Her hand slid down the seam of my leg. Lila pulled back slightly to say, "We should probably wait."

Horror washed over me. *Is this God? Patience? Teasing? Are the balls of God blue?* "Yeah, that's fine," I responded.

"Well, we don't have to completely wait." She pulled back my pants.

The night wasn't young, but it was alive with electricity, energy, a god I had yet to know. We tested our limits as the city hummed along. She gave me a release that night, but I had a feeling something else was happening—a thing much bigger and more important—a break in the tide, a shattering of the tension that had wrapped us up so tight during this unbelievably "hot" summer? I wasn't sure if I knew the course, but there we went.

* * *

The next morning, in the upstairs conference room, Todd, Abby, Ozzy, and several members from the pre-pared-foods department were gathered in a semicircle around me. The only person who wasn't seated was Todd, but at his height he was only a little bit taller than me when I was sitting down. I began to feel beads of perspiration on my forehead. They stared in silence as I began my opening statement.

"I would first like to thank Todd, Abby, and every-one in prepared foods for the opportunity to inter-view for the supervisor role in the department. Dream Grocers has taught me many things during this trying time of life. I can do . . . I am ready to step up and create a positive environment for customers, coworkers, and myself in this role."

When I ended my opening monologue, people were jotting down notes. Sweat was soaking through my shirt, and my throat was raw.

Abby looked at me and smiled with assuring, soft eyes that made me feel more at ease. Each person asked several questions about some aspect of the job. Todd fidgeted about silently in the corner, with an intense burrowed stare, as if he were stockpiling ammo before unleashing the unthinkable on me after everyone else had asked their questions.

A quiet came over the room, and I got the sense that everyone was waiting on Todd. And at that exact moment, when the tension had been built, he stepped forward and said, "I have just one question." With an undeterred seriousness, he asked, "If you were a spice, what would you be?"

What in the actual fuck? I thought. That was the question he had been waiting to say all this time? By the look on his face, I couldn't tell if it was a serious question or if he was trying to be lighthearted. But it completely threw me off. You never knew what you were going to get with Todd. The monster or mouse was just around the corner at any moment.

"I would be cumin." I replied.

VIII

"**I** think you are done with the 'training,' Daniel. How do you feel?" Achilles asked.

"Like I have learned nothing."

"Perfect. That's how we roll here at Dream Grocers. Straight into the fire."

A teaser of panic crawled up my spine. "Are we really done? That's it."

"Yeah. We end the shadowing tonight."

"Jesus Christ."

"Look, you are going to do just fine."

"Fine? Not great?"

"Oh, honey, *great* is a stretch for anyone in this role. We run a difficult store. And you have learning to do. You've never even worked in a restaurant before. It's not a bad thing. In fact, that says a lot about you that we picked you. We all talked about it and selected you because you seem like an everyman and a fighter. Like, I know we made the right decision by working with you for the last couple weeks. But be forewarned; it's gonna get worse. I get the feeling we are at a high point, and lows are coming. Just wait until the corporate comes through."

"I can't tell if you are trying to encourage me or scare me."

Achilles laughed. "You're gonna do fiiiinah, seriously. Just take it one thing at a time."

I'd been following Achilles around for the last two weeks. During this time, we had gone over the checklist of tasks to do, and most nights, every formal task would fall apart or someone would call out or quit, and maybe a freezer would break right at the end, and we would have to improvise. There was a frenetic pace to the whole thing that was fun in a way, but I dreaded the idea of going it alone. On top of my duties as a manager, I would still have to put the load away. A staggering amount of work had to be finished every night. And it wasn't like the corporate world, where I could leave things until the next day. What I would learn later was that sometimes shit didn't get done, like, ever. It was the nature of the job. I had to accept my fate every night and do the best I could with what I had.

Achilles and I counted the stock on the wall of prepared foods. I said the numbers. He wrote them down. I enjoyed working with him. Hell, I was starting to enjoy working at the store in general.

* * *

"Remember, you have to show authority. This is your crew," Tony said with a clenched jaw, then walked away.

Achilles strolled up and asked, "What's his deal?"

"He's having a long day," I said. "Think the crew is being stubborn. Abby told me that he got turned down for a promotion."

"Aww . . . bummer. Well, he shouldn't be such a dick. Then he might have got the job."

There was a pregnant pause, and I asked, "Is he really that bad?"

"I mean, he is just difficult sometimes. Maybe more than most. I am too. We all are. This is a pretty high-stress job. I feel like a burnt and discarded match most days. Tony is a good guy, though. Don't worry about it."

"Alright. I will kill him with kindness."

"Ooh-kay . . . let's not get crazy here, ya weirdo. Have you received the load yet?"

"It's not here."

"Cool. Want to cover Janice on the Chef's Case for a bit? I need to talk to her about something."

"Is she in trouble?"

"Eh. I shouldn't say right now. I'll tell you later."

The Chef's Case was the front desk of our department. It was a long glass dome-like structure that housed a billion different bacteria not mentioned on the menu, and many of the products or full dishes we made in-house, such as chicken teriyaki, grilled chicken, and tandoori chicken. Or we might have had something such as rice pilaf, fried plantains, stuffed peppers, beef lasagna, Swedish meatballs, or bacon meat loaf, but there were always salads, salads, salads, all types of salads—broccoli, chicken Caesar, garden salads. The food would remain in there for a few days, eroding down to an ugly alcoholic version of its former self. Think of the pizza you left on a plate uncovered in the fridge for a few days. It would be edible, sure, but it would also be a test of endurance and intestinal fortitude.

Janice smelled like orange juice and mouthwash when I told her that Achilles needed to talk to her about something. No judgment here—whiskey's dull knife was burrowing into my skull at that very moment as the excesses of the night before oozed out of my skin and mustard-gas breath rolled out of my mouth, hot and slow, for all who dared to get close. There was a good reason that I smelled like shame and wished for death. Last night, we had celebrated me overcoming the struggles of my time at Dream Grocers. My neighbors and I had gathered on the patio and drunk ourselves into a furious stupor. It had been the right thing to do, and it had been par for the course during the summer of 2020. Everyone I knew was on a mission to oblivion or staggering abundance or somewhere in between. A half bottle of whiskey had remained when Jason, my favorite neighbor, had begun talking furiously about the state of the world.

"All I want to do is go to a concert and take acid and people watch," he said.

"Me too, buddy," I agreed. "I can't wait until concerts come back and the world begins to right itself. I am desperate to get back to the way things were."

"I'm not entirely sure we will ever get back to that," he responded. "There seems to be a permanent shift happening, in real time, right in front of us."

"This isn't something we can subconsciously forget, I think."

Jason swigged the whiskey and said, "You're probably right. I'm sad that we may be in a permanently altered and quickly forgotten state going forward."

"I really wonder when being a human was 'normal,' ya know? Was it when Pizza Hut had a badass buffet, or do we need to go back to a time before we were born? I guess I'm more bummed that we're missing out on these years of our lives."

Lizzy interjected, "There is a deadly virus raging out there, and people are dying, guys."

"People were always dying, Lizzy," someone said.

A roar of laughter cascaded across the group. We were very drunk. But she was not wrong. I just didn't know the extent to which I should be afraid. The things that concerned me were that of sex and freedom.

"Dude, I think it's awesome you are pushing for a goal even while the world burns. That's goddamn morose and inspiring."

"Thanks, man. It's the only thing keeping me tethered to reality. Oh, and this girl, Lila, I've been seeing at work."

"Oooh, details, please," Lizzy said.

"What do you want to know?"

"Do you love her?"

"Not yet."

"Are you two in lust?"

"I guess you could call it that."

"Good. That's all you need for now."

* * *

"Ruff, *ruff*!"

A disheveled man with bushy gray hair on his head and face and a tube going up to his nose came into focus. His wild eyes met mine. His mouth opened to make the "Ruff!" sound, just like a dog.

What the hell was that? I thought as I shook my bones loose to see if I was dreaming.

"Ruff!"

That fool was barking at me like an abused dog who didn't know what to do when someone tried to hand him food. I paused for a moment. He leaned on the case and pointed, "Two pounds of the lemon salmon."

"Uhh . . . okay. Sure," I said, then placed the salmon in a plastic bag and set it on the top of the case.

"Ruff, *ruff*!"

I came to the quick realization that he must have Tourette's syndrome or something. But then he lunged toward the case. "Look, sir. I'm not trying to be a pain here, but I don't like those pieces."

"Oh, okay. Well, what pieces would you like?"

I grabbed the tongs and pointed to the pieces as he chose which ones his heart desired.

"Ruff, *ruff*!"

I stood up to hand him his fish. "I need more things. I want to pick out the pieces," he demanded.

My hangover was getting worse by the minute, but nonetheless, I crouched down while he hand-selected green beans and shallots, meat loaf, crab cakes, rice, etc. All the while, he barked away and told me what he wanted.

The man and his wife finally walked away with maybe $120 worth of precooked food that had been made two days ago. Achilles walked up to me with

Janice at his side. She looked like she had been crying. "Can you help that customer, Janice?" he asked.

"Sure. No problem."

When she was gone, I asked, "Everything alright?"

"Yeah, I think we are good," Achilles responded.

"You didn't tell me we had a barking customer," I said.

Achilles burst out laughing. "I'm glad you got to meet him on your first night. He is a fresh nightmare sometimes."

"Very picky and rude on top of the barking. Does he have Tourette's or something?"

"That's what I thought at first, but I have watched him as other people helped him, and it didn't seem compulsory. He definitely picks who he barks at."

"So why does he do it?"

"No idea. I think he just likes to fuck with us."

"Umm . . . that's so bizarre."

"I know, right? I have never understood it. I just try to avoid him and walk in the back, but sometimes it's impossible, and you are stuck helping the rich dog-man."

"I guess so. Oh, and he left thirty dollars' worth of salmon here to rot. He wanted different pieces."

"Damn. That comes directly out of your pocket. Sorry, buddy."

"What?!"

"Just fucking with you. Write it down, and throw it out."

"We seriously throw this out? That's crazy."

"Yeah, man. We can't put it back in the case, and the company won't let you take home shit like that to eat.

Just wait . . . the amount of waste you will see here will leave you breathless and enraged that people starve."

"Interesting. I guess I'll see tonight when I clear out all the old products when I write production. Besides Janice, who do I have working tonight?"

Achilles smiled. "Well, you have Jamie, who is great, and . . . Pedro, our prodigal son."

"Hey . . . we'll get it done, my friend," I said.

"That's the right attitude," Achilles said. "Some nights will be worse than others, but you'll get through it all and be better for it."

"Really?" I asked.

"Oh, hell, I don't know. That's just what I tell everyone."

"You are *so* kind, Achilles," I said.

"Thanks, puddin'. Alright. Did you need anything else from me? Remember, you only have a couple more hours. Text me if you need anything." He turned to Janice. "You gonna be alright, hun?"

Janice's skin was blotchy red, and her eyes were tired from a lifetime of whatever she'd witnessed. But she had a good smile and a charm. "Yeah, I think I'll be okay. I'll just talk to Daniel if I am having any issues."

"Good, good. Okay. Well, Daniel, I am out of here. Go with god."

"We are the cockroaches of retail, Achilles. They can never kill us."

Achilles laughed. "Whatever you say, bro. Just give it a few weeks."

* * *

An hour later, while I wrote production, Janice walked up to me with sore red eyes and a slight tremble. The ambrosia of mouthwash pierced the air a bit more this time. She hadn't uttered a word, but I knew something was wrong. I took stock of the situation: I had one other person on the case (Pedro), and Jamie was at the pizza station. That was it. Those were all the people I had to close for the night.

"Daniel," she whimpered.

I tried to play it cool like a manager should. When really, I had no idea how to act. "Hi, Janice . . . how are you doing?"

"Well, I don't really know."

"Okay. How can I help?"

"I just started freaking out while I was helping a customer."

I looked back at the counter. "Like, you started yelling at a customer?" I replied.

"Oh no, nothing like that. It was inside my head. I get anxiety attacks."

"Ah, yeah, I understand. I get those too sometimes. Do you want to take a breather?"

"Could I go out and smoke a cigarette? I won't take a whole fifteen."

"Sure. No problem. I'll help watch the counter."

"Thanks, Daniel."

"No problem at all," I replied and went back to counting the in-house kettle-style potato chips.

"Daniel?" Janice asked.

"Yup, yup," I said and looked at her momentarily.

"You have kind eyes. I think I'm going to enjoy working with you."

"Thanks, Janice. I think I am going to enjoy working with you too. Let me know if you need anything, okay?"

She replied, "Alright," with a slight smile on her face and walked away.

* * *

Production wasn't complicated, but it *was* time consuming. I counted each item in stock and then used a spreadsheet to forecast what I needed my team to produce during the next few days. This process devoured the majority of each shift. I was incompetent and slow at first—methodically going over each item, making sure I got it right. With time, I would find my identity with that element of my job. I would start to obsess over the wall. I would *need* the holes to be filled. But what I would learn was that it was nearly impossible to do the work because we would either not have enough cooks to make the food or not enough people to pack out the items. And because of this dynamic of supply and demand, I would be doomed to forever chase that goal like a dog chasing a car it would never catch.

* * *

A couple of hours passed, and Janice hadn't returned. That left us with two people and myself and several hours until we closed. I followed Achilles's advice and went upstairs to see what a manager might advise me to do about the situation.

Assistant manager Richard was leaning back in his chair at his desk, eating macadamia nuts out of a little plastic bag. He licked the salt off his fingers after smashing a handful into his face, then stared at me with little lumps of coal we normally called *eyes* as he waited for me to ask my question.

"So," I said with trepidation in my voice. "We have an employee that seems to have either wandered off or left for the day without telling me. Looks like she's been gone for a couple hours."

He shot up from his chair. "Why didn't you tell me about this earlier?"

"Honestly, I have been busy writing production and didn't notice. The other employees didn't say anything. Probably because they are busy too."

"Daniel, I need to know these things right away."

"Sorry, I didn't have time with everything going on."

"Who left?"

"Janice."

"How long has Janice been gone?"

"She asked to go on her break about two hours ago."

"Well, this doesn't look good on you, Daniel. As a new manager, I would expect you to be more attentive."

"Again, I'm sorry. What should we do here?"

"What do you think *you* should do?"

"Can I close down the sandwich station?"

"That's a possibility," he said, then casually scooped more macadamia nuts into his mouth and chewed loudly.

"Richard, I could really use your help. It's my first shift on my own, and I've been slammed. Both of the employees left need their last break."

He dropped the bag from maybe a foot above the counter, and the nuts nearly spilled everywhere. "Do what you need to do, Daniel."

"Okay. I'll shut down the sandwich station and close up an hour early."

Richard turned around to his computer without saying a word. I stood for a moment, unsure if I needed his permission or what exactly was happening, but I finally decided to walk out.

* * *

The department was in a state of disarray when I arrived downstairs. Jamie was organizing his station. Pedro was cleaning areas that were already shiny. I gathered them for a quick chat.

"Alright, guys. I don't know what happened to Janice, but we will need to start closing up shop piece by piece so we aren't here all night."

Jamie squinted with a lack of understanding and said, "What do you mean by 'happened to Janice'? She's downstairs getting supplies."

"Really? I looked down there. I looked everywhere, and I couldn't find her."

"I don't know, man. But she's here."

"Well, maybe she was playing hide-and-go-seek or my mind is playing tricks on me. Either way, I don't think it would be a bad idea to get this place tidied up and start getting ready to close."

Excitedly, Pedro asked, "That mean we can shut down the sandwich station now?"

VIII

"Since we have Janice, I don't think we should close it all the way. Maybe just prep it to close, but be ready to make a hamburger if a customer comes up. How does that sound?"

"Eh. Whatever, dude. We have been slaving away all day, and you have been off wherever doing some bullshit. I think we should be able to close some of the stations early. What do you say, Jamie?"

Jamie shrugged. "Whatever Daniel wants. I have plenty to do."

Flustered by Pedro's sudden rebellion, I said, "I haven't been doing 'nothing.' I've been doing my job. I'd say go ahead and start preparing for close, but be ready to throw a burger on if someone swings through."

"Sure," Pedro responded and walked away.

"You good to go, Jamie?" I asked.

"Psh. Yeah, dude. Ignore him. He's just one of *those* people."

"What kind of people?"

"The miserable and lonely kind."

"If you need anything, let me know—sound good?"

"Works for me," he replied.

That's when I saw Janice walk out from the back room with a sleeve of napkins and a sleeve of plates. Knowing that I needed to be delicate in order to make it through the night, I teased, "I thought we lost you for a minute."

A disoriented or feigned shock came over her face. "I would never just leave you, Daniel. I had to talk to my boyfriend for a bit because the cops were at our apartment. We were both calming each other down, and I walked off behind the parking garage and lost track of time. I'm sorry."

"That's okay. Just let me know next time. Is everyone safe at home?"

"Yeah. Everyone was fine. It was something about the neighbor's dog biting him, and they will have to put him down."

"Your boyfriend?" I said.

"Shit, I wish," Janice said, and we both laughed.

* * *

As I entered my production numbers into the computer, I checked the case area and pizza section. Pedro was "cleaning" and closing down the stations, Janice was helping customers, and Jamie was working away by straightening up the area. The line of people coming up to the case was steady for the next couple of hours. Pedro walked over to me. "Dude, this is what I'm talking about with listening and paying attention to your employees. Janice and I need our breaks."

"Sorry, Pedro. I was busy doing production. You can go on your final fifteen, and I'll help the front catch up."

"Did you even hear the part about listening to your employees?"

"Pedro. Is there something you need to get off your chest?"

"What I already said. Jesus Christ, man."

"So I'm not sure what exactly I did here, but you can go on your break. If you need to talk to Abby about your issues, we can set up a meeting."

"Nah, dude. We don't need to involve her. We can talk man to man."

"Okay. Well, we both have work to do, so maybe later."

He slouched back and looked toward the ceiling slowly, then said "Whatever" and walked away.

I looked out at the case, and Janice had cleared a line of people and was cleaning and closing up shop. I eased back into my drafting chair, and my feet sighed from sweet release. Every clump of muscle and ligament between my toes, feet, legs, and back screamed at me as I sat in isolation and finished typing numbers into a spreadsheet I barely understood the purpose of. Our desk was located in a normally busy hallway by the stairs behind prepared foods. People walked through at all moments of the day, but it was night-shift-hospital quiet that night. A refrigerator fan kicked on in the main cooler. Hinges from a door upstairs screeched. The sound of keys click-clacking away sung with the glory and pain of making it through a day doing something new. I reflected on the misery and compatriotism of the people who worked with me.

Pedro made it back from his twenty-minute break.

"I'm finished with my work if you need to talk still," I said.

"Nah, dude. I'll get Abby involved."

"I thought you wanted to talk to me 'man to man'?"

"Honestly, I don't think anything will change if we do it that way."

I was too tired to fight. "Okay. Sounds good. Can you do me a favor and ask Janice to go on break, and we will start closing up? We have about a half an hour left."

"Yeah, dude. Whatever."

I was proud of my resolve not to punch that fucking idiot in the throat. Something about his passive-aggressive attitude made me feel a bit of pain for him. Maybe his mother had refused to hold him because she thought men could tell she was a young mother when she would go out with friends and drink. Or maybe she had neglected him while spoiling him at the same time, like, "Here is a new gaming system; go play. Mommy's busy." I found it entertaining to think of the scenarios that might have made Pedro into the sad sack of shit that he came off as. Failure backed up behind his eyes like water at the Hoover Dam. He wanted everything but wasn't willing to work for it. If he was younger, I would have given him a break, but he had to be close to forty.

In my journey through management, I would run into people like him over and over again. They lacked the imagination to understand why people didn't like them and why they never seemed to get ahead. My doubts as a leader came into play here because I loved to talk to people about their lives and give what advice I felt qualified to accord, but Pedro was past that point. The conversations we did have consisted of conspiracy theories and his shortsighted observations about the world where he blamed others or cocooned himself into his past life, unwilling to change.

I started doing some of the dishes and cleaning the removable countertops when Jamie popped up with all the pizza equipment. "What's up, dude?" he asked.

"Not much, man. Just finishing up some dishes before I do the department walk."

"I can finish up here," he said.

"You sure?"

"Yeah, dude. Easy peasy. Plus, you are taking too goddamn long."

I laughed. "Yeah, I am kinda learning as I go with this stuff."

"You haven't worked in a kitchen before, have you?"

"I can barely cook for myself, dude."

"All good, man. How did you get into management, then?" he asked.

"Ha. That's a good question."

"Sorry, I don't mean to be rude. I'm just surprised they put you here if you didn't have experience."

"Nah. You are fine, man. I guess you could say I was pretty much the only one that applied. But really, I just wanted the job, I work hard, and I'm pretty likable. I wanted to prove it to myself."

"I can't speak to the first one, but you seem like a reasonably nice dude."

"Awww . . . thanks, Jamie. That's so sweet."

We both laughed, and I said, "Well, I think I'll let you be. Enjoy."

I smiled as I walked away because I liked what Jamie brought to life: he was a straight shooter, friendly, affable, helpful. That was the kind of person I wanted to work with. He would have his moments, but we all did from time to time. The distance between Pedro and Jamie could not have been further. I decided that I needed to check the Chef's Case, but Janice was still there.

"Didn't you have another break?" I asked her as I walked up.

"No. I basically took thirty minutes before, so . . . I'm good."

"Oh, okay. How are we looking up here?"

"Surprisingly smooth, but where did Pedro go? He was here for a minute. Asked me to take my break, and I told him what happened earlier. He looked annoyed, then said he was going to talk to you. I'm so sorry. I don't mean to cause trouble."

"You are fine. No worries at all. I would say that going forward, just keep it between you and I if we have issues like the earlier one."

"I will. I'm sorry," she said with a whimper.

"No need to be sorry. And I'll help you until he gets back."

I looked around for a few moments, and Pedro wasn't within sight.

I grabbed a mop and began to clean the floor. A finger tapped me on my shoulder. I looked up, and Janice was pointing at a selfie with her and a young man on her phone. "That's my boy," she said. I gave it a close examination.

"You look like a good mother."

"Oh, I am," she announced with faux bravado.

"No, really. I think he looks like he loves his mom. That's good."

"You really think so?"

"Yeah. I really do," I replied.

"Good. Sometimes it's difficult to tell how people feel about me."

"People are hard to read. Experiences can be even worse. Sometimes you just need someone to tell you what's up, ya know?"

"Yes. Yes, I do." Janice replied with a smile.

My phone vibrated from a text message.

Lila: 🥒 🧄 *Tonight?*

Me: 100%

Lila: Bout time. 🙂

162

VIII

***

Our skin glistened as salty legs twisted together like pretzels, and we lay entangled at dawn smelling like a hormone ocean gathering our postorgasm breaths. A cold front signaling the slow movement from fall to winter had moved in overnight, and the heater in my apartment had failed again. We huddled under a blanket. Lila had a contented smile painted on her face, and I was a very happy man. It'd been a long time since I had fucked, and there I was, back in the saddle, so to speak, reclaiming my manhood. The pandemic had been a long, lonely stretch for many people. But I had managed to finally find someone who liked me enough to share these moments.

She looked at me with gentle eyes. "That was pretty good, huh?"

"It was. You're amazing," I replied.

"You're not so bad yourself." She combed out the longer pubic hair to the sides of my groin with her fingernails. "I wanna do that again. Can we?"

"Yeah, of course. Can we wait just a little bit? You know, I'm not as spry these days."

"You're so silly. You act like an old man in the strangest moments. If I thought you were too old, I wouldn't have hit on you. I don't really care about that shit. I go for who I'm attracted to."

"That's nice to hear."

"Good. Now fuck me again."

"At your request," I said as I rolled over and slid between her legs. Her breath shuddered a little. I was diamond hard as I began to move in and out. The moans banked off the walls, rising in pitch until, I think, she climaxed. I was still unbroken. She looked at me. "Did you cum?"

"Of course," I lied and sat up.

"So are you worried about the holiday season?" she asked as she lay on her stomach with her head in her palms.

"Should I be?"

"Not really. It's just a busy time of year. It gets over-whelming in prepared foods."

"I guess that's what I signed up for with this man-agement thing."

"I think it's sexy that you have ambition."

"Oh really?"

"Extremely. Even with your age showing, I think we should do this again. What do you think?"

"I'm available allll week."

"Good," she said as she grazed my dick. She stopped. "Are you hard already? How is that possible?"

"I have good vascular strength."

She grabbed it a little harder than I would have liked and asked, "Did you take Viagra, dude? Like, this is the second time you 'came,' and, like, you have the boner of a teenager."

The gig was up. "Um . . . if I said yes, would you be mad at me?"

She laughed. "Well, why do you need it? You're only in your thirties."

"I guess I was just nervous is all. At my ripe old age, I need some time to get situated. Ya know?"

"I guess, but why didn't you say something? Instead you just lied to me like it was nothing. Now I feel weird that I can't satisfy you."

"Oh no! That's not it at all. I promise."

She sat up quickly, slid off the bed, and began putting on her bra. "That promise changes nothing. You lied to me, and I know it."

I scrambled to my feet with my stone pillar swaying side to side in the cold air. "I'm so sorry. I didn't know it would offend you."

"Dude, you are in your thirties, and you have no idea that lying is bad?"

"It's a lie that got you off, though, right? That has to say something."

She paused for a moment, then threw her purse strap over her shoulder. "In fact, it does. It says our connection—that orgasm—wasn't real."

"Oh, come on now." I backtracked because I was invalidating her feelings. Therapy had taught me not to do such things. Especially in moments like that. "Can we please just talk about it? Can I explain myself?"

"Maybe another time, but right now, I need to go."

And just like that, she was almost out of sight. She even left the door wide open, and I didn't get a kiss good night. I covered my junk and jumped to close the door. I sidestepped to the window, pulled the slats of the blinds apart, and watched her storm down the stairs and out into the night. My dick was soft and sad. All my steam and confidence were gone. But they had been built on lies, so it didn't really matter. Nothing had sustenance anymore. There was nowhere to go except the emptiness I had conjured up through my own anxieties. I knew I had ruined a good thing all because I had wanted to rise to the occasion—literally and figuratively—and turn Lila into the person I'd envisioned. She wanted honesty and companionship and fun, and I'd thought our foundation was built solely on lust. I didn't need that little blue pill. A robust and honest conversation with myself would have gone a long way. I needed time. She turned me on; I knew this. Soon I realized I was just peering out the window in hopes that she would come back and I could apologize. But that—that ship had sailed. I wanted to cry as I stood stark naked under a popcorn ceiling and desk-lamp lighting with toes digging into the dirty carpet. I let the blinds swing, then turned the light off and walked through the darkness of my apartment, feeling lonelier than a man marooned on a desert isle.

When I slid into bed, I could smell her on my sheets, and my arousal came back with a vengeance. I turned onto my back, pulled her pillow onto my face, and thought about her hips moving—I could see my failures from tonight as I finished at the edge of a lie and desire.

IX

Day 1

Six a.m. opens my eyes with a battering ram. I slide out of bed with forced enthusiasm, throw on what work clothes I can find, and brush off the week-old dirt and grime. I have an allure consisting of stale frying oil, dried sweat, and the road less traveled. No time to settle in with my French-pressed morning routine. I pour my leftover coffee out of the thermos and throw it in the microwave for thirty seconds, then put it right back in the to-go mug—I'm desperate. No shame. Add cream, and sip the bitter end of a rushed morning.

I'm out the door and on my Schwinn before the caffeine hits my bloodstream. The asphalt is damp, but there isn't any ice to speak of, so I peddle faster and let cold air crack me across the face like a baseball bat. I rise from the ashes immediately. Eyes widen; focus narrows. Here we go.

By the time I reach the store, my face feels like a warm pond of blood covered by a layer of skin frozen to the touch. The line that has stretched around the building since the beginning of the outbreak is more tense than normal. It's the week of Thanksgiving. And from what I have been told . . . God doesn't visit the store this time of year. No forgiveness of sins. No understanding. Just the devil all the way down.

I clock in, grab my chef's coat, and head down to the kitchen. The department managers had a meeting this week, and we are about to have our own. Tony, Achilles, Sarah, and Liam are buttoning up their jackets, getting ready for Abby.

"Where is she?" I ask.

"Think she is printing some stuff off. But we've all been through this before, so I wouldn't worry about it too much," Achilles says.

Liam laughs. "Sure, dude. It's always a madhouse. Every year."

"Shut up, Liam. I'm trying to encourage our little Daniel. I don't want him to quit."

"Just so you can sexually harass him."

"Oh, is someone getting jealous?"

"I have two kids, Achilles," Liam responds.

"So did Ted Haggard."

"He has a point," I say and smile at Liam.

"Goddamnit, Achilles. I told you to stop talking about my uncle," Liam says.

"Wait a minute! Your uncle is Ted Haggard?" I ask.

"No. He was the prostitute smoking meth with Ted."

"Really?" I was shocked to hear such juicy news so early in the morning.

"*Yeah, but I told Achilles that in confidence. Damn you, Achilles.*"

A hush came over the five of us, and then an eruption of laughter burst out of the seams.

"*You had me going for a second,*" *I say.*

"*We know. And it was fun,*" *Liam says in between breaths.*

Abby arrives from the stairway. "*What's so funny?*"

Tony is laughing the hardest out of anyone. It's the first time I have seen him show joy of any sort. He tries to explain between the laughter. "*Liam . . . meth . . . prostitute . . . uncle.*"

Abby squints at him. "*Maybe give it a shot later when you catch your breath. Alright, gang, are we ready to start the meeting?*" *We compose ourselves and face Abby.* "*Thank you all for showing up so early. I know that for many of you, this day will be very long. Hell, this week is gonna be grueling for all of us. I appreciate you being here. Remember, we are approved for as much overtime as needed. Here are the checklists. I put you into pairs. Sarah and Liam, me and Tony, and Daniel and Achilles. Look over your lists, and get back to me. Achilles and Daniel will be busy with receiving all day today. But the meal-prep work will begin tomorrow.*"

"*Dude, this is a long list of things to do,*" *I say to Achilles.*

"*And it's only one-third of the things we need to do to be ready,*" *he replies.*

"*Jesus Christ.*"

"*I told you last week that Mr. Christ takes a vacation every year on this week.*"

"*And to think I was about to become a believer.*"

"*There are no atheists in a foxhole, and this week is a fucking foxhole. You ready to hit up receiving? We are due a few hundred turkeys here shortly.*"

"*Let's go.*"

Ozzy is standing at his desk. "*What up, fellas? You ready for this shit or what? Truck just arrived.*"

"*Born ready,*" *I respond.*

"*That's sad,*" *Achilles says.* "*We should all be doing anything but this with our lives.*"

"*Someone has to do it,*" *I respond.*

"*I should have gone to art school,*" *Achilles says.*

"*There's still time,*" *I reply as the dock doors raise like the eyelids of a drunken god, only to reveal the pain and misery of a lifetime of indiscretions. Boxes are stacked on pallets to the very edge of the truck. The driver comes in through the side door and warns us with his southern drawl,* "*Y'all are in for a treat. A couple of these pallets tipped over in the back. No way to tell what's salvageable until we get them unloaded. And we have a full load today, boys. Twenty-eight pallets on this truck, and another fella should be waiting with the same amount.*"

"*Is all of it ours?*" *I ask Achilles.*

"*Yes sir. The second truck too. Are you ready to pop that cherry?*" *the driver replies.*

"*Do I have a choice?*"

"*Not today, my friend. Not today.*"

The driver begins unloading the truck. First, we have ten pallets of turkeys stacked eight feet tall. Next come fourteen pallets of hams. Finally, the four remaining are rosemary chickens. The next truck will have the remainder of selected meats. We begin to unload box after box after box onto U-boats—forty, fifty, sixty pounds

170

apiece. Boats are full. Elevator down. Unload. Back is stiff; my joints crack and hate me with every movement in this young man's game. Elevator up. Load the boats. Achilles is still downstairs straightening up the room and clearing space. Heave boxes. My body bends and twists and pulls. What did they say in training? Ah yes, lift with your legs. But how? Not possible at these angles and in these positions. Beads of sweat bubble my brow and begin to soak my black hat. I take off my chef's coat. Sweet relief. Muscles start to warm. Blood pumping. My back is less starched now. Warming up and getting a rhythm. Throwing boxes with fifty pounds' worth of ham above my head. Two U-boats loaded. No sign of Achilles. Pull one and push one to the elevator. Sink into the earth. I find Achilles sitting down. He hurt his back. Shit. I clear one boat, and we sit on the elevator ride up.

He is wincing in pain. "Dude, I don't know how it happened, but I'll need to sit for a while. I'll talk to Abby and see what we can do to get you help."

"I will be alright," I reply, motivated.

"You sure?"

"Yup. Just rest up so we can close the store properly."

"Okay. I'm sorry."

I am alone now; the chipped-paint mosaic that is receiving expands and contracts, breathing and tightening, constricting. At the back of the truck, I find that the product didn't actually fall over all the way. It leans against the wall of the trailer. "Man, sometimes you just get all the luck," the driver says unironically. He is thinking only of his situation, of course. In a moment he'll be gone.

The second truck is lining up as I get in the elevator. One door closes; another one opens.

I begin to unload the last of the first truck into the cooler. It's not a large room, and the space is shrinking with every box. I wonder how everything will fit in this tiny space. The sweat accumulating on my neck gives me chills and freezes in place.

Cases of holiday-related products are lined up all the way to the elevator door. I can barely sneak through. This load consists of more ham, but the majority are frozen sides such as green beans, yams, corn . . .

The items weigh less, but there are many more boxes of all shapes and sizes. I will need to make more trips on this shipment and drop them in many different coolers. My fitness level is deplorable. I begin to cramp. I ignore the biting pain, remembering that I can work through this sort of thing. I press on. I'm making good time. I worry about Achilles, and I wonder if anyone will be coming to help, but I change my tune and focus on the task at hand. Cartons of god-knows-what are stacked up, up, up, and they won't put themselves away. I remember earlier in my youth—the vital years—I thought I hated physical labor like what I am doing today. It seemed unnecessary, punishing, even, but now I'm struck with a sense of relief and joy. I am actually doing something instead of typing away on a keyboard connected to the abyss. My corporate life is far behind me now. There are obviously trade-offs in this situation, but I am stoned happy with the changes I have made despite much of world limping along outside this grocery store. Even though I face the public daily and a virus is running through our society—and shootings are happening at other grocery stores—I feel secure at the center of it all. Like the eye of the storm. It's calm, and the people I work with are generous. The customers are

. . . well . . . some are kind. Others are here to exercise the emotional pain they live with in public. Their shame has no bounds. I've moved into management. Onward and upward. I'm making Mother proud. I even like how I can let my mind wander and not lose track of the work. I couldn't do that at the office. Sure, I would spend large swaths of time surfing the web, but I was chained to that desk, that life. Here, working in receiving, I feel untethered, at least for now. I want to say that doing work with my hands is the truth. It's what we are supposed to do. Our trajectory, as a species, is low and fast, dangerous, and ultimately unknown.

As I finish up the second truck, I massage my shoulders and dig at knots in my back with the corner of shelving. I try not to voice my joyous pain. I wish things hadn't gone south with Lila and she was here—ready and willing—to make my body feel better. She is good at that. We've been talking here and there. Maybe there is a chance to revisit the magic. I look at my phone. No texts yet today. Strange. Maybe that was my one and only shot. I dragged it out so long that I'm surprised she waited for me at all.

I shelve these thoughts for a bit as I bring the final U-boat downstairs. Every corner of the holiday cooler is filled with the holiday meal components. We will unpack everything and assemble them this week, cook the turkeys, and provide joy for nearly a thousand well-to-do families. The price tag ain't cheap on our meals, but at Dream Grocers, we make them with "love"—so say the commercials. It's time for lunch. I have never been so ready for a meal.

I check again to see if I received a text from Lila, but my apps for social media are going crazy. I put my phone back in my pocket and enjoy the little vibrations reminding me of my growing fame over the last couple of days. Frankie is established and forging a life of his own.

Achilles is walking toward me slowly. "How's it going back here?" *he asks.*

"I'm almost done. Feel like I just got jumped by five dudes in a dark alley, but I am surviving."

"Oh my! What did they do to you?" *Achilles says with a smile followed by a wince.*

"Unspeakable things," *I reply.*

"Please . . . do tell."

"Not on my darkest days."

"Even after I threw out my back for you?"

"Even after you threw out your back . . . ahem . . . for me."

"See if I ever help you again."

"You can barely walk and still talking shit. You're relentless," *I say.*

"You know it's entertaining. Don't lie, babe."

"Fair enough. How is the back?"

"It's tender. Every step hurts," *he replies.*

"Jesus. What are you going to do with yourself for the rest of the day?"

"Well, I know if I leave, then we'll be fucked later in the week, so I'll do the prep work best I can."

"Have you talked to Jake about getting you some pain meds?"

"I don't need to become a pill popper, Daniel."

"I was thinking edibles, but you know . . . if you need some heroin, I got a guy."

"What?! The fuck you do. I ain't having you get high on that shit."

I'm laughing. "I'll stay away from the hard stuff, just for you, Achilles."

"That's right, mijo. That's right."

"You're so thoughtful."

"It's my gift."

"Okay. So I'll finish up and get something to eat."

"Have fun, mijo."

Upstairs, I sit, slumped over the table, holding my phone with dry, cracked fingers while shaking my legs periodically to remove the numbness. It's a strange place, this world. I'm both pleased and distressed at the moment, tired and alive, waiting for my follower count to update. Piece-of-shit smartphones can barely keep up. Frankie's Instagram and TikTok and other apps are popping off, and the follower count is growing too. Everyone is locked up and bored, and a grown man in a panda costume who jabbers into the abyss and drinks espresso martinis constitutes entertainment. I look at the time, and my break is already up. I don't know why I hold myself to such strict timelines, but I feel like I am cheating the system if I take longer than my allotted fifteen minutes.

Lila and Jake are walking down the hallway, smiling, and laughing with that youthful exuberance and flirtation that comes only from fucking. They don't notice me. That's okay. I don't have time to be jealous.

* * *

Wisps of snow hit the piss-colored streetlights and coat the ground. The sound of crunching snow masks the cracking in my knees. I check my phone. There is a text from Lila. I think we should talk.

I don't answer. It's 11:30 p.m., and I don't have the energy to think about dating or sex or anything. A younger me shakes his head in shame. Head hits pillow. Falling away. A hand tries to save me. Nothing left. Day one complete.

* * *

Day 2

Morning comes too soon. My muscles have congealed to look normal but have been stretched and contorted and extended to their max capacity. I am clay waiting for someone to mold it into a life worth living. Some might wait for God to help them. God isn't here. I sit up in my bed and place my feet on the jeans I wore yesterday. A plate of crumbs and pizza sauce sits on my nightstand next to a glass with maybe a thimble of scotch left in the bottom. These are reminders of blurry, overworked nights and the cascading effects they have on my life. I don't know if my body and spirit will be ready for another round. I need something, anything, to make me feel alive again. I walk into the kitchen and pour a cup of coffee. Pour a little Bailey's in and stir. Here we go. Nothing happens. No jolt. No paso nada.

I walk out the door, struck with the realization that yesterday was only the first day. Denver carries a hefty burden as I wander through my empty, frigid city—for I need its spirit to lift me, but there is only a carcass of a former self to help me across the finish line.

* * *

Abby is far too chipper for any normal person. "How are you feeling today?" she asks.

"Ugh . . ." is the best I can come up with.

"Pssht . . . I love this time of year. The energy is surreal. Everything happens so fast, and we're providing for our community in a way they will never understand or appreciate. We save the holidays every year."

"But who saves us?"

"Ha. No one. We are the unsung heroes in this part of the American story. I think it's pretty cool. Even more so with the pandemic going on. People are desperate for anything, and anyone, to help ground them in such turbulent times."

"I guess so."

"You'll see. By the end of it all, you'll want to spend the holidays in our jungle every year. I promise. Anyway, we'll be assembling meals tonight, and another shipment is coming in."

"Another shipment? I thought that we received it all yesterday."

"God, no. That was just the biggest one. We get stuff every day of the week. And you still have the regular shipment."

I visibly shutter.

"Isn't this fun?" she says with a clenched-jaw smile.

"Maybe for the masochist in me."

"See . . . I knew you would be right for our team. The load should be arriving soon. For now, will you help out the front and restock the shelves?"

"Sure thing."

Since there aren't any people standing at the case, I decide to take a walk around the store to avoid work and breathe in the sights and sounds of a grocery store in a high-end neighborhood bursting with holiday merriment.

The lights shimmer a bit more as I stroll past the meat department and wave at the crew. A woman is making demands about an aged lamb roast she purchased. She seems upset as she points a long, gnarled finger in poor Billy's face. Billy is a climber and hard worker. He changed his life in the last year and went from cart boy to management seemingly overnight. He was the guy who brought me in from my meltdown outside. He told me not long after the incident that I'd scared the shit out of him. He didn't want to get to that place. I tried to tell him that I was okay, but he was still worried. Now, some months later, he is burning, burning bright as the line of restless customers is being held up by some old biddy who long ago shed any sense of decorum. My heart is full of both fear and love for the path I abetted, even if only in the smallest way.

In the dairy section, a woman scolds her daughter for running off while the store is so busy, but in doing so she brings a pathway that's already a narrow squeeze to a complete standstill. I slide in between her and a massive refrigerated column of greek yogurt. She doesn't notice me, but I can hear her desperate tone, as if the child were playing in a war zone rather than the grocery store of an affluent neighborhood. Eventually the girl will grow into a woman and make up her own mind about what and who her mother was in this moment. It might be interesting to hear her conclusions. People are pushed to the brink. The goddamn scene is teetering on madness. Everyone is wound so tight as they wait for their prime rib dinner or whole king crab. I look back at the cattle chute this woman is causing with her rage right before I turn the corner and forget about it forever.

I check my phone and see that it's time to receive the load. I'm not entirely sure where the hours went. Once I return to the case, I find a line of angry customers, and Abby is helping another employee clear them. She looks at me. "Where have you been, Daniel?"

"I just went for a walk to get a better understanding of this whole thing."

"I'm not sure what you are talking about, but that must've been a mighty long stroll, because you've been gone for over an hour."

"What? No, I haven't. I just got here."

"Check the time. You'll see."

Sure enough. I've been at work for three hours. "Damn. Umm . . . well, I don't have a good explanation for that one. Looks like the load's here."

"Take care of it, and we'll talk later."

I walk back to the dock, and sure enough, all my pallets of regular food and holiday goodies are waiting for me. I look around for U-boats to go to war with, but I can't find a single one. I walk downstairs to see if some are in the coolers. None to be found. A similar desperation that the woman yelling at her daughter had begins to seep in, and I realize I have wasted too much time. I should have grabbed some boats at the beginning *so that they wouldn't be taken by other employees. The boxes of chicken, holiday hams and turkeys, and other raw ingredients are sweating and slowly warming up to room temperature. Soon they will spoil. I finally find a cart. It's much smaller than normal, but I begin to load the most important items first. I feel they are close to the brink. I grab a temp gun and check the product. I am still good to go. I need to pee, so I head off to the bathroom just around the corner. When I return, Tony is standing there with Richard.*

"Daniel, how long has this product been sitting here?" Tony asks.

"It's been there awhile. Sorry. It's been a crazy day."

"It's getting dangerously close to temp."

"I know. That's why I am trying to get it done ASAP."

The assistant manager, Richard, looks me up and down and points behind me. "Where were you just now? This needs to be a priority. Not talking with ladies."

"I was in the bathroom. There weren't any ladies to talk to in there."

"What kind of smart-ass remark is that?" Richard replies.

"What kind of line of questioning is this, given the chicken is about to expire?" I reply.

Todd turns the corner. "What's all the hubbub about?"

Richard quickly changes his tune. "We were just talking about getting this chicken in the cooler."

"Okay. Well, carry on, then," Todd replies before he walks off.

"Here. I'll help you," Tony says.

Richard walks away without a response.

"Sorry, dude," Tony says. "I didn't mean to throw you under the bus. Richard just puts everyone on blast."

"All good. Let's get this shit done. We still gotta assemble meals, and I need to write production."

"Damn. Good point."

We are done receiving the load in short order. Tony says to me, "I'm sorry about earlier, man."

"Eh . . . don't worry about it. I slipped up and got back here late anyway."

"Nah, nah. Everyone slips up, and I know you're working hard. I should've explained that to Richard."

"Damn right you should've. Fuckin' asshole," I say with a smirk to let him know we can move on. We've had a rocky start to our working relationship in general, so I think pure shit-talking seems like the best approach.

"Now that's the right attitude," he replies with a laugh.

I sigh in relief that I might finally have a fun coworker instead of just a grumpy dude to work with.

We walk back to the desk to find Abby and Achilles standing at the computer, chatting.

"You two finished with the load?"

"These two finishing loads?" Achilles teases. "Bah . . . they got nothing on me."

Tony puts his hand on my shoulder. "I don't know, Daniel might give you a good run for your money."

The universe cracks with the uproar of laughter that comes from all four of us. Coworkers walk by with curious eyes. Even Pedro, who just got done clocking in for work, cracks a smile, although I can see he is taking it personally or thinking, How can they have such fun when nothing is going right around here?

My face hurts from laughing. I'm not sure if I actually think it's that funny or if it was just the timing, the pressure of Thanksgiving week, and the idea that I am finding a pocket of real humanity among all the madness that has befallen our times. Not the type where my feelings aren't going to be hurt or I won't be tested but more of a cocoon of struggles and situations where I can be myself and where I can find purpose and valor even in the smallest things. True joy washes over me. I look up, and Abby, Achilles, and Tony are staring at me, wide eyed and worried.

"Are you alright, Daniel?" Abby asks.

"Yeah. I'm fine. Why?"

Achilles points at my face.

I turn and look in the reflective cooler mirror. Dollops of joy and saline solution are pouring. I wipe down my face and turn back to them to say, "I guess I'm just happy?"

Abby brings everyone in close. Tony resists.

"Come on, big fella," I say. "We have two more days. Then we are scot-free."

"Until Christmas," Tony replies.

"Tony, stay positive." Abby says.

"Now let's get through this shit."

"Bring on the whiskey," I say.

Everyone agrees.

"I know we are trying to have a moment here, Abby, but this is kind of corny," I say.

"I blame you, Mr. Cries-in-Public."

"Hey, these are modern times. It's okay for men to cry. I think I even saw an article about it on the cover of the New York Times."

Abby rolls her eyes. "Oookay. Well, let's make sure all the employees are set up here; then we can get to packaging up the meals. Most of the pickups are tomorrow."

We disperse, and I decide to check in with Pedro and Janice.

"How are you two doing up here? Anything I can do for ya? You all set on breaks?"

Janice has a flushed and energetic face. There isn't a tremble to her hands. She probably had a swig of medicine before work, but she showed up, and I think that is one of two elements that matter most in regard to my employees. The other part is being willing to work the whole shift and staying positive. Janice does that well. Despite her struggles with the devil's sweat, at least when she is here, she tries.

Pedro is present also, but that may be only in spirit. He looks upset. I don't have time for him tonight. But I'll give him the benefit of the doubt, because he is also here, just like Janice.

Janice replies, "We both just took our breaks."

"Yeah, but Janice took more than her normal time," Pedro replies.

"Excuse me?" she replies.

"Well, you did."

"Oh, did I? What time did I leave, and what time did I come back?"

"I don't remember exactly. But I know it was at least twenty-five minutes."

"Fuckin' liar."

Pedro holds up his hands.

"Hold up, you two." I intervene. "Pedro . . . follow me."

"Why would I do that?" he asks.

"I need to talk to you."

"Nah, dude. I'm good."

"Okay. I'll grab Abby, and we can talk."

"Wait, wait . . . we can talk."

"Follow me." I stop by our desk in the hallway since we don't have an actual office. "What's going on, man?"

"What do you mean?"

"Well, you just accused Janice of something serious in public. If there is an issue that you notice, the best thing to do is talk to a manager in private. Can you give me some more detail so that I can talk to Janice about taking long breaks?"

"Nah, dude. I'm good."

"So now, in private, you don't have any comment?"

"Yeah, dude. I said what I needed to say. Can I go back to work?"

"Yeah. Go ahead."

Achilles walks out from the cooler and says, "Looks like someone pissed in your Cheerios there, bud. Wanna talk about it?"

I shake my head. "You know, man. I want to throw hot grease in some of these assholes' eyes and watch them thrash about on the floor as I stand and make pas-sive-aggressive remarks about their frailty."

Achilles stands open mouthed. Then bursts into laughter. He puts his hand on my shoulder. "At long last, someone said what we have all felt."

A smile spreads like raspberry jam across my face, and I let go of a kernel of hate.

Achilles continues, "I can't tell you how many times I have thought the world would be better if some of our employees were hit by the bus on the way home. I think that is a core tenet of being in middle management. I don't know why Abby hires these people. I have talked to her about it before, and the best response she can give is 'I will take what I can get. No one wants to work for what I can pay them.'"

"That's a pretty good excuse."

"I know, right? It's goddamn sad. That's why we need to unionize."

"You should talk to Jake and Oz."

"Oh, really? What about you?"

"What do I think about unionization?"

"Yes."

"I'm on the fence about it. It's hard enough to get rid of assholes like Pedro without a union backing up his shit behavior."

"Damn, that's a good point," Achilles replies.

"I guess it is all a matter of trade-offs, right? Also, a union might be able to guarantee pay raises for us, but it also might cause stagnation on ambitions and magnify laziness. Just my thoughts."

"All good points. Shit, I forgot that Abby wanted us to head down and start putting the holiday meals together. Do you think you can come down with me?"

"I think so. I'll tell Janice where we are if they need anything."

"Okay. Meet us down there when you can."

There is muffled yelling coming from the front. I realize that I haven't written production yet. My heart begins to pound. Pedro is walking away from the Chef's Case, swearing. He cruises right past me. I see a line of maybe ten people waiting to be helped. Janice is nowhere to be found. I still need to help downstairs.

My chest feels like it's gonna explode. Stomach acid is crawling up my throat.

Every customer I interact with has a distinct edge to their voice. The stress has burrowed inside their brain. The holiday season is upon them in all its aggressive pageantry. Dark swaths of skin droop below their eyes. Children tug at their shirts. The noise—oh, the sounds of exhausted parents at the end of their rope—and it's only the week of Thanksgiving. There is still a month-plus of this bullshit left. God help them. God help me. Wait . . . I almost forgot God takes this time of year off.

My day ends just like that . . . with no resolution. I didn't have time to help downstairs. The lines never stopped. The saloon doors to the kitchen flapped about all day like wings on a bird landing on water. People taking orders. Customers yelling. Demands, demands, demands. A rising tide of ego, pressure, money, and groceries swept me away. The whiskey tastes mighty fine on my walk back to my apartment. I am struggling to see the reward Abby mentioned. It's hard to keep the faith. I am wondering what the purpose is in it all.

* * *

Day 3

The COVID-induced line outside that I stare at every day is frothing and foaming and purging with an air of panic and hostility I haven't seen in months. Inside, I hear a voice from somewhere in the aisles screaming:

"All hands on deck! Aaallll hands on deck! And if you didn't know . . . well, you're gonna learn today."

The outer rim of my toes and fingers are frozen windshields from the bitter cold walk. Abby asked me to work a twelve-hour shift today, again. She sold me on it by telling me that her overtime in years past was enough to pay her rent. This will be day three of twelve-hour shifts. I've had maybe two hours of overtime every night for the last few weeks. I am separating out the money to see what vast luxuries I can afford when it's all said and done. I'm not sure about her rent promises. She's a Gen Xer and may have fantastical memories of Denver's past, when rent was cheap and wars were short and the world wasn't as steeped in madness, but I fall for the same nostalgic trap as a millennial—I know I do, but I could use the bump, a shot of adrenaline, anything, really. I might just use my overtime money for a bagful of bumps. This job doesn't pay what it should to consume the kind of drugs that stick to you, but it's nice to escape for a while. Even if illicit activities were not involved, this job would still pay far too little. The amount of work we do as managers or even regular employees in general seems criminal at the pay rate in a city booming with opportunity, for a company having record years, and with inflation on the rise.

All hands on deck! All hands on deck! All hands on deck! All hands on deck!

More of my people are coming up the stairs and down the hallway to give their lives to this place. Each face more solemn than the next until a familiar face pops out from around the corner. Neal is here.

"What's up, dude?" I ask.

"Yo," he responds with a slump and whimper.

"You alright, man?"

"Tired as all hell. The front end has been a war zone of quiche, pumpkin-pie filling, and the angriest demons you have ever met. I'm happy for you that you got out."

"Damn, dude. But I definitely didn't 'get out.' We do all the prepackaged box meals for the lazy rich families. But Abby says we save Christmas!"

He laughs. "Oh, shit! That's right. I'm sorry, dawg. At least Turkey Day is almost here and gone."

"Almost is the key word there."

"You getting the fear yet?"

"The fear?" I ask.

"Yeah, man. It's that stark feeling that you will die doing this. That you will never truly enjoy Thanksgiving again."

"Oh . . . I hadn't started feeling that until right now."

"Good, good. It's good for you. I have been doing this for a few years now, and it's not a way to live."

"It's almost over, though."

Neal places his hand on my shoulder and says, "For now."

"Thanks, Neal. You're wise beyond your years."

"I know, brother. God's words to your ears."

I am grateful for these people. They make all the difference. But the moment ends quickly as Abby rushes past, then stops. "You clocked in yet?"

"Just did," I answer.

"Great. Can you help Tony bring more of the dinner sides from the basement? He is heading down right now."

"Sure thing," I respond, but she is almost to the end of the hallway.

"Thanks!" she yells, but it's barely audible.

"Good luck, dude," Neal says.

"Thanks. You too."

I walk past the break room toward the back stairs that will get me closest to the coolers in the basement. The walls are chipped, fading black with the orange Dream Grocers logo printed above the middle landings between levels. The floors have gone unwashed for at least a decade. I wonder for a moment how many souls have hopped down these stairs to help out on one task or another. Down, down, down. I reach the bottom, and Tony is loading a U-boat.

"Abby sent me," I say. "What do you need help with?"

"Every goddamn thing."

"Wanna point me to one of these goddamn things?"

He points to a pile of boxed green beans and says, "We are damn near out. Buncha savages stripped us clean to the bone."

"How much should I grab?"

"All of it."

"Jesus. Alright."

I pile up a U-boat and push it down to the freight elevator. Tony is waiting for me. "Let's go, brother."

"Must be serious, huh? You never call me brother, like, ever."

"It's a zoo. Straight-up animals at every turn asking for this or that—they didn't order ahead but demand we do something for them. Emergencies, wildfires, holiday cheer, overconcern, babies crying, weeping and gnashing of teeth."

"It'll all be over soon, homie," I say, trying to calm him down.

Once we reach the correct floor, Tony removes five boxes from the U-boat and says, "I guess so." His right foot slips, and all the boxes go tumbling down. The bags inside crescendo across the floor, ripping open.

"God fucking damnit!" Tony exclaims.

None of the customers notice, and I want to laugh because it's the only reaction that feels right, but I don't. It's the wrong moment. I gather all the beans and boxes, write down the quantities for tracking, and throw them in a trash can. We unpack what we have and head back down to the basement.

In the cooler, Tony sits down on a stack of pallets, pulls out a tiny flask, and has a taste. He offers me some. I take a sip, and the corners of my mouth sear like oil in a hot skillet. We quietly pose under the flickering light of a cooler, far away from God. I have been at work for only an hour.

The peace is short lived. I receive a text from Abby. We are out of a couple more items. We finish loading up the U-boats and head upstairs.

When we arrive, people are running in every direction. "Where the hell have you been?" Achilles barks at me and Tony as soon as we enter the room. "Oh, never mind. Don't answer that. Will you bring those into the walk-in? We have a line of twenty people waiting for their fucking turkeys and fixin's." I look out the window of the kitchen entrance, and sure enough there is a massive line that is separate from the Chef's Case line. We bring the sides to the cooler. "I better get some more," Tony says.

"Sounds good," I agree. "Achilles . . . what do you want me to do? Help up here or get more sides?"

IX

He looks at me with pity and love. "Here, bring this to the whales out front. I am afraid an earthquake might start if they start stomping around and yelling again." He smiles.

I grab the boxes, throw them in a cart, and head out to the floor. "Wait, hold up," Achilles says. "That's only half of it. They have two turkeys."

"My god."

"This is the third of four two-turkey meals we have handed out today. Pretty sure there are like ten more."

"Maybe they have a bunch of people in the family."

He scoffs. "Maybe, Daniel. Just maybe. I'll let you be the judge when you get out there."

A whole shopping cart barely fits their meal. Achilles is wrong in his assessment, because the man and woman who stand before me are not whales. Whales are beautiful. The couple "stands" before me with translucent, malnourished skin, varicose veins popping from liver-spotted legs and arms leaning on their carts, wheezing on oxygen. This isn't beautiful. It makes me sad. I pity them. "Where the fuck have you been?" the woman barks.

"Sorry, ma'am," I say. "We were getting your sides."

"That's no excuse, son. We have been waiting for an hour."

"Again, I am very sorry. Here, would you like some help to the registers?"

"If that's all you can fucking offer, sure. This is the last Thanksgiving I shop at Dream Grocers. Every time we come here, it's the same goddamn story. I think we should go to Country Market next year."

"I understand where you're coming from. Country Market makes great stuff. Honestly, they are less

expensive than us too. Since you have a huge family to feed, you might be able to save some money there too."

"Huge family? What the hell are you talking about, boy?" The fat man labors to stand independently of the cart. "This meal is for my wife, me, and two cousins from my side. That's all. Nothing extravagant."

I look at the mountain of food. "Oh, wow," I say out loud when I shouldn't.

"What the fuck is that supposed to mean?" the woman says.

"Nothing. I was just thinking of something else. Anyway, did you need help?"

"You're very rude. You know that?"

"I guess so."

I feel a sudden pull on my shoulder. I turn around. It's a woman with Cartier sunglasses perched on a daggerlike nose. "Where is my meal?" she asks.

"Ma'am, if you let me finish with these customers, I will help you next."

"She wasn't next. I was!" a man with rat eyes and a beaded brow yells at me and lunges forward in front of the dagger-nose woman.

"No sir, you were not," she retorts.

"I was too, goddamnit!" he replies.

She shoves him, and he falls back onto a table filled with holiday cookies.

I feel a pull on the cart. I turn around. It's not the whales but some other woman. "I'll just take this one. I need to get out of here."

"Hey!" yells the original customer. "That bitch is trying to take our meal."

"You only need one. You fat fucks," she responds.

I let go of the cart. The woman begins to walk away. The whales take aim. The female shifts her great frame and shoulder checks the lady taking her groceries. This petite woman crumples to the ground. More noise is coming from behind me. I turn around and see a full-scale brawl has broken out. Over the loudspeaker I hear, "Security to prepared foods. Now, please! Security to prepared foods."

"Hey, man."

I turn around again. Chaos all around.

A pencil-thin man with a plaid shirt and yellow-stained teeth is standing there, smiling. "Since they all seem occupied, do you think you can help me?"

* * *

Thanksgiving
We rest.

X

The phone rang several times before Janice finally picked up.

"Hey, Janice. It's Daniel. How are you? Are you doing okay?"

"How sweet of you, Daniel. I'm doing just fine." Her voice sounded cheerful but distant, like she was only half with me on the phone.

"No problem. Just wanted to check when we might be seeing you at work?"

"Work? I don't work today."

"You're on the schedule."

"Shit, shit, shit . . . I completely forgot."

"That's fine. Just get here as soon as you can."

"I don't know if I should do that."

"What's going on?"

"I'm very drunk right now."

"Oh, yeah. Umm . . . definitely don't come in if you are drunk."

"I'm so sorry, Daniel."

"You're fine."

"It's not okay. I let you down." I could feel the painful truth in her voice.

"Don't worry. I'm going to transfer you to Abby. She will need to talk to you."

"Oh, alright." I could clearly hear the slur in her voice now, with a deep sadness in tow.

My heart began to melt at her pain. "Janice, you are a great employee. Just talk to management, and we will see you in the store soon. Okay?"

"Alright. Thanks for being so sweet."

I was starting to feel like I had crossed a line in being encouraging. I was out of my depth, but the holiday help had left after the new year, and we needed to keep all the people we could. The schedule was stretched so thin, and so were all the employees. Management was a strange beast. You just had to make do, and no one gave a shit. You had to suffer well, so they said.

A small wave of panic crept up into my already crowded mind as I realized that I had called her on my cell phone. I had broken protocol. I hoped she wouldn't call back.

I called Abby. "Hey, Janice is on the phone. She is calling out of work. I think she should talk to you."

"Alrighty. What's up?"

"Well, she openly admitted to me that she is drunk."

"Like I-partied-too-hard-last-night-type admission or full-blown-alcoholic-type stuff?"

"The latter."

X

"Oh god. Alright. Thanks for letting me know. And so you know, when people tell you shit like that, you should immediately transfer them to HR. They will handle it. Don't get involved."

"Yeah, she started admitting things right away, and I cut her off."

"Good call. Sorry, dude. This happens more than you might think."

"That's heavy."

"Agreed. So I'll get her over to HR. I'll be down to look over your schedule for tonight to see where we can fill in the gaps since Janice can't make it."

"Sounds good, boss."

She paused for a moment, then said, "It's gonna be alright."

"It always is. This is just a new way for me to lose a person for a shift."

Maybe ten minutes later, Abby came downstairs to the kitchen. "We are all set. HR is gonna talk to her. She agreed to come in tomorrow on her day off to help us out. Hopefully that happens."

* * *

The next morning came barreling in hard and fast and ice-fucking-cold with a polar weather front engulfing our great city. Denver was a lonely, miserable mess that January. I'd been up late, drinking with neighbors and talking about how Janice couldn't make it into work. I'd wondered out loud several times if she was up late drinking like us. I hoped not. Closing shorthanded was always brutal but especially with Pedro bringing us

197

all down with his special brand of toxicity. Then I asked my friends if I was really being empathetic to her situation or just concerned about my well-being. They didn't have much to say. We concluded that it was a little bit of both but that I was entitled to the mixed bag of emotions. Drunk pandemic therapy sessions had kept me sane during those months of indiscriminate craziness.

Abby was staring into her computer screen like she was a scientist discovering a black hole when I turned the corner into the kitchen/office. "Goddamnit. Who can we get to fill in?" she mumbled into the abyss, not having noticed me yet.

"Janice didn't show, did she?"

"Not sure about that one. Pedro called out."

"Shit. What was his excuse?"

"I don't know. He didn't say, and legally we aren't allowed to ask."

"Damn. Did Jamie call out too?"

"No, he's here."

"Thank god. Does that just leave the two of us? We might as well shut the whole thing down."

"Well, Janice hasn't come in yet. She should be here shortly."

"I'm praying."

"I'm praying for you. I have an appointment tonight and can't stay. One good shred of news is that we don't have a shipment tonight."

"So no receiving?" I replied.

"Yes sir. You got lucky."

"I think we have different definitions of luck."

"Well, I would take it where you can get it. Sometimes it's way worse."

X

"Not doing the receiving kinda bums me out. I actually like that part of the job," I said.

"Really?"

"Yeah, I get to hide away from the world. It's purely physical."

"Oh, I see. Well, that's good. I'm glad you found some sort of respite from the grind. Being a manager can be stressful. But, hey, you are doing a great job, and I feel like you are a well-seasoned vet at this point."

"Am I?"

"Of course. Most of this job is a test of your endurance."

"I'm not sure how I'm supposed to feel about that."

"I think there is a reward in perseverance."

"I think so too. But usually I associate the value of sticking it out with something noble."

"Isn't it noble to tell yourself that you *will* do something, then you do it . . . no matter what?" she replied.

"I don't have a rebuttal to that."

"Good. Oh, look who's here."

I looked over my shoulder. Lo and behold, it was Janice.

"Hey, hey!" I said as I raised my arms in celebration. But I immediately knew something was off by the look on her face. Abby and I glanced at each other. There was a scent of Listerine hanging in the air, and her skin bordered on translucent with flame-red cheeks. Her eyes were sunken back, with deep shadows underneath.

"When is the last time you slept?" I blurted out but immediately knew that was an inappropriate question.

Abby put her hand on my shoulder as if to pull back my question and asked, "How are you feeling, Janice?"

"I feel fine," Janice replied with a wobble.

"Are you sure you're ready for work?" Abby asked as she reached for her phone.

"I'll be fine," Janice replied.

"I think I should call Todd or Richard," Abby replied.

"Please don't, Abby. I promise I'll be okay."

"I just think you need to rest, hun."

"Please. I'm rested. I promise."

"I'm sorry, Janice, but we need to go up to HR."

Immediately, Janice began to cry. "I need this job. Please. I need this job."

"You aren't going to lose your job, but we need to have you talk to HR."

With slumped shoulders, she softly replied, "Okay."

The two of them walked out the door. From that moment forward, Janice would work day shifts because the store management recommended that Abby keep her close to make sure she wasn't endangering herself or anyone else.

* * *

A couple of weeks later, I was finishing up the production planning for the evening, and the crew was preparing to close. Zzz . . . zzz . . . I looked down at my phone and saw that a number I didn't recognize was calling me. I ignored it and sent it straight to voice mail, assuming it was a spam call of some sort, and I went back to the production schedule. Five minutes or so passed. Zzz . . . zzz. It was the same number. I decided

to answer, thinking it was something serious. I picked up the phone.

"Hello?"

"Hi, Daniel."

It was Janice.

"Hi, Janice . . . what's up?"

"Oh, I don't know." She began to cry. "I just don't know what to do, ya know?"

"I'm so sorry to hear that, Janice. Have you talked to HR about what's going on?"

"I tried. They didn't answer."

"Ah, well, make sure to leave a message."

"Daniel, can we talk for a moment?"

"Honestly, Janice, that would probably be inappropriate. I'm sorry."

"I get it. I'm so drunk right now, and I don't know if I will make it to work tomorrow."

"Oh, okay. Well, I will write down a note for Abby to talk to you in the morning."

"Daniel."

"Yes?"

"You are one of the sweetest managers I have ever had. I just wanna tell you that."

"Aww . . . well, I appreciate that, and I enjoy having you on the team too."

"Daniel . . ."

"Yes, Janice."

"Don't let them corrupt you. Don't let them take your soul. That's why I am where I am today, because I let them win."

"Umm . . . Janice, are you alright?"

"I . . . I am fine. I just wanna know dose things."

"You sound very drunk. Do you think I should call someone?"

"Naaah . . . I'm fine. Oh . . . I gotta go. Byeeee."

"Wait, don't—" The phone went dead. I immediately called back. No one answered. I tried again. Again, no one answered.

Jamie walked through the door to the front. "Hey, dude. A customer has a question."

"Okay. I'll be right there." I looked back at the phone briefly and headed to the front.

I walked out to face a woman sporting shoulder-length, faded-from-red-dye hair. And by the look on her face, I knew she would be a Linda in every way possible.

"Excuse me, sir. Are you the person in charge here?" she asked.

"That's me. How can I help you?"

"I just bought this tuna salad, and it has cranberries in it."

I paused for a moment, then asked, "Can I see the box?"

She handed me the clear plastic container. I examined the label. It read: *Cranberry Tuna Salad.* "Ma'am. It's labeled cranberry tuna salad."

"I know what it says, you idiot. It was in the wrong spot on the shelf, and I didn't look at the label because I *assumed* you would have the product in the right place."

Pedro chimed in with "Well, you assumed wrong."

I fought the urge to burst out laughing and said, "Not now, Pedro."

"What the hell did he just say to me?" the customer demanded.

I changed the subject back to the salad. "So how can I help you with the salad?"

"I just want to know why it was in the wrong section, aaand I want a new one."

"Well, of course we will get you a new salad, and I apologize for product being in the wrong spot. Sometimes customers put the product in random spots, and we don't see it right away."

"I have a hard time believing that's what happened. The incompetence here is pretty mind blowing. I don't think I'm going to shop here anymore."

"I'm sorry to hear that," I said without thinking.

"*You* are *sorry* to *hear* that?! That is not the right response in customer service. You know that. You are supposed to ask me what you can do to change my mind. This is ridiculous. I need to speak to your manager now."

I was grateful to be excused from this conversation. "Yes, of course, let me call and see if I can get ahold of him."

I walked to the back room and dialed the extension to the manager's office. Richard picked up.

"Hello?"

"Hey, Richard . . . a customer down here wants to speak to you."

"About what?"

"Cranberries in her tuna salad."

"Please try to offer one or two for free. I am in the middle of something."

"I already did. She insists on talking to you."

"Goddamnit. Alright."

I found it strange that a manager who seemed so uptight about everything would be so candid. Richard was awful to the employees, but maybe that was because he was just miserable in the life he'd chosen.

After he hung up, I looked at my cell phone. No new calls. I thought for a moment that I should reach back out to Janice, but now I had another problem to handle. She would have to wait.

Richard arrived downstairs. "Where is she?" he asked.

I pointed through the door window at the loose-skinned energy vampire.

"Wait here," he said.

I watched them talk for a little while. The gaunt, angry woman flailed her arms. Richard talked with her calmly, but I could tell she was going to win the battle. It was inevitable. I began to prepare for Richard's wrath. I knew that even my minor indiscretion would not go unpunished. I dared to feed the beast.

Their discussion went for a little while; then Richard returned with anguish and concern plastered on his face. "Did you really say that you are sorry to hear she won't be shopping here again?"

"Yeah."

"Why would you say something like that?"

"Because she was getting way out of line. She called me an idiot for asking how I could help her. There is only so much you can do with some people. I offered her free food. I was polite and let her vent. She just wanted to scream at someone."

"Even if she's that way, there is no reason to tell her something like that. I expected more from you, Daniel. I think we are going to have a sit-down with Abby about

X

your behavior. I'm going to need you to go out there and apologize."

"What for? I did nothing wrong."

"Yes, you did. Now, go apologize, or I'm sending you home."

"You're serious?"

"Dead serious."

I stared at Richard for a few moments as I seethed in primordial rage and thought, *This audacious fuck stick.* I wanted him to feel every ounce of hate I had for him. He should know how this changed everything. I would never go out of my way to help him again.

"Let's go," he said.

It took the weight of not being able to pay my rent to walk out there and apologize.

"I'm sorry."

"You should be," the customer responded. "Thank you for apologizing."

I turned around and walked away. "Hey, Pedro . . . I'm going on a break."

"I haven't had my break yet, boss," he said in that stupid, whiny tone.

I ignored his reply and walked through the kitchen and out the side door of the building to the break area. My hands trembled in anger. Cars whizzed by as I sat quietly on a bench. I thought back to my corporate life, where I'd toiled away for years until I'd known I needed to break free of stupid assholes on power trips like that Linda I had been forced to apologize to and the Dave waiting for her at home. As I climbed up the corporate ladder at a grocery store, I would inevitably deal with those people and be sucked back into that life *again*. And here I was, yet *again*, staring out from a park bench, contemplating my decisions. My mother had always said that I had trouble making up my mind. She'd lectured me about how I was doomed to repeat myself over and over again. I was becoming a poster child for a generation that many considered widely confused and inept. One that wanted all the stardom but none of the work to achieve glory. I realized then that I needed to break my cycle. I needed an out.

I looked down at my phone. I had gained something like ten thousand more followers across Frankie's various social media on that day alone. I thought maybe, just maybe, Frankie could be my ticket to a different life. I had done some research, and I was close to being able to monetize his social media. For once, I had hope. I thought about Janice then, and I wondered if she thought about her future. What was she living for, you know? She had a son she was very proud of, but was that enough to pull her through? Thinking of her also reminded me that work was almost over and beer was waiting for me at home.

There I was, turning into an optimist before and despite my own eyes. We had a big meeting scheduled for tomorrow that I'd been told I should care about, but I felt confident in how I was going to move up and out of my circumstance. We would just have to see how this job played out. A smile came across my face as I realized that within the infinite complexity of human life, among the political and corporate wolves, there lay the opportunity for a man to live out where the wild things were, working in a grocery store but moonlighting and holding influence online, dressed as a panda. I walked back inside to finish my work for the night.

XI

Not every meeting was created equal. And many of them were utter bullshit. I'd learned this in the big companies when I'd worked in cubicles, and it transferred over directly to any gathering of more than four people in *any* setting unrelated to your own personal well-being. Most were meant for other people to complain or feel like they were important. I had felt imposter syndrome in every one of those company masturbation sessions I had ever been a part of—from team huddles to company earnings calls. I would never get it. But the meeting that happened on this particular day was important, apparently. We were there to talk about our department scorecard and corporate walk. But not just any corporate visit. The CEO and the VP of Food Services were coming all the way from a coastal city to look at our store and judge our ability to put together a functional copy of what they envisioned for our department.

Abby paced back and forth for the first five minutes of our meeting while the rest of us sat quietly, looking at each other and wondering what the meeting was all about.

Finally, after what seemed like ages, she said, as if only to herself, "We have to be ready for them. Our jobs are on the line."

We all looked at each other but said nothing.

"I'm serious, guys. We need to knock this one out of the park. We need to reel in the big one. We need to *crush. This. Shit.*"

"What exactly *are* we doing?" Achilles asked.

"Shit. That's a good point; the details matter," she replied with a flustered look, then continued, "The CEO and the VP of Food Services are coming to walk our store and specifically *our* department. Isn't that exciting?"

I figured she was hoping for a more dramatic reaction from the supervisors, because she let her sentence hang out to dry, but no one was interested.

"I don't know if I would call that exciting, but it sure is *something*," Tony said.

"Oh, come on, guys. It will be good for us. Like Todd says, 'Pressure is privilege.'"

"Yeah, but we all hate Todd," I responded. Everyone laughed. Even Abby.

Then, with an exasperated look, Abby said, "Now, he's not *that* bad, Daniel. Come on now, you guys, ya gotta give me something."

There was silence until I asked, "Why this store? I mean, I am fine with it. I'm just curious as to why this store, right now? We have been short staffed for so long by their budget that it seems like unnecessary pressure . . ." I stopped. "I almost forgot. Pressure is a privilege."

"That's exactly right," Abby said. "Look, I know it's gonna be tough, but I believe in you guys."

"This was Todd's idea, wasn't it?" Achilles said.

"Actually, I insisted," Abby replied.

"You do know that Todd didn't come up with the 'pressure is a privilege' thing, right? It was Billie Jean King, a pioneer in women's sports. It's the title of her book. She is a badass. Todd's a phony," Achilles added on.

I nearly spit out my water.

"Okay," Abby continued. "I think we need to stick to the problem at hand. I have a list of tasks that we need to make sure we do daily so that when they do arrive, it will be easy just to sweep up real quick. We only have two weeks before they arrive. I have assigned tasks for you to give to the crews. Mostly, they will need to do it at night."

It was always the night crew's responsibility to do this sort of stuff, and since I was the closing manager, it mostly fell on my lap.

"Looks like it will be the night crew's job, *again*," I said.

"Daniel, that's not true. We will assign things during the day, but we are slower at night, so you all will have more time."

"We still do have to close, and people call out weekly."

"Good point. Well, how about we rotate another supervisor in there with you?"

"That would be helpful," I replied.

"Achilles, I will put you on close this week and Tony next."

"Oh, thanks, Daniel," Achilles responded.

"It's gonna be great," I replied with a smile.

"Alrighty," Abby said. "I'm gonna go to lunch. Let me know if you have any questions. I'll be around for a couple hours. Then it's off to salsa lessons."

"You take salsa lessons?" I asked.

"Yes. Do you know how to salsa?"

"Won three state championships in high school."

"Really?"

"No. That's ridiculous. I have no dance skills."

"Dammit. You had me going there."

I smiled and told her that I was taking my break.

On the table in front of me lay a list of additional responsibilities along with my phone. I could have started plotting my nights and maximizing my time. It was the perfect moment to get organized, but instead, I jumped on Frankie's' Twitter and doom-scrolled through the news about the pandemic and riots and all the things wrong with the world. I trolled a prominent politician and gained fifty followers in those fifteen minutes. Frankie was truly gaining a life of his own. My escape vehicle was intact. And before I could blink, I was heading back downstairs into the furnace with my chef's coat that gave me imposter syndrome every day draped over one arm. At this point, I had been the night supervisor for over nine months and still felt like I didn't belong.

I jumped on the computer to check for any new emails. Of course, several notes regarding our visit from the CEO were flying around. I half read through them, looked at my white coat, contemplated wearing it, and ultimately decided to hold off until further into my shift. The thought of wearing that heavy wool jacket irked me since I still had yet to receive the load and check over everything else. My first alarm went off: Check Temperatures. I grabbed the clipboard and headed out onto the floor.

A symbiosis connected the customers to the store and me. Or at least that was what I wanted to think as I was met head on with a wall of productive and important sound. Families casually strolled through the aisles. Fathers and mothers imparted advice upon their adolescent children as they decided on meals for the week. Grocery stores were the kind of place where parents might actually talk to their children and ask, "Where do you want to go to college?" or "Have you asked out that girl yet?" or "How is history class going?" I'd never thought about it until I worked in a different position besides the cash registers, but those types of conversations were tendons between muscle and bone—the structure and motivation that ultimately created that thing we called *family*. I'd had many expounding conversations about life with my mother while I'd picked out Totino's pizzas and the cases of Dr. Pepper that had fueled my summer. I guess it had been a free moment where parent and child could connect over food. It was intimate in a whole different way than one might normally surmise.

As I checked the temperatures on each station, I heard a commotion start behind me. I turned around to see two younger boys running up and down the hot bar station. The HB was an area where prepared items would sit in metal bins over heated water for hours. It was a place where you could get meat loaf, green beans, and sliced peaches all in one. People would load random items into a box for lunch or dinner. All the items fell under one price that was measured by weight. It wasn't cheap, and the food was mediocre, even though our team worked hard at what they did. Customers would tell me how much they loved our food. I just couldn't see it anymore. I was jaded. Once you saw how the sausage was made, it forever altered your perception.

The boys ran back and forth without regard for any of the other customers around. I looked for the parents, but there were none to be found. I walked over to the kids and asked, "Hey, guys, this really isn't a great place to be playing. Can you please stop running? Maybe move toward the cafeteria?"

"Fuck off, old man," one of the children said.

"Old man?" I asked. "I'm in my thirties."

"That's fuckin' old."

I smirked at their brazen disregard for authority. I was reminded of my youth. "Fair. But I'm going to need you two to go play away from the hot food. It's not safe here."

"We can play where we want."

I looked around for the parents again. No one was found.

A woman came up to me and asked, "Can you help me find the Bucknell rosemary-infused cherries?"

"Umm . . . never heard of them, but I can—just hold on one second." I turned around, and the kids were gone. I sighed in relief. "Okay. So you are looking for infused cherries, right?"

"That's what I said."

"Alright. Well, they will be on the other side of the store if we have them. So follow me, and we will try to find someone who knows."

"Oh, so you don't know?"

"Sorry, no, I don't. I work in our prepared-foods area, and that would be a grocery item."

"Fine," she bellowed, and we walked toward the grocery department.

I could feel irritated energy as she walked behind me. *What the hell is that item? It sounds completely made up.* I wanted to tell her some random location, but I'd been caught in that lie too many times, and I could use a better attitude when I interacted with the world. A younger, less seasoned employee might have just pointed and sent her on her merry way, but I guess I was just trying to be better. I didn't know, honestly, and I regretted it immediately because of her shit attitude. I'd even been trying to remove the word *Linda* from my vocabulary. But with every sigh and snort, this lady was earning her Linda title.

"Ah, Oz! What up, man?" I said as I went up and gave him a fist bump.

"What up, brother!" he responded.

The woman interrupted. "Could we skip the pleasantries and tell me where my cherries are?"

"Anything you say, Linda," I snapped.

"Excuse me. What did you call me?" she said.

"Sorry, I thought your name was Linda."

"Well, it's not. And I don't like your attitude."

"My apologies, ma'am. Oz, can you help this woman find . . . what kind of cherries were they, again?"

"Bucknell rosemary-infused."

"There you go. Well, Oz will take care of you. Have a good day."

Ozzy rolled his eyes a bit followed by a clenched jaw and an ice-cold stare. The woman said nothing, and I walked back toward my department.

When I rounded the corner to my section of the store, I immediately saw those same two kids fucking around near the hot bar station. As I got closer, I noticed one kid had a handful of mashed potatoes, and the other kid was holding a baguette. He was about to swing it like a bat. The pitcher launched the ball of mashed potato, and the other batter hit it square, causing it to explode everywhere. They cheered like they had won the World Series, with their arms in the air.

"Hey! Hey, what are you two doing?" I yelled. They looked at me and ran off again.

Mashed potatoes and spaghetti were splattered on the floor, and it looked like those little shits had dug into a dozen or so dishes. I was almost impressed with the level of a food fight they had been able to pull off in such a short time—and with no one seeing them throw down like this. But now I had to figure out how to clean this up and get my other duties done. Tony was downstairs in the kitchen, and all the other managers were done for the day.

I called out to one of my employees named Ziad. "Hey, can you get a mop and bucket? And grab Brian while you are at it."

Ziad and Brian walked over a moment later.

"Thanks for getting here so fast. Can y'all clean this up? I need to get these temps taken and production ready."

"Sure thing, boss," Brian replied with sincerity.

"You two are the best," I said as my panic subsided.

Dependable and genuinely helpful employees made all the difference. They were the rebar that kept the foundation intact. I wasn't sure how or why I deserved to have such good people in my life, but alas, I'd found them. Or really, they had discovered me and saved me.

I checked the temperatures, then began writing production—crouching down to pull out a small tuna salad or PB&J hidden in the back, counting the number of items still left on the wall, helping people periodically, putting items back every ten seconds until over an hour had gone by. Sometimes just the simple task of calculating all those items in one of the biggest stores in the region took a damn long time.

I was only two sections in on the ten-part wall when Ziad came up to me. "Hey, Daniel, sorry to say it, man, but it looks like those kids put their hands in everything. I can't tell what was touched and what was not."

"Shit. Has anyone eaten from it yet?"

"Not yet."

"Okay. Well, I guess let's pull the whole hot bar and throw it all away. Do you think salads are okay?"

He shrugged.

"Umm . . . pull the salads too, then. Just don't throw them away. Might as well do it all at once. I'll look for a manager to explain after I am done writing production."

"Sounds good, boss."

"Thanks, Ziad."

"Anytime. At least it's some variety, ya know?"

I laughed. "Yeah. Mixing it up with calamity."

"Embrace the chaos, amigo. That's what I tell myself with four kids. You just gotta lean into it and learn from it."

"Very wise of you, Ziad."

"Those kids age me too."

"Shit, I bet," I said.

"Do you have kids, Daniel?"

"Oh no. Not yet. Maybe never."

"Never?! That's foolishness, my friend. You would be a great father!"

"Maybe one day."

"You just need to find a nice lady," he said and raised his eyebrows.

"Yeah, that would be nice."

He leaned in as if to whisper because people were around. "I heard you are dating Lila."

"How did you hear about that?"

"I am a man of the people, Daniel. They confide in me."

"I assume you don't even know Lila. There are so many people that work here."

"I don't. I was only told her name and saw her when someone pointed her out. She is very pretty, my friend. Strong hips to birth many children," he said, then motioned as if he was humping.

"Allllright, Ziad. I think we'd better get back to work."

Ziad winked at me and said, "No problem, boss."

The evening crowd was larger than normal. Ziad and Brian barely had time to put the hot bar away before a line of customers formed that they needed to attend to. Nothing was closed down, really, but the area was sealed off with "Closed" signs. I made an executive decision and just filled in my best guess on the production list and ran to the back to get some gloves to put the hot bar away.

I returned to find an elderly man filling up a container with mashed potatoes. He had moved the "Closed" sign and decided just to go for it.

"Excuse me, sir," I said. "The hot bar isn't open anymore."

"Why the hell not? I'm hungry."

"We had an incident with . . . umm . . . food safety."

"What?! Why wasn't the food removed?"

"That's what I was just about to do."

"I mean, this really shouldn't have happened. What if you hadn't come back in time?"

I didn't really know what to say. My nerves were fried. I stood in silence.

"Well, are you going to answer for yourself, son?"

"What did you want me to answer for, exactly? I was on my way to clear all the food, and you moved past the 'Closed' signs to eat. If you want to set down that box of food, I will have this all cleared out so we don't have to worry about it."

"I would appreciate that but would like to see a better attitude from you. Do you think that will get you anywhere in life? I owned a chain of grocery stores for nearly twenty years, and terrible things happen all the time. You just have to deal with it."

The nerves were now unbuttoned, and soon the emperor would wear no clothes. I needed him to leave. I imagined him engulfed in flames, running around the store but still managing to stop and scold some employee for the incredibly difficult circumstance he or she was dealing with so that he could feel the superiority he thought he deserved.

"Son, I hope you learned your lesson here today," the man said. He set down the box and walked away.

Whatever lesson was to be learned burned up in my hatred for sanctimonious attitudes. His "wisdom" fell on deaf ears. And it made me wonder why people thought that shit worked. *In what world does telling a stranger to suck it up during an extremely rough moment help in any capacity? And to think that man ran businesses. Did his time in the industry melt his brain? Jesus Christ.*

The night began to bear down on everyone in our crew. I wasn't getting enough done with my duties, and I was way behind. Production was counted but only half-written. The line of customers seemed to only increase as the night wore on. It was nearly 9:30 p.m., and we were about to close, but there were still people waiting to pick up the chicken scallopini or Yorkshire beer pasta salad. The large line was pulling Ziad and Brian under. We had been assigned to double down on cleaning the ovens and restocking the floor with every-thing, even smaller items we had ordered just enough of to fill holes or had transferred from another store, to make sure we looked fully stocked.

Tony was unaware of these problems. He was helping the kitchen staff catch up. Cooks from both the morn-ing and night shifts had called out. "We're doomed," he'd said after we had each taken a swig of whiskey and before he'd headed downstairs. "Good luck with the wall," he'd said and offered the bottle again.

"I better not," I had replied, realizing I had been drinking a shot or two almost every night. I didn't want to slip into a lifestyle I couldn't recover from, but it sure made my life easier.

Abby had been working to fill holes on the wall for some weeks. We had rearranged items to clear out prod-ucts that weren't going to be in for a while. The only problem with this approach was that we would have to move it all back afterward, *and* we hadn't ordered the product we needed. The model was designed to blow our loads with this visit but sacrifice the future sales. Abby had said, "We need this!" all week. Sometimes she proclaimed it to herself while she restocked the plastic lids.

I enjoyed working for Abby. She was friendly and had a killer sense of humor. I could tell she cared about the employees as much as she could. But in time, I'd learned that in order to head up a department within Dream Grocers, a person needed to go to the corporate water fountain, overflowing with enthusiasm for a life of servitude, and drink as if their life depended on it. You had to love the grocery world. You had to be *all in*. There was potential reward for a life dedicated to something you believed in. But you always ran the risk of never being good enough or being passed over by someone who played the game better or had more luck. Usually, it was a combination of luck and hard work. From what I had seen in my life, if you put in the time, better opportunities would come to you. Don't quote me there, and you'll see a similar turn of phrase on the internet with a quick search, but I wanted to believe in it, and Abby thought I would find something that was fulfilling. I just didn't think our department was the answer.

It reminded me of my father's plight. He had been a pastor at a small church when I was growing up, and he'd served with all his heart. "The Lord will provide," he'd say, and our family was dedicated to the service of God. It was pretty simple for my parents—the kids, not so much. We were under the watchful eye of believers. In that community, pastor's kids were supposed to be examples on how to live. Being perched on a pedestal is no way to live. Believe me. I don't know how people do that shit on purpose. I didn't care for it. I never was much for participating in organized anything besides sports, and there was glory in that, but in church, I'd watched internal politics play out over time. When you dedicated your life to something, whether God or corporation, the same things could happen to you, and you could fall out of favor.

People had eventually turned against my father, and they had taken other people away from the church. The attendance had dwindled down to nothing; then the doors had to be shuttered. A life of service had left him out in the wild to grapple with his completely destroyed path. But his choice had been to serve an omniscient God who'd known his failure before he'd ever started. God hadn't rewarded him, as was promised in the Bible. That was not *agapao*. It was cruel. It was human. It was corporate. It was a human resources department for a major grocery chain. And for some reason I thought Abby was hoping that God would take care of her. I was too, in my own way.

Two weeks passed like two hours in a DMV. Slow and painful and all-encompassing—and when you're leaving, you feel violated as you stumble out into a foreign world.

I walked home through the snow that night thinking I was completely unprepared, and the reality was that I wouldn't see the walk-through. Nihilistic thoughts weighed heavy inside my mind. Everything was beginning to be too much. Even my burdens carried burdens. I felt a pressure to be great but thought there wasn't a chance in hell I would accomplish it. But I decided to ignore my thoughts and enjoy the snow crunching under my feet as I smoked a joint and lay my troubles down

on the frozen earth. I walked away from any worry and
floated all the way home.

XII

The big day came. Our white chef's coats were bright like white lines of pure cocaine. The energy matched the coats with a mix of anxiety and self-absorption. I told Achilles this metaphor, and he looked at me like I had some serious issues. He wasn't wrong, but we had done drugs together before. So I knew that he immediately thought about little white lines. I laughed at the fiendish coping mechanisms of the grocery-store world.

I wasn't scheduled to work, but Abby had insisted that I come in and get overtime since I'd put in a ton of work to get us where we needed to be for the walk-through. I appreciated her attempt to show recognition for the hard work. She knew it was a war zone most nights.

We all stood in a line in the back hallway. Jake and Ozzy walked by and started gesticulating like they were in a photo op. "Look at these fancy mothafuckas," Ozzy said. "Daaamn sexy, if you ask me," he replied to himself. They winked at us. Achilles and I winked back; then the boys walked away.

Abby was brushing off Tony's jacket. "How's everybody feeling?" she asked.

"Like I need a drink," I replied.

"You always do," Abby volleyed back.

"I need one too," Achilles said, then motioned toward the parking garage. "I have a bottle of peanut butter whiskey in the car."

"No. You can't do that. It's seven a.m."

"Do we really need to mention that it's five o' clock somewhere?" Achilles responded.

"It's not five o'clock here."

A wonderful idea popped into my head. "I say we make some waffles after this shit show of a walk-through and put chocolate sauce and whipped cream on top to soak up the peanut butter whiskey."

"Jesus, that sounds good," Tony interjected. "I'm in."

"No, that sounds disgusting. And you better not do that shit at work," Abby said, now showing real concern.

I didn't say anything, but when Abby turned around, I looked at everyone, and we nodded with the understanding that this would happen at some point. But it never did.

"Okay. So you all look fantastic! They should be here in about an hour. Let's each go over the sections and make sure this place looks goddamn incredible. What do you say?!"

No one responded. Apathy lingered like the smell of an old cigarette. She looked around for reassurance. We all nodded to feign agreement. I knew some in the group meant it more than others, but we all had a sneaking suspicion how this was going to go.

We broke off to our different assigned sections. Abby wanted me to clean behind a cooler. I tried to tell her that I thought it was pointless. She stared at me until I turned around and walked to the cooler with a mop and bucket in hand.

There were a great many things that one could learn when they stood in the corner of a cooler at seven thirty in the morning scrubbing an area so hard that they began to sweat—one being: the idea that . . . suffering gladly as an absolute good is bullshit. Some asshole who worked in a skyscraper four states away was coming in to judge our work and was about to judge my work, and there I was polishing the unseen corner of a place no one would look at except the people who cleaned it regularly. I wondered if that was what gulags were like, and I laughed. I scrubbed for a short while until Achilles walked in.

"Dude, I'm cleaning the refrigerators that I already polished three times," he said. "And no one uses them, so they look the exact fucking same."

"Well, I'm scrubbing my way to hell."

"I think you got it all wrong. You see, we are already there. You're scrubbing the floor in hell," he replied. "Daniel, I don't think we are supposed to live like this."

"I don't think so either."

"I just wanna be far away from this godforsaken tundra, on a boat that's anchored a short distance from the beaches of Sardinia, drinking mai tais with my hubs, screaming 'hot boy summer' out at the crystal-clear ocean."

"That's wildly specific, but I'm down."

"Oh, Daniel . . . you couldn't hang."

"Oh, yeah?" I pulled out a little snifter of coke. Achilles's eyes widened.

"Well, okay. You can come along, but you have to bring friends. We can't be entertaining you all the time. We are going to be busaay, if you know what I mean."

"You never are one for subtlety. Deal. I'll bring friends. Now take a bump, and let's get back to work."

"Daniel, you're the best."

He handed it back to me. I took one more snapper to the face and looked at the work I'd done. "Does this look clean to you?" I asked.

"Oh god, it looks amazing, Daniel. Now let's go see if there are any other bullshit tasks to do." He looked at his watch. "Looks like they should be here now. Woo-fucking-hoo!"

"Praise Jesus!"

"I don't believe in Jesus, Daniel."

"Hmm . . . well, just humor me and give him a shot."

"Well, alright, just this time."

"Let me hear you say it."

"Praise Jesus. Are you happy now?"

"More than you'll ever know. Now let's go out and see the world. I am ready to rock!"

Achilles laughed, and we left to find Abby.

* * *

The store was buzzing like an overheated hot plate when we walked out to the Chef's Case. Abby stood, leaning on the glass with one arm, rhythmically tapping her fingers.

"Where the hell are they?" she said. "I saw them walk in, and Todd looked flustered a moment ago when he walked by and told me to be ready."

"Did he remind you that pressure is privilege?" I offered as the first thing that came out of my head, but thankfully, Abby ignored my snark and went right back to her concerns. "I want them to come to our section first before the normal Saturday destroys everything we did. Why the fuck did they have to choose a weekend, anyway? These bastards never have any decency," she said to herself.

"It's all good, Abby," I replied. Achilles was standing behind us, shaking his head at me and motioning for me to stop.

"We don't know that yet, Daniel."

"Told you," Achilles said to me.

"Told him what?" Abby replied.

"Nothing. I just knew they wouldn't come to our section first," Achilles said.

"Maybe you should have told me."

"It's all good, Abby," I said again, for no particular reason. Probably because I was high.

She looked back at me. "You just said that. What are you, high or something?"

Panicked, I looked at Achilles. He shrugged and turned his head to the side to giggle.

"What?!" I said.

"Oh, I'm just kidding, Daniel," she said as she leaned in and brushed some whatever off my jacket. "Okay. You don't smell like alcohol. That would be an issue." Then she laughed.

"So we are both done with the cleaning. What else did you need us to do?"

Her body language was tense from the last two weeks, and without a single ounce of love, she said, "Nothing. Everything is set in motion. Just look alive and keep yourselves busy."

Achilles and I looked at each other and scampered to the back and headed downstairs to get away from the strange scene before us.

"This shit is wild. I don't really see the big deal," I said.

"It's like a big deal on paper, and the CEO will stop by eventually, but if I had to guess, I would say that he'll walk through and say some nice things, but he won't linger. He has bigger things to do. We will have worked our ass off for two weeks for five minutes of banal huffing and puffing. I've gone through two of these. Same shit every time."

"Do you think they just use it as an excuse to make us work harder for a short while?"

"Oh, for sure. Thing is that they will have a normal inspection right after he leaves. And that's probably where we will get dinged by something. So again, we work harder for some extended period of time. Do you see the pattern here? It's the slog of capitalism. By the force of our mighty paychecks, they make us keep pushing that rock up the hill like Sisyphus. That's why we need a union."

"How would a union help us with that?"

"I don't know; I just heard you are not fully on board with unions, and I'm sitting in a cooler, doing bumps of coke to pass the time. It seemed like the right thing to say."

"Do you want a union so you have a lower likelihood to get fired for sitting here doing drugs and neglecting our duties as managers?"

"Oh, probably, but that's beside the point."

"Is it, though?"

"Stop trying to play mind games with me, Daniel." Achilles handed back the little beaker of drugs. "Let's clean this cooler, eh?"

"We cleaned it two days ago!"

"Okay. Let's reorganize it."

"I think that will confuse people who need to grab stuff."

"Goddamnit, Daniel. Goodness, this stuff is fiya. Anyway, what should we do to kill time?"

"Let's go to the receiving docks. Maybe Jake or Oz are there?"

We walked up the stairs to find Richard and Todd in the warmth of embrace. Achilles and I stopped just out of sight and watched for a moment. Todd leaned back and said, "We did it, my friend."

"I was worried for a moment, boss," Richard replied.

"There was never a need to be concerned. I will always protect you. Now, listen to me. We cannot go easy on them during and after the regular inspection. You know what that means. You understand what we must do. Remember what I said to you? This is where you must make your stamp in life. This place is our legacy."

Richard wiped the tears of joy from his face, and between clenched teeth, he said, "Oh, I will."

Achilles and I turned back around to look for Abby and Tony and to tell them about what we had seen.

Abby was sitting at our manager's desk. Tony stood like a tree, leaning quietly against another desk as if in deep thought.

"Well, we made it through the big one," Abby said. "Well done. Now, we just need to get through the normal inspection, and considering how much we prepared, I think we will be home free."

"Think again," Achilles said. "Daniel and I just overheard Todd and Richard talking about how they are going to be extremely tough on each team in the inspection."

Abby replied, "Shit? Really?"

"Really," I said.

"Well, I have worked here for twenty years. They won't be able to pull a fast one on me."

Achilles scratched his chin. "They seemed pretty determined."

"We'll be fine."

"When does it start?" I asked.

"In about an hour?"

"Is it cool if I take my break?"

"Yeah."

"I should probably take mine too," Tony said.

"Sounds like we are going on a date. Where are you taking me?" I responded.

"There's a dumpster out back if you're interested."

I put my hand on my chest. "Well, I do declare . . . Tony, you sure do know how to treat a man."

He chuckled. "Dumbass."

"Tony, Tony, Tony . . . why would you use such harsh language?"

"Will you two just go?" Abby said sternly.

Tony and I walked up to the break room together.

"Do you think we'll pass?" I asked.

"I don't know. If they are looking for something, they will find it. And some things are just impossible to fix in an old kitchen that doesn't get the support it needs. The rest of the departments will probably be fine."

"Why would they try to fail us on purpose?"

"Todd—and, well, Richard too—talks about the vision and the mission for this company often. They take it more seriously than others. Far too serious, in my opinion. Like they are win-at-all-costs sorts of people."

"Why do you think that is?"

"I guess maybe people just need something to focus on. They need a purpose and power, even if it is a grocery store."

"Over the last year and a half, I learned that the store is pretty goddamn important. I hadn't thought of that before, but it is a vital resource in our cities, towns, and neighborhoods."

"You're right about that. People still gotta live, though. There is no need to torture the plebs because you need a purpose and you enjoy power."

"All salient points. We never really talk, ya know. This is nice."

"Fuck off."

"Tony! Don't leave me now."

"You're fine. Just no sentimental crap, okay?"

"I swear from here on out, it's all bullshit or serious talk."

"Thank you."

"Wanna see my alter ego?" I asked.

"I swear if you show me your dick, I'm gonna throw you down the stairs."

"Damn. Well, I guess I will have to show you my other alter ego. You ready?"

"As long as you keep Little Daniel in your pants, yes."

I handed him my phone with Frankie Bombay's social media on it. "What do you think?"

"What do I think about what?"

I pointed to the phone.

"Oh, you are asking if I am interested in your kink where you dress up as a panda. Umm . . . not really."

"Oh no? Look at the follower count on that one."

He looked closer at the phone. "Jesus Christ! You have three hundred thousand followers! How long have you been doing this, and what do you do when you are in the suit?"

"I have been doing it for a long time. And I just talk to the camera and drink cocktails. Nothing too crazy."

"You can't be serious. You just talk to the camera?!"

"Yeah, dude. It's weird, I know. But people have connected with what I'm saying."

"I will never understand this generation."

"Wait, which generation?"

"This one. Whichever holds the keys to the current thing. I can't imagine sitting there listening to a stranger talk into a camera with a panda costume on. That blows my mind."

"I don't understand why people like it either, but that doesn't mean I won't have a better idea later on down the road. I like to think that I'm learning as I go."

"I'm just an old-school chef with a checkered past. I don't have time for these things."

"Oh, I want to hear about this checkered past."

Tony looked at his watch. "Shit. Looks like we are already late. If you buy a bottle of whiskey, we can kick it, and I'll tell you about my past. But no whiskey, no deal. That's the only way I can dig into that shit."

"Deal."

We turned the corner from the stairs to find Achilles looking nervously down the hallway.

"What's up, homie? You okay?" I asked.

"They started the inspection, like, right after you two left. Richard and Todd look like they are on a mission."

"Odds are we're gonna be alright, dude."

"Ugh. I know, Daniel. I just don't care about this place enough to have to do extra work because some small-dick power-tripping assholes wanna ruin our life."

There wasn't much to say there. I carried with me the exact same sentiment. I had no interest in what might come if they failed us on purpose. I looked at Tony—a man buried deep inside his head. A furrowed brow of concern sat heavy on his face, but I knew that he would carry on no matter what came of this inspection. This was his life now after whatever crazy shit he'd gotten into earlier on. His tattoos, shaved head, and bullish mustache kinda said it all.

The minutes seemed like hours. Finally, Abby came around the corner and waved for us to come her way. We walked into the cooler that Achilles and I had done drugs in and cleaned earlier. It looked spotless in my eyes, but Richard and Todd were rummaging around. "So when was the last time this cooler was cleaned?" Richard asked.

"Achilles and I cleaned it earlier today," I volunteered.

"There is dirt on the shelving. We are going to have to deduct for that."

"What dirt?" Achilles asked.

Todd pointed to a smudge on the side of one rack. I stared in amazement. They were actually doing it. They were railroading us. Weeks of long hours and double the work on half the staff, and they were going to fail us on purpose. They were failing us to prove a point— the power lay in their hands. The two men went back to their clipboards. All four of us knew what was happening. We looked at each other like doomed people, like death row inmates who had been fighting for years, knowing they were innocent, but in the end it was futile. The gig was up. Evil had won.

We walked around for about another half hour. They pointed at things and wrote down words on their powerful clipboards with their tiny hands. Lies slithered out of their mouths like snakes in the Garden of Eden. I began to zone out and think about anything besides being publicly flogged for all the store to see.

I wondered if there was any hope for me and Lila. There was a decidedly quick *no* that came to mind. I fought it for a short moment but knew my soul was right on that one. I tried to remember there was a life outside of that place. And before the pandemic, we knew about the outside world. My experiences at Dream Grocers were a juxtaposition of insulated interactions and raw nerve exposure to the madness of the time. I dealt with the worst kinds of people, but I had the best folks to back me up. I couldn't work from home, but I was glad to still have a paycheck. As I watched customers fall apart in real time, it allowed me to build actual grit that survived harsh conditions. The burden we all carried during 2020 and 2021 was ever present, but being so close to the flame gave me strength.

A finger tapped me on my shoulder. I turned around to see the saddest Tony in the world. "Abby wants us to meet at the outside break area."

"Isn't it a bit too cold out there for a meeting?"

"Yeah, I guess, but she is on her third cigarette in a row, and I told her we could have the huddle out there to save her a little bit of stress."

"Alright. Let me get my coat."

We stood in a semicircle as the cool spring pummeled the ragged crew. Looking back on it now, everything seemed a bit too dramatic for what was simply a bad review, but when you were in a moment where careers were at stake and the ego got in the way, life could seem ridiculously intense.

Abby had her legs crossed. She inhaled a prolific drag of her cigarette while she stared off, then blew it out to say, "This is gonna be a long quarter. We got a C."

I was the newbie to corporate visits. We'd had smaller versions from the regional manager but nothing from the top of the company, and I didn't know exactly what that meant, but there was an audible sigh from Achilles and Tony.

"What does a C mean?" I asked.

"It means we are fucked," Achilles replied. "And not in the good way."

Abby lit another cigarette. "It's kinda worse than what Achilles said. We will be getting fucked for three months straight. Weekly visits from corporate. Additional cleanings and assignments every night and day for everyone. Constant scrutiny. This hasn't happened before at our store, and we are one of the biggest in the region. Hell, it hasn't happened in our region for maybe five years. So *everyone* from the regional office will be in our—mainly my—shit all the time. But we'll get used to it. The team will not be happy about the additional duties, but they are going to have to get used to it, and we will have to make sure they do them. It's a hard road ahead."

"What did we do that was so wrong?" I asked.

"Oh, they got us on probably ten very small things."

I looked at Achilles. "They did it to us on purpose. Todd and Richard. They wanted to teach us a lesson or some shit. Achilles and I saw them practically putting fingers in each other's asses, and we heard them say that. I mean, is there any recourse?"

"I remember you two saying something, but there wasn't enough time, and no, there isn't any recourse. The only action is to get ahead of it and make sure we get the things done they wanted."

I began to tremble in anger. "We have been short staffed the entire time I've worked in the department. They add new things to our list every week. We are a top-tier store in the region and insanely busy. We work our goddamn fingers to the bone, and they fail us out of spite? To teach some lesson that we are supposed to learn from two incel losers who obsess over this place because they are empty inside? Jesus Christ, what a toxic mentality."

Abby put up her hand to stop my rant. "Guys, we need to stay positive about it. This could be a very cool learning experience for all of us."

"*Very cool* is a strong choice of words," Achilles said.

"Tony . . . what do you think?"

"I think we will just do what we gotta," Tony said. "It's not like we have a choice. God hates us. It's fine."

I couldn't help but laugh. "Tony is always bringing that positive heat," I said to the group.

"I mean, what else are we supposed to do?" he asked. "The struggle is real. Life is suffering. I've been through worse. Whatever cliché you wanna use to sum it up."

"Was prison sex worse than this, Tony?" Achilles asked with a laugh.

"Fuck off, Achilles. We didn't have sex; we made love."

The tension left the group.

"Wait, I don't think I've heard the prison-sex story. Please, do tell," I said.

Tony put his hand on my shoulder. "I told you, man. Over whiskey."

"Glorious. Prison rape is key to any good hang sesh," I replied.

Tony opened the door to go inside. With the glow of the store at his side, he said, "I told you. We made looove."

I looked at Achilles and asked, "Is that true?"

"You're just gonna have to sit down with him. He's had a wild life."

Abby stood up. "Oh, that's right! Hey, hold up . . . I forgot to mention what we are doing next." We all stopped and looked at her. Tony was already inside. "I'll get some plans together this week, and we'll have a meeting next week to discuss how to fix this bullshit."

"Sounds good, boss."

"Hey, Daniel—hold up a second."

Achilles went inside.

"So your one-year review is this week."

"Oh, yeah, I was wondering when that was coming up. Is there anything I need to do?"

"No, just wanted to give you a heads-up."

"Well, I appreciate it. Oh, and, boss—"

"Yes?"

"Despite this place and the madness within, you're a good manager and, more importantly, a good soul."

"Well, thanks, Daniel. I appreciate that."

I opened the door and stepped inside the building. The night wore on like the brutal days of my adolescent years. I teetered on the edge between joy and pain. I was lost but also understood. I worried about one of the coolers going down because of a rattling fan in the AC unit. The sales floor was an utter mess. Lindas were inevitable. Daves were probable. Pedro was passive aggressive. Janice didn't show up for work. Jamie was solid. We were short staffed but getting all our work done. We had been born to survive. And I did. And we should, given those were tiny sufferings in comparison to what could be. Burning out on the city streets of this life, losing control, finding a grip, and we were doomed to repeat it over again and over again and over again.

XIII

Fluorescent bulbs hummed disco in the background of the room bathed in a godforsaken, harsh white light. My eyes watered as they sat perched above the face mask in a steam bath consisting of hot breath and coffee. I thought I had moved past the masks, but not in that moment. They were back with a vengeance. I'd been sitting here for ten minutes. My index tapped reflexively on the chair as Abby searched for my year-review paperwork. I was starting to grow impatient with the length of what I considered a transactional meeting. My left ass cheek was going numb, and my back was beginning to hurt. I fidgeted and stretched, but it did nothing, so I pulled my mask down. "So did I pass or fail, boss?"

"Don't be silly. You did just fine. You know this is just a formality," Abby said as she dug through papers—acting more flustered with every movement. "But I can't find that thing anywhere."

"Is this where I get to review your organizational skills?"

She looked up, rolled her eyes, and said, "I guess it might be." Then she continued to search around the desk, opening drawers, looking increasingly lost with every passing moment.

The atmosphere in the room was stale with the dust of the 1980s and long overdue for some new air filters. The spring weather had swung back to a warm day with chilly winds. Every minute or so, the air conditioner kicked on, and sweet relief hit me but quickly stopped and brought me right back to the DMV waiting room disguised as an office. The oscillating temperatures caused beads of sweat to stack up on my freshly starched chef's coat. The heavy wool didn't allow my skin to breathe. It was a good-looking jacket, but at this point, I took no pride in it. But maybe I should, since both men and women at work had said I looked sexy in it—in fact, it might have played a role in gettin' me laid in the past, but all sense of accomplishment was gone. I was met with only discomfort and the increasing notion that my work was piling up downstairs in the bowels of Dream Grocers.

As she searched frantically for the paperwork that was full of disappointments, I meditated on the fact that it was not exactly her fault this moment had come down to a flurry of disorganized frustration. We'd had an awful walk-through, and we'd been short staffed due to budget constraints for as long as I could remember. Our department leadership team was worn so goddamn thin that it was hard to keep the world stitched together. You could patch only so many holes with drinking on weekdays. It was a miracle if I smiled some days when

I walked in. And that was not how work should be. It wasn't because of the people. It was the organization and the situation. There was a framework in place that didn't call for this to be a career. I kept pulling at this fucking mask. I wanted that fabric monstrosity to be out of sight and out of mind, but it was back. My beard made it itch while my eyes slowly cooked like pork carnitas. All for the inevitable, boring, commonplace result of this meeting.

"Oh, here it is. Are you ready?"

"Well, before we start, can we take the masks off? Just for a moment. We are probably whatever distance the CDC says we should be, and there is great circulation. And something seems disingenuous about the moment with masks on."

Her eyebrows raised. "Umm . . . sure. I guess. You aren't feeling sick, are you?"

"Of course not," I responded.

"Yes, that's fine."

We both removed our masks, and the staggering intensity of the scene fell away. "That's much better," I said as I inhaled the dusty office air.

"Okay. Now are we ready?"

"Sure."

Her body language begged for me to play along.

"I mean, hell yes! Let's do this!"

"I did mention in your review that your sarcasm has exceeded expectations during your time at Dream Grocers."

"Does that increase my raise?"

"Daniel, let's be serious for a moment."

"Fiiine."

"Do you want the positives or the negatives first?"

"Umm . . . there are negatives?"

"Well, yes, but only because I have to write something down."

"You shouldn't show your hand like that."

"What?"

"Never mind. I'm just messing with you. Start with the positives."

"Okay, here is what I wrote down. Daniel has been exemplary in his meteoric rise in our company."

"Hold up . . . you actually used the adjective meteoric in your review?"

"Yeah. Why?"

"Nothing. That's just an excellent adjective choice. Please continue."

The muscles in her face slumped, and her eyebrows raised in semiexhaustion. She adjusted her placement in the chair. "Daniel has shown himself to be an essential part of our team. He is always willing to help others and put in the extra time to get what we need done. As a result, he has moved up twice in our department in just a matter of months. Daniel has embraced the Dream Grocers Code of Conduct and leads by example. He has been an exceptional leader during a difficult pandemic where we have made constant adjustments to our ever-changing circumstance. He has handled the transitions with grace."

She paused a moment and looked at me.

"Is that all of the positive things?" I asked.

"No. I am just making sure you are still listening."

"Of course I am still listening."

The ego padding continued.

"In an example of his exceptional leadership, Daniel ran several shifts with only two people to work with. They managed to keep each area running without incident, and he wrote our nightly production. He has been an invaluable leader in our Dream Grocers kitchen through the darkest of times. It's because of these and other accomplishments I am recommending that he receive the maximum raise for one year of service."

There was a pregnant pause. "Well, thank you for the kind words," I said. "Now, what are the negatives?"

She looked at me for a moment, then handed me a paper. "Here, you take a look."

I flipped the paper over. It was blank. "Umm . . . what's this?"

"There weren't any bad things I could write down. I mean, we all have areas to improve, but you are doing great."

"That's awesome, but didn't you say that you had to write things down?" I responded as I slumped in my chair.

"Yeah. I said that because I wanted you to be surprised. None of this matters anyway."

"That I know," I said as I cringed, freed from the awkwardness.

She leaned back in her chair for a moment and said, "But there is one issue here."

"What's that?"

"You don't look happy anymore. I feel like that fire in your eyes has slowly dimmed."

"Is it that obvious?" I said with a laugh.

"It really is. I mean, what changed?" she responded.

"Everything."

"Like, when, though? It seemed to come out of nowhere."

"It did? I feel like everyone has changed during the pandemic. Ever since the 'incident,' I have been on a journey—you know, one of those vision quests of self-discovery or whatever. My sense of self has been slowly melting and restructuring since that day. I feel like a brand-new person."

"Wow . . . I had no idea. But did that lead you to be unhappy? Or was it something else? Because we are all going through that same shit. Yours was just a little more extreme. I didn't really know you or anything, but word around the store was that you wanted to kill yourself that day."

I raised my hand to stop her and defend myself, but I changed course. "Yeah. Everyone jumps to conclusions. They judged me before knowing the whole story."

"Well, yeah. That should be expected. We all do it. But now that I've gotten to know you, I don't think that anymore. Like I said, we were and still are going through some shit. That's life. And I mean that for the people like you and I that have to go into work right now. When I say we are all in this together, I don't mean everyone in the world—I mean the group of us that didn't get a choice to stay home."

"I'm not entirely sure if I'm unhappy. I think that's a permanent state of being for me."

"But, Daniel, that can't be it, or at least that can't be the whole reason you lost the fire. I didn't meet you until after your distress call at the outside break room."

"I guess that's true."

"Well . . . indulge me, then. I'd like to know where your head's at."

XIII

"Okay. Yeah. Sure. Fine. But first, can you tell me what my raise will be?"

A look of motherly understanding washed over her demeanor as she said, "Five percent is your raise."

Despite knowing that was coming, I grew enraged and blurted out, "That's why."

"Huh?"

"That pathetic raise. I knew that was coming. For over a year I knew that's what I was worth to this place."

"Well, wait. I'm not saying that's what you are worth to this place or to me. That's just the most I can give you. And if you knew that's what was coming, then why stay here?"

"I didn't have much of a choice given the pandemic. No one is hiring."

"That's fair. We are all stuck at the moment. It's a tragedy. Is that why you are unhappy?"

"It's a tragedy for sure, and maybe that's why I'm miserable, but let's not get off the subject at hand. You know what that raise equals out to at my current pay rate?"

"No, I didn't look," she said, embarrassed.

"If you factor in inflation, my raise is more than nothing—I am making less than before." As I spoke, a strong urge to stand up and raise my middle fingers to the sky and proclaim "Fuck this place!" crawled through my brain like a soldier in the jungles of Vietnam. My legs tensed up, and I used my arms to lift my ass off the seat, but she stopped my heroic act of defiance and reckoning.

"I don't think that's true. That can't be. Are you sure?" she asked.

"One hundred percent. I make eighteen dollars an hour. A five-percent raise is ninety cents more. Inflation hovered around two and a half percent per year in early 2021, last I checked. That dissolves half of my raise. My rent went up by one hundred dollars. I'm bleeding out, looking for a lifeline in an economy that doesn't let me find another job that pays better. This raise is an empty gesture. So you see, I appreciate the kind words. But this job is way too much work for little to no real appreciation. And I think you know this. But I really do accept the sweetness in your honesty and hopeful attitude. They are thoughtful, and I enjoy working with you. I am paid to do the work, but this is also crushing my soul."

"Why didn't you tell me before? Maybe there's something I could do?"

"Come on now, Abby. We are being candid here. Don't try and bullshit me. You know this place. You know how it works. Just yesterday we watched Richard and Todd railroad two weeks of hard work because they want to prove a point."

"Well, that's rude. I wouldn't put you in a bad situation on purpose. I honestly had no idea that you were in such a bad place."

"I'm not saying you did anything on purpose, but look, deep down inside you know that I work really hard and the raise they are willing to give me is a slap in the face."

She nearly choked on the swig of water she had in her mouth and lurched forward in shock over my bold yet completely obvious assessment. But she settled back in her chair with a contemplative look. The situation simply demanded examination, and I appreciated her attempt to understand as she sat in silence and I waited.

After several air-conditioning rotations, she finally came to some sort of conclusion and asked, "So does that mean you are quitting?"

"I don't know. I mean, not yet . . . maybe. I don't know what possessed me to be so honest, but I needed to say that. Look, I'm not saying I'm a victim here, because I am not. But the weight of my day-to-day duties paired with the exhausting circumstances of the last year have led me to this point."

"I get it. Believe me; I get it. No need to apologize. Do you want to know something? I feel trapped too."

"Really?"

"Yes, but not in this job, though. Not here, at this store. In the past. Now, I'm in a great position with the company. I think you just need to dive into your work more. Talk to the right people. Make the right moves."

My jaw sat agape as I tried to wrap my head around what she had just said.

"Umm . . . I don't want to be rude, but you are in a middle-management position with heavy stress. And I thought that's what I have been doing this whole time, making the right moves," I said.

"Maybe think about it more."

"You just told me I am an exemplary employee."

"Well, maybe that's not all you need to be doing to move up in your career."

I had nothing but a blank stare to give her in response.

Her voice turned worrisome as she said, "I don't know. Maybe I'm not explaining this right. You're doing great, but maybe there is more you can do, ya know?"

Annoyed and disgusted, I asked, "Okay, what should I do?"

"Daniel, don't get snippy with me. I am just being honest. You were honest with me just a few minutes ago."

"That's fair, but it strikes me as more vague than honest. But maybe that's how it works here?"

There was a sharp change in mood, and I didn't understand quite how we'd gotten there. The room turned into a claustrophobic and unsettling space. What I had thought was a simple conversation had turned sour and complex. I hear a voice behind me say, "How's everything going in here?"

It was Todd. The gel in his hair glistened as he stood strong and authoritative with a slight hint of arrogance. "I heard you guys from the hallway, and it seemed like a lively conversation."

"Hi, Todd. We were just having a conversation about honesty," Abby said.

His face contorted with concern, and he dragged a metal chair across the floor and sat down. "In what context?"

Abby motioned for me to talk.

"Well—"

"Hold on," he interrupted. "Why aren't y'all wearing masks?"

"We wanted to have a more candid conversation, and we are both over six feet apart," Abby replied.

Without hesitation, Todd removed his mask and said, "Great idea. Now, back to the conversation."

My heart thumped against the side of my rib cage. I thought about what Achilles and I had witnessed in the hallway and the results from our walk-through, but I held my tongue for the moment. "Abby said she was being honest with me about what I need to do with my time here at Dream Grocers, and I said that was more vague than it was true."

Todd leaned back and scratched his chin. His beady little eyes moved back and forth as he contemplated my words in silence. I looked over at Abby, and she shrugged, as if to say she didn't know. Again, another person was taken back by my honesty—they were startled by my apparent brazen truth seeking. My heart flushed with pride as I told Todd how I felt. Relief swam through my veins. Would it pay off, though? Had I gone a bridge too far in my forlorn quest to get meaning out of this shit job? I trembled with anxiety because in my heart of hearts I knew how it was going to play out, or so I thought. The air conditioner clicked back on.

"Daniel, is the truth always obvious?" Todd asked.

"Well, no. But—"

"That's right; sometimes you have to search and search and search for the truth, and you may not find it at all. Hell, it might not exist."

"Umm . . . Todd . . . there is always a truth in any given situation."

"You don't know that," he replied.

"Yes, I do," I snapped.

"Be careful with that attitude, Daniel. I'm being relaxed here, but I won't be insulted."

"What?" My throat began to tighten.

"I am your superior, Daniel. I will not be insulted," Todd said as he thundered down on his chair with an open-faced hand.

I hated that term, superior, in reference to management and the authoritarian undertones it carried in tow. I fucking despised Todd and his little-man huff and puff.

He was a pitiful sight in his lack of accomplishment and tragic in his bitter response to success.

An employee of mine named Edmund had called me his superior all the time, and it had given me the creeps. Todd fixed his lump-coal eyes in my direction. Panic spread through my chest like bronchitis. He was waiting for an apology, but I wasn't going to apologize. It was time to lean in and say what I needed to.

"Look, I'm not trying to insult you; that's not my intention." I paused for a moment and reframed my direction. "I think we have gotten way off track with this conversation. All I was really trying to do was find out why I got such a low raise. I have worked my ass off in this place. I have done everything you've asked of me. And now we are going to have even more work after last night's sham of a walk-through. What I am saying is that I can't see what incentive you provide for success in management here at Dream Grocers."

Fear gripped me as I realized what I'd said about the walk-through last night, but Todd continued on with the conversation in his head that he was already thinking about. "Well, the truth is that we've talked about your raise." He pointed to Abby. "And we both decided that what you need isn't a bigger raise. You don't need more money."

"Jesus, really? What do I need?"

"A better attitude."

"And you expect me to change my attitude after a ninety-cent raise."

"No. I expect you to change your attitude in spite of it. Pressure is privilege."

Jesus Christ! That trite bullshit again? Dude, stop reading leadership books, and actually fucking lead,

XIII

you goddamn fucking troll. A night crawler–size vein emerged on the side of my head, and raging clarity snapped into view like a DMT trip. I put my hand up, and the room went completely silent, even the air conditioner. "You know what? Consider this my two weeks' notice."

"Wait, what?" Abby and Todd asked simultaneously.

"I'm putting in my two weeks' notice."

"Like, for real?" Abby asked.

"I understand you're upset, but don't do anything rash," said Todd.

"Look, I'm not doing anything off the cuff here. Well, maybe a little avant-garde, but I need the catalyst, and this fucking place is not it. I just came to an important observation about our futures here at Dream Grocers."

Todd folded his arms and asked, "And what would that be?"

I contemplated if I should say it. And I did. "I saw you talking to Richard in the hallway last night before our walk-through. I heard you say you were going to be very harsh, because, and I quote, 'They need to learn our ways.' You failed our team on purpose."

Todd's muscles spazzed. But he sat there in silence. The whole room collapsed on itself while Abby and I waited for his reply. I'd told her about his shady dealings last night, but she had not been expecting this turn of events.

After quite some time, Todd shifted toward me in his chair. "So you think I said that because I am vindictive? Is that what you think of me after all this time, Daniel? I brought you in from the front end. I saw the possibilities in you, but apparently, I was wrong. You can't see the

251

bigger picture. You aren't able to grasp the vision I have for you."

"That's the fucking thing, man. Your vision for people isn't what matters. That's not what a leader is supposed to do. You should try to foster our visions."

"What is your vision, then, Daniel?"

"I envision a job where managers don't absolutely crush their employees because of their ego. Where the work we do is appreciated. I know what you are going to say. You are going to tell me that you were trying to help us be better, but really, you and Richard just wanted to look good in front of your superiors. Keeping us held to the flame makes you look like you are doing something. If there was ever a trickle-down effect, it's in how management is approached here. From the top of Dream Grocers on down, it's a punitive system that focuses on 'pressure' instead of thoughtful and nuanced motivation."

Todd was even more relaxed. "Daniel, I want you to think back on how our interactions started. How could I be more nuanced and thoughtful than plucking you out of the front end after you nearly commit suicide to try and give you a better life inside of the organization? I wanted to watch you grow and thrive."

"That, or you just felt bad or obligated to treat me better since you made the wrong decision about not calling an ambulance."

His jaw dropped. Abby's mouth was wide open. I knew it was over for me there.

"Hold on a minute. Can we just stop for a second? I think we all need to cool off," Abby interjected.

I decided to take control of the situation and leave him holding his ego in his hands and exit on a high note.

"I've made up my mind, boss. After this whole fucking disaster of a year . . . I just can't do this shit anymore. This is my official two weeks' notice."

"Well, after that little tirade, I don't think we want you here," Todd said. "But I can appreciate the honesty. If you apologize, I'll let you stay."

"What would I apologize for, exactly? If you appreciate my honesty, then we should be good."

"There were some exaggerations and false statements in there."

"What did I say that was wrong? It might have been mixed with my opinion, but it wasn't false."

Todd looked off into the distance.

"I'm exhausted. Can I go now?"

"Are you sure you don't want to make this your last day?" Todd asked.

"No. I'm giving you my two weeks. Then I'm done."

Todd paused for a moment. "What if I just decide this is your last day?"

"I guess that is something I will have to live with," I replied.

Rage was building in his tubby, rounded face that glistened with moisturizing lotion, but Todd didn't give in to his lesser nature. He glanced to the side, took a deep breath, and slapped both knees. "Well, if there is nothing I can do to change your mind, then so be it. But just so you know, once you put in your two weeks, that is final."

He said one and meant another with such regularity that his words rang hollow. The truth was etched into the lines of his face like hieroglyphics. I knew they needed me. There was no one to directly replace me, and they always dragged their feet on hiring new people. It was part of the business model. Do more with less.

"I can live with that," I responded.

Todd didn't acknowledge my answer and walked toward the door, "accidently" knocking some papers off a desk onto the floor as he left.

I looked over at Abby, and we both smirked awkwardly. "Well." She tried to move on. "Where were we . . ."

"We had moved on to casual conversation about anything but work because I put in my two weeks and the whole dynamic of this meeting is irrelevant."

She laughed. "I guess you are right. So how about them Broncos?"

"They are a tragedy in my eyes." We both chuckled, but there wasn't much to talk about anymore. I didn't need to be here. Neither did she.

"I'm going to miss you, dude," she said, to my surprise.

"Really? I mean, do we talk that much?"

"Uh, yeah we do. Well, more than most people. I mean, I know that you are writing a novel."

"See, that's how little we don't talk. I'm actually shelving the novel for now. I'm going to focus on Frankie and see where that goes."

"What's Frankie?"

"He is a character that I have developed into an online influencer. I've got several sponsors already."

"Oh, really? That's awesome. But why give up on the novel?"

"Who reads books these days? I can make more of an influence with Frankie."

"Is that what you want? More influence? I thought you wanted to create a meaningful piece of art."

"Frankie can be meaningful."

"Don't influencers just party on boats and take selfies?"

"Not all of them," I said sheepishly.

"Well, I think you should write a book. That would be super cool."

"I'll think about it."

"Good. I hope you aren't just taking this influencer route because you are at a weird crossroads in life. I think that happens with all creators from time to time. Like writer's block or something."

Where had her in-depth perception come from? "Yeah, I suppose. But that's not it. Entirely. I don't know."

"Well, what was your book about?"

"It's about this place."

"Oh! Really? Am I in it?"

"Yeah."

Abby's face turned red. "For real?"

"Who knows, really? Maybe I'll write about this conversation, or maybe I'll talk about it on Frankie Bombay's social media. Who knows?"

She began to look uncomfortable and shifted in her chair.

"I'm just fuckin' around, boss." I wasn't, but I didn't want to ruin her day.

"Well, let's just say I would be flattered if you wrote about me and the team in a book, but I don't want people blathering about me all over the internet."

"For real? I mean, about the book thing. Not the internet thing. I won't talk about you on Frankie's social media."

"Yeah. Of course. Don't you think it's flattering to be immortalized?"

"What if it's unpleasant information?" I replied.

"Doesn't matter to me. Most of our lives fall like sand through a sift. No one—not even loved ones—will be remembered forever. And if it's factual, then I will just sue you," she said with a great big don't-you-dare-type smile.

"You have a good point there, boss. I didn't expect this conversation to be philosophical."

"Well, I didn't expect such a good employee to quit."

"That's fair. I kind of dropped that on you, huh? Hell, I sprang it on myself."

"Do you want to take it back? You can if you'd like."

"I can? Todd just said that I can't."

"If I stick up for you, he will be fine with it. We can chalk it up to misunderstandings."

"Well, I really appreciate that, but I'm pretty set on it."

A comforting voice with a southern drawl broke open the silence in the room to say, "Hey! Y'all done here yet?" I looked behind me to find the old leather flask holder that was Jeanie. "We got the leadership meeting going on. Shit, it should've started five minutes ago if y'all weren't neckin' so much."

"Dammit! That's right! I almost forgot," Abby blurted out. "Can we pencil in a conversation about your future in the next few days? I really want to hear about it."

"Of course," I said with a nervous smile because I didn't know where to begin. That feeling of failure crawled all over me like ants, and I didn't actually want to talk about it because I might second-guess myself. I turned around to see Jeanie standing close.

"Where is your goddamn mask, puddin'?" she asked.

I laughed. "I guess I am just breakin' the law like you did back in the day."

"Shit, sweetie. You don't even want to know."

"Oh, I do. Shots of devil's water later after work?"

"You know it, kiddo. Now, get out," Jeanie said.

Abby walked over. "You should put your mask back on, Daniel."

"Do I still have to even though I'm quitting?"

"Yes, you do," she responded with a flat expression.

"You're quitting?!" Jeanie yelled.

"Well, yes, long story," I said. "Devil's sweat later. We can talk it over. We can grab the whole crew."

"Perfect."

The room began to fill with managers of all shapes and sizes. Their faces were replaced by graphite scribbles as they talked. It was strange. I should have known everyone, but I was at a loss. My hands began to tremble. The loneliness of the moment was getting to me. I felt like I was stepping back from something, but behind me was a cliff, and I really had nowhere to go. The hum of the AC was drowned out by discussions of meat specials for the week and tasks of the day and sales numbers and the ugliness of middle management. I stood by the door, trying to hear the details, and I knew what they were saying, but I couldn't understand the words, like being a second-year Spanish student in a crowded market in Madrid. Everything exploded into the static on an old television. This was upsetting, and I was trying to care about it, but I couldn't. I wouldn't even fake it anymore. My stomach turned at the idea of giving another moment of my life to this place. I was glad I'd put in my two weeks, even if it terrified me. I didn't know what I was going to do, and I couldn't afford to take the time off like I had before this job. It was a requirement to care. I didn't remember there being so many managers. The room was packed to the brim. Everyone was facing the front of the room, and I saw only black baseball caps. I couldn't even see Jeanie or Abby anymore. Where were Todd and Richard? They usually led that meeting. I decided that it was all too much for me and stepped out into the hallway and shut the door behind.

Short-Timer

XIV

I stumbled to the front of my apartment as one fist pounded away at my door and another railed against my temple. The light of midday spring nearly put me on my ass. "Oh, what's up? Jason."

He rocked back a bit and said, "Woah, dude? Looks like I missed out on quite the evening."

I shook my head to clear the cobwebs and said, "Yeah. I mean, it was a good time."

"Looks like it."

"I'm looking a little rough, huh?"

"You must still be drunk. Have you looked at yourself in the mirror?"

"No. What's up?"

"You're wearing a panda costume."

I looked at my hands and touched my head, and sure enough, I was in full panda garb still. "Ah, yeah, I was doing some videos for Frankie Bombay's social media with coworkers, and it got a little carried away. Twas a celebration, and I feel like the remnants of a roman candle."

"I wish I was there. Last night, when I was leaving for work, you told me you put in your two weeks at work. Is that true?"

"Yes sir."

"Well, then I think we should celebrate."

"Agreed. Whatcha thinking?"

"Do you still have those magic mushrooms?"

"Ohhhh yeah. Sure do."

"Fuck yes. Let's eat some and have a park day."

"I love this idea. You wanna go now?"

"Give me an hour. I gotta run to the store."

"Sounds good."

After Jason left, I opened my dirt-stained off-white refrigerator with little to no items of nutritional value within, grabbed a Coors Light and two string cheese, and sat down on my seventies-style flower couch. I pulled out a wooden box where I kept drugs of all types. Underneath some more illicit substances was a nice little baggie of those silly little things that looked like turds so old they'd turned gray. I shook them around and admired the swatches of deep-blue psilocybin stained into the stems. To the touch, they were only Styrofoam Cheetos, but inside, there was the magic known for millennia. Those unassuming little morsels may have had a part in the evolution of humans—the stoned ape theory, coined by Terence McKenna. The tiny caps at the top seemed disproportionate to the body, causing the whole thing to look phallic. Jake had told me the strand of mushroom was called "Penis Envy," and it seemed wildly accurate. This wasn't my first rodeo with those mushrooms. Hell, I'd been experimenting with hallu-cinogens for almost the entire pandemic. What a fun and ever-expanding way to observe a world completely turned upside down and inside out. A world that pitted brother vs. brother. A world where the real virus was fear, and people in high places were doing everything they could to leverage our uncertainty and insecurity into a more entrenched power source of which they held the keys. They promised empty inflatable lifeboats that leaked at the seams.

Tripping was therapy, most nights. How else was any reasonable person supposed to deal with the terrify-ing reality before us? My only option was to let all the unknowns and knowns hit me like a wave of radiation. I felt like an open nerve to all humanity when I took LSD or mushrooms or Molly. When I tripped, it was like I opened up the curtains and let some light in on my dusty old hovel; then I observed it for what it was, and if I felt the urge, I'd rearrange the furniture inside the liv-ing room of my mind, slowly, making damn sure I was comfortable and free in the strange life I lived.

I drank another beer and ate more string cheese. My mood and general disposition improved. I popped a small stem into my mouth. Maybe ten minutes passed where I thought about almost nothing at all as I sipped my beer. I looked at my phone. Jason would be back soon. Then we could get on to the real shenanigans. A slight breeze crossed my skin even though I was inside with all the windows and doors shut. There was a shim-mer to my otherwise off-white/mustard-colored walls. The mushrooms were acting faster than expected. Jake wasn't lying. They were premium. The lift was nice. My feet were sore from a long day. I looked around the disheveled room and wondered how I could live in such a shit hole. Was my destiny to live in squalor? I lay down on the couch for just a moment. I was thinking too much. But as soon as my head hit the pillow, I heard a knock on the door. Jason had arrived.

"What up, dude," I said with a smile. Jason was a good friend, and I always enjoyed spending time with him, but I was even more excited to see people in the flesh during those days as the framework of our society crumbled.

"Hey, man. Sorry I took longer than expected."

"You're late? Time is imaginary, homie," I said, hoping he would laugh, and he did.

"Are you on your way to the moon already?"

"Yes sir. Here, join the party." I handed him the bag.

"Ooh, these look nice!"

"You want a beer?" I asked.

"Please."

I grabbed two Coors Lights and handed him one, and we sat down on the couch.

"Has work gotten better since you decided to quit?" Jason asked.

I laughed. "Define *better*."

"That's fair. But at least you aren't going to have to deal with that shit anymore, right?"

"I don't know how to convey my emotions properly in regard to the amount of joy I feel."

"That's awesome, dude. So what's the new job?"

"New job?"

"Yeah. Like what are you going to do now? You didn't quit your job before having a real thing lined up, right?"

"Define *real thing*."

Jason's face tightened up with concern. "Dude. You quit your job without having a real job lined up? That's wild!"

"Jason, dude, relax. First off, you know me. I'm a survivor. Like a cockroach in nuclear winter. But I already have an online presence established as an influencer. Well, Frankie Bombay does, but he is me, and I am him. So I guess we are in this together?"

"The panda guy is going to be your job?"

"Yup. I made enough off promotions to pay the rent this month."

"No shit? That's wild, homie. Well, good luck," Jason said as he chewed away on a magic stem. "I guess sometimes ya just really gotta let go."

"I've given it all up and let Frankie take the wheel," I said, hoping to change the subject to something that wasn't anxiety inducing. I was starting to feel like I was touching a nerve that I shouldn't in that moment.

"In Frankie we trust," Jason replied.

I was grateful we were moving on from the uncertainties of my future for the moment. "The one and only," I said.

"Are you sure you should give him that much trust?"

"I mean, he seems like a nice fella. If things go sideways, I'll shut him down and start an OnlyFans."

"Good point. Speaking of which . . . how long have we been wearing these masks?" Jason asked, holding his chin diaper in hand.

"It feels like an eternity."

"For some reason—stay with me on this—I feel like we have always been in the time of COVID. We just never realized it."

He held the bag up and looked inside with great concern, trying to select the right piece.

"What do you think about this one? I don't want to go too overboard with these things, ya know?" He held up a mushroom to show me.

"Looks like a space probe if I've ever seen one. I say go for it. I'm already at about three pieces that size."

"Shit. I'm game. What were we talking about again?"

"You had just brought up that we have always been—"

"Ah, that's right—I mean, I don't think we have *always* been in the time of COVID. I remember the late nineties—that gap between twenty-year wars in the Middle East, when we had CDs to give access to dial-up internet. Bill Clinton was sleeping with interns, and Marilyn Manson was the only real threat to our children."

"The white children."

"Good point."

"I get what you're saying, though. Our early years of life were a time of great prosperity, at least in the United States. We made some huge leaps in short order as we emerged out of the eighties and sailed through the nineties; then 9/11 happened, and as a country, we went into a war that we know now we were cowed into by powerful people. Young men and women in our generation died for it. It's even worse in those countries we invaded. I'm sure we both have friends that saw things they never needed to see. As a species, we are homogenized by fear."

"I gotta say, Daniel, this conversation turned serious pretty damn fast, and it seems you are higher than me right now."

"You're right. I'm sorry. I've just been overwhelmed by the world recently. And putting in my two weeks' notice, betting less on myself and more on the times, has my head spinning. These are the last couple days of my traditional life. I need people to talk to in an open manner—one that's conducive to solving big problems . . . I'm just trying to understand. No one talks to each other anymore. I look around and see people doom-scrolling, masked, muzzled, and burning the whole thing down." A sudden urge to cry came over me, but my tears turned into balloons full of inertia and ramble. "Should I throw on a record?"

"Actually, why don't we go outside? The springiness is screaming for us to explore while the warm sun blesses us on this fine day."

"Yeah, I'm down. But is there something wrong?" I asked Jason.

"What do you mean?"

"Never mind. I think the drugs are kicking in."

"Aye-aye, Captain."

"Let's go for a walk. How does Cheesman Park sound?"

"Sounds fantastic."

I rounded up the supplies we needed: sunglasses, backpack, blanket, bottle of gin, blueberry lemonade, and the rest of the mushrooms.

"What kind of snacks should we bring?" I asked.

"What do you have?"

"Nothing, but we can stop by the store."

"Deal."

"Wait a second. How do you feel about pork rinds?"

"Well, I'm not indifferent to them, if that's what you are asking."

"That's not exactly what I'm asking."

"Are you asking if I like them?"

Puzzled, I stopped for a moment and said, "I believe that's what I'm asking you?" I began to giggle. Jason followed. We convulsed for a few moments in pure joy. As the waves of absurdity and calamity pulled back, I was reminded how I should laugh more, even at stupid things and for no reason at all.

"I'm glad we cleared the air because I fuckin' love pork rinds," Jason said and nearly fell into another fit of laughter.

"Do you now?"

"Yes sir."

"That is great news because I love pork rinds also."

"Do you have any pork rinds?"

"God no. But I think we should get some, though."

"I agree."

At the store, we found the fried pigskin we desired, peach rings, Gatorade, and water. A man with Jesus on his name tag was smiling under his mask as he rang up the items. "Thanks, dude," I said to him as we left, and I contemplated how awkward I sounded.

"Did I sound weird saying goodbye to Jesus?" I asked Jason.

"Huh? Why would that sound awkward?"

"I don't know. I guess I'm a concerned fella at the moment."

"You need not worry, my friend. If you sounded awkward, well, Jesus forgives."

"Good, good."

Our spring day expanded out with the universe, and the sun peppered our stroll on the disheveled sidewalks of Cap Hill. Within the city limits of Denver, this neighborhood was my home. I loved it for all the leftover bohemian discontentment it provided. The mishmash of architecture ranging from 1800s' mansions to edgelord conceived, modern bungalows and shiny skyrises to homeless encampments strewed about made for an interesting and diverse cross section of humanity.

Cap Hill was located in what I considered the throbbing vein at the center of the city, where transients and old neoliberals found their nests. Brick houses were converted into four separate apartments on the streets lined with old cedar and aspen trees sprouting in unintentional areas. Down the alleyways, you may find a burned mattress leaning against the electrical panel of an apartment building or a junkie shooting up in a tent. But there still remained children playing in front yards and hipsters walking to Thump Coffee and dive bars offering cocktails to go. The old juxtaposed with the new and the bleak with the infinite possibilities. It was where I found myself in tango with the genetics of our city—smashed together like Play-Doh of the gods and piled high like kindling.

As we walked and talked and moved around a homeless man leaning over into a trash can, I noticed the weather was good natured in comparison to many spring days in the Rocky Mountains. The sun was shining, and the birds sang the praises of someone more important than me. From March to May, Colorado could be found having a midlife crisis of sorts, where half the time we were covered in snow, and the other we were cursed with heat. The weather was God's adolescent confusion at not getting what it wanted, but on that day, I was grateful for the easygoing mood.

We reached the edge of the park, and a slight cross-wind hit both Jason and me like a force field as we stepped past the shelter of the houses on each side of the street. I lowered my sunglasses and looked over at Jason. He looked back, and we both understood the moment. A gong thundered at the base of my skull, and the reverberations skipped down my spine. I shivered.

Jason leaned toward me and said, "It looks like an impressionist painting in motion."

"They glisten and pop like exquisite 3D animations," I said.

"That's called real life," he responded.

We both laughed. He wasn't wrong.

"I mean, yeah, kind of, but have you ever seen so many people walking all alone with masks on? Look at that guy over there, sitting on a park bench—not another soul for fifty feet, and he is wearing a mask with a face shield on. What's the point of being outside if you can't experience it?" I said.

"People are scared. It's an escape room, but the only way out is through compliance. I mean, I don't blame them. It's not their fault," Jason replied.

"Whose fault is it?"

"It's Jesus's."

"The guy at the gas station."

"The one and only."

"That's not fair."

"There is no 'fair' in a pandemic."

"This is true. Where should we sit down?"

"Let's find some shade and pour a drink."

It was midafternoon on a weekday. The park was abnormally busy—almost to the point where it was crowded. Packed, even. I didn't know if it was the quantity of humans or if it was that people were trying to stay six feet from each other and everyone took up more space with a dot matrix composed of "social distancing." People scribbled an arbitrary circle around themselves, and everyone needed to stay the fuck away. The world became a very lonely place. But I got it. That was why we were there too. It was the only respite from a life locked in homes and boarded up.

Jason and I weren't making any extra efforts to stay six feet away from each other. Like, I wanted personal space, but I wasn't going to make an ordeal out of it. There were enough things to concern myself with in this life, and not hearing someone because we were too far away was not going to be one of them. Even a year into the void that was the pandemic, I had friends who were very worried. They wouldn't hug people goodbye or visit family, and they were losing touch with reality.

We weren't wearing masks either. As we walked through the park, I saw a few people doing the same— living a maskless life—and it made me happy. Weird that something so incredibly normal was suddenly a unique, inviting sign of life. It was also awkward as people glared in disapproval. *How dare you live and put us all at risk?*

We found a sunny spot near a cluster of pine trees. The ground was chilled from the spring thaw, and I was grateful we each had brought nice thick blankets. We spread out our territory, and I poured gin into two cups, followed by blueberry lemonade, and handed Jason his drink.

"How are you feeling?" I asked.

"Wild eyed and bushy tailed," he responded.

"Sounds like we have a spring chicken here."

"We definitely have something springlike here. How are you feeling?"

"Like I am watching a movie based on a movie about making a movie."

"Rad."

"Yeah. It's not so bad. Here, let's get some tunes going."

Jason's brow furrowed with worry. "Not too loud. We don't want to be those people and draw attention to ourselves."

"Agreed. What should I play?"

"Something spicy? 'Lamb of God'?"

"What? No, dude. You're a musician. I was expecting more from you."

"Well, then maybe you shouldn't lead life with expectations."

"Good point. I'll play some Pink Floyd."

"No complaints here," Jason said.

The eerie bells of a grandfather clock crawled out from the beginning of "Time" as I leaned back on my elbows. The building of drums and keyboards filled the entirety of our space. I looked up in the sky to see the sun turned into the orange clockface, with the hands moving at incredible speeds. Everything else was still. But perceptions were wrong. Anxieties were high. I looked to my left. "Shit," I said. "Why do I know there is a Linda walking our way?"

"My god. I think you're right," Jason replied.

"She has a cunty radar built in. She sensed we were enjoying ourselves maskless from three miles away."

"Damn. Maybe she is just walking by."

"Doesn't look like it," I replied.

Linda arrived. "Hi. I know everyone is having a rough go of it, but do you think you could wear a mask? The vaccine is so close to being released to the public, and we are trying to avoid getting sick."

My eyes were full-size dinner plates behind my sunglasses. I remained baffled within my psychedelic terrarium, and I remained silent, hoping that she would give up and move on. Jason didn't say anything either.

"Did you guys hear me? Do you think you could wear a mask?"

"Umm . . . yes, we *could* wear masks."

"Well, then why don't you?"

"We're outside."

"Yes. But people may walk by."

"So?"

"So . . . the virus is airborne."

"And everybody was fine staying the hell away from us until you waddled over here."

"Well, it seems unnecessary to throw insults."

"You came over here to harass us with your bullshit." I noticed some people were filming as I became inflamed with rage. I knew this could end badly, and I would be the bad guy. Before my lower primate brain took over, in a calm but stern manner, I said, "Listen, you need to leave."

"You know, I just think—"

"Fucking leeeeave!"

"This is just really—"

"Now!" I said, pointing in the direction from which she had come.

She stormed off.

Jason and I looked at each other. I lifted my drink to my lips and said, "Jesus Christ, man. That was way too intense."

"No kidding. What has this pandemic done to people? Did you see how she was trembling?"

"Yeah, dude. It was so strange. All the hairs on my body are standing on end right now. I don't know how I can recover from that negativity."

Jason lifted both arms toward the sky. "We shall endure," he said.

"That we shall."

"What makes someone believe they can tell others what to do?" he asked.

"They are weak, feebleminded fools. Someone on the news told them what to believe, and they believe it's their duty to tell people what to do as the arbiters of truth. The people in power—the ones that encourage that woman to do what she just did—poisoned the goddamn well, and I don't think we can go back. We can't undo this mess. Speaking of permanence . . . did you see that person filming?"

"I did. Maybe we will become internet famous."

"I already am," I said.

"Whaaa? Really? How so?"

"I told you about it already, broheim. Frankie Bombay. Here, look." I showed him my phone.

"Oh, yeah. There you are in the panda costume. Damn, dude. You have a shitload of followers."

"Told you. And you doubted me quitting my job."

"I'm sorry. I don't doubt your ability to make whatever work. I was just surprised. I guess I am old fashioned. The idea of quitting your job to entertain people online sounds bizarre to me. But anywho, Frankie Bombay, huh? Interesting. What does he do?"

"Define *do*," I replied.

Jason gave me a look of exasperation and said, "Do you always have to be so esoteric?"

"Only when I know it will annoy you."

"It's working."

"I'm just teasing."

"Fucker," he replied.

"Well, it all started by way of pure, blinding boredom. I was drinking a copious amount of gin, sliding deeper into the darkest parts of my soul with no one to listen to my thoughts, so I started recording videos of me on my phone. It started as a great scream into the void, but I shared it on the web, and people started to follow me. One night, I was a half bottle deep and decided to throw on my old Halloween costume. And when I put on the polyester ceremonial garb, my god, I saw lightning strike twice. People were in search of anything to lighten the stress of being locked in their homes. And I was there for them. I'd rant about lockdowns or daily habits. I philosophized and waxed poetically about the life of a panda, of which I could only imagine as a man in a panda costume. I even started an OnlyFans."

"Holy shit! Really?!"

"No, I didn't. But should I?"

"Probably. I mean, what's the difference if it's anonymous?"

"Good thinking, Jason. So, anyway, it's been my saving grace. And from the emails I get, I guess it's gotten others through the hard times also."

"I guess we all have our ways of coping."

"This is true," I said. "Dude, she is coming back."

"Ah, fuck . . ."

This time she was strutting back with two other Lindas by her side and a camera pointed in our direction. We braced for impact.

"How do you feel about endangering everyone around you?" she said.

"Ma'am. This is public property, and you're harassing us."

"You're right that it is public property, but I am performing a civic duty, and you two are dangers to society."

"Don't you have some rich-white-lady things to do?" Jason chimed in. I looked over at him. His eyes weren't covered, and one of his hands was shaking. He wasn't looking too good.

"Typical misogynistic tropes. We will not stand for it," the first Linda chimed in, and the two other women responded in agreement, their phones pointed in our direction.

"Listen, you three are the ones breaking social-distancing guidelines here," I reminded them.

"Maybe, but it's in the name of justice."

"Is it justified when you kill your parents, your children's grandparents?" I asked.

"How dare you! We all know this situation is about you two and *your* dangerous behavior!"

"Look, you can tell yourself whatever bullshit you want, but we aren't moving, and you are wasting your time."

"Well, we won't leave either. In fact, more are coming."

"Shit. I mean, why not. Let's have a superspreader event. Why are you even wearing a mask?"

"It's the responsible thing to do."

"And harassing innocent people in public parks is 'responsible'?"

"As a citizen of the world, we should look out for each other."

"Who are you looking out for, exactly?"

"Well—"

"You are looking out for your fucking self."

"No I'm—"

"Yes, you fucking are. Now, go back to your thousand-dollar strollers, Mercedes-Benz B-Class Minivans, and sheer panic-filled lives to await the realization that you're dead inside and no one will ever really love you."

The eyes of all three women were wide and bright and full of sadness from a life of neglect and unmet promises. But to their credit, they said, with sheer determination of will, "We have nothing. We need this."

Shocked, I looked at Jason and asked, "Did they just say what I think they said?"

"Yeah, dude. I think they did."

I turned back around, and they were halfway across the field. The people filming us were laughing and uploading videos and doing what these modern kids were prone to do.

"That was so strange," I said.

"Yeah, dude, but I am glad you stood up to them."

"I did?"

"Yeah, man."

"What did I say?"

"You don't remember?"

"Nah, dude. I'm so high right now."

"Oh, yeah. I almost forgot. Well, you flattened them and told a truth they had never heard before."

"Really? Shit. Good for me." We both laughed.

Despite our encounter with the three Lindas, I found magic in a day free of walls and ceilings, masks, and politicians—full of vitamin D and a sense of freedom that seemed to be slipping away. I didn't really know if I had an opinion on the state of the world at the moment, but I understood that the sunshine was seeping into my pores, and I was wrapped up in the reminder that I was alive. The mushrooms were starting to tone down, but the alcohol was going strong on that uncanny, pleasant day.

"Do you want to eat more of those things?" I asked.

"Sure. What have we got to lose?"

"Everything."

"But that's true all of the time. We could die at any moment," Jason proclaimed. "Speaking of which . . . how are things with Lila?"

I sighed.

"I'll take that as not great."

"For all intents and purposes, we are over."

"Just a flash in the pan, eh? I'm sorry, dude."

"It's okay. I think it was supposed to end just like my time at the store. Just like this pandemic will come to an end."

"I'm not sure that the pandemic will end, but relationships are tough."

"No truer words have been spoken. She was young and hot, and I am a nervous wreck. I don't think I deserved it."

"Nah, dude. Don't be so hard on yourself. We are the realized failures of our fathers. It's okay. There will be others."

"You're right. I guess I just need to sit in it and take a breath."

"Exactly."

The sky moved fast and furious like it had somewhere to be or something to do. I sat up and saw that the folks who had been filming us were staring in another direction with their cameras out. I followed their line of sight and began to tremble. "Jason, look at that."

"Woah. Umm, should we get going, dude?"

"I don't know. We aren't doing anything wrong."

"They don't care. I think we should go."

"But then they'll win."

"Not everything is a zero-sum game," Jason replied.

"It is when my freedoms are involved."

The Lindas had regrouped with more Lindas, Daves, and even one Norman. There were at least twenty-five people walking in our direction with aggressive and heavy body language. Their faces were covered by home-made masks with fancy patterns and favorite sports teams' logos. The cameras of bystanders multiplied. I decided that was a great idea. I needed a record of the interaction. I pulled out my phone, turned on the video function, and reached out toward Jason. "Dude, make sure to get this whole thing on film."

The crowd came closer. "Are you ready to do this, man?" I said as I looked behind me. Jason was putting all our stuff in the backpack.

"Dude, I'm sorry," he said. "I'm not staying for this. It's not worth it."

A wave of fear washed over me. He was right. My freedoms were less at stake. I needed to keep my sanity, especially on mushrooms. I smiled at the irony of staying sane on boomers. A hand grabbed my shoulder. "We gotta go, man." With that, I began to run without looking where I was going. Jason was my guide, my hero. My legs were churning. I heard cheering in the background. *Shit, they think they won.* I stopped and turned around to see my enemy.

The breadth and scope of the park hit my eyeballs all at once, and the world pulled in close. The green and brown, the undecided sky, cracked, splitting life as I knew it right in two, between blue and bearded white clouds, the earth, the sun, the chin-diaper zombies strolling past—the whole kit and caboodle could fit inside a fleck clinging onto the ridge of my eye. I couldn't see the Lindas and Daves anymore. I looked inside, and for a moment, I didn't see myself either. But I was there to stand strong for however long it took.

What I did see, however, was the last bastion of nature left in the midst of a concrete jungle—a preservation for the human animals trapped in the city. I saw the walls were closing in. There were tiny pixie-like angels hooked into my skin, pulling me apart by the billions. My epidermis rippled across my body in waves of electricity. Wild thoughts floated past me like boats as I pushed them off into the river of existence. The west had been won by those who sought to define their own existence, by those who *chose* to stand, as I did, and to live and die by their own volition. The groceries must be sold along with my soul. The people must eat and be merry. But what was left for me, there, in the absence of meaning and purpose?

When my legs stopped moving, I stood—half-panda, half-man-in-the-wild-west—with the sun dipping into the mountains, and Indian paintbrush orange bloomed behind the foothills. Jason and I decided to sit on our community patio and unwind. "Were those Lindas real, or did we just freak out?" he asked.

"If we both experienced *that*, then it actually happened, right?"

"I guess. I mean, yeah, that makes sense," he replied and now seemed more at ease.

We listened to the cars pass. "Do you remember sitting on the patio with Levi and his girlfriend when the pandemic started? We howled into the night and listened to neighbors fuck and fight."

"Yeah, dude. Those were weird, lovely times that I'll never forget."

"I haven't seen Levi for a while. Did he move out?"

"Yeah, dude. He moved out a month or so ago."

"Why is that?"

"I think the pandemic has worn us down. Living with other people is tough. His girlfriend practically moved in, and it was all too much. Evenings turned uncomfortable. Bridges were probably burned." He shrugged and took a sip of his drink.

"Well, that's a shame."

"I agree. But it also makes sense, ya know? Relationships are being put to the test all the time, but the pandemic is maybe the biggest figurative minefield of our lives."

"With both external and internal relationships."

Jason sat quietly for a moment. "There is too much truth in that last statement. The totality of the internal wars being waged inside all the humans is far more destructive than all the conflicts in physical world history. But now that I think about it, that's always been the case."

"True and true, but now people only cling to doom-scrolling and fools dressed up in panda costumes jabbering on about the world."

"Then I guess that's what we will take."

XV

It'd been three days since anyone had heard from or talked to Janice. We weren't scheduled together anymore because of her flaky behavior. I couldn't afford to have someone show up only half the time. The only problem was that they hadn't replaced Janice on the evening shift. Once again, I was short staffed, and their only offering was to place a manager to work alongside me at night. This was something I could handle because I got to work with Tony or Achilles on nights, and we joked around enough to make it all tolerable for my last couple of weeks.

The opening and midday crews were finishing their tasks when I walked into the kitchen. Abby sat quietly at the desk as she stared off into the distance.

"Hey, boss!" I greeted her.

"Oh god! You scared me, Daniel."

"Sorry, didn't mean to." I noticed she had been crying. "Hey, so . . . what's up?"

"Do you know if Tony is here yet?"

"I saw him upstairs. He should be down any minute."

"I'll tell you guys when he gets down here."

"Ah, okay." I put my chef's coat on and brought my backpack to an area I knew was out of the way. I'd grown tired of having our office in the hallway, where everyone walked by with ample opportunity to grab our shit. For once, I would like to be treated like a human and not like an afterthought.

When I got back to the desk, Tony had arrived, and he was looking at Abby with the same concern. "Is something wrong?" he asked.

"Let's go outside. Sorry that you put your coat away, Daniel."

"No biggie." I walked back to get my jacket.

The dim city lights intermingled with the fading shadows of the day. Dusk in a big city lacked imagination sometimes, but at other moments the concrete split by growing trees and the broken infrastructure that would be there long after we were gone was magical to the point of disgust. Abby sat down and lit a cigarette. "I don't know how to say this lightly, so I'll just go for it. Janice won't be coming to work anymore."

"Damn. I know she needed this job. I'm surprised she quit," I replied.

"She didn't quit."

"Huh?" I asked.

"She killed herself."

And with those words, Abby put the world on mute. A gregarious group of teenagers walked past, but I couldn't hear a word they said. I could think only of Janice and her family. The thoughts of pain and suffering consumed that moment. She'd beamed with life when she'd talked about her son and his accomplishments.

"How'd it happen? I mean, are they sure she committed suicide? She was so proud of her son that it's strange that she would kill herself."

"My brother-in-law knows her, and it looks like she took a bunch of pills and drank a lot of vodka, and, well, she left a note. I shouldn't know this, and I *definitely* shouldn't be talking about it with you two, but I am freaking out a bit. You have to promise to keep this to yourself. Deal?"

"Silence is violence," Tony said.

"Huh?"

"I'm just kidding. Trying to break the tension."

"Now is not the time, Tony," Abby said.

"Oookaaay, fine. And yes, I won't tell anyone," Tony replied.

"Thanks. We good, Daniel?"

"Of course," I said.

"In her letter she talked about the pandemic at length. It wasn't specific besides that she felt so isolated and lost. She said the free world wasn't so free anymore. Or that maybe it was an illusion all along, and in either case, it didn't seem like she was helping anyone by being here. Her son most of all. She thought he would be better off with her gone. I'm sorry if this is all too dark. I just needed to share. The mind is a scary place. To think she could imagine her life was both so important and inconsequential at the same time is something I'm struggling to understand. Her burden must've been great. Then you drink yourself to delusions of grandeur and worthlessness. Her poor son must be devastated. Oh, and she said . . ."

"What did she say?" I asked.

"About what?"

"You trailed off at the end. What were you going to say?"

"Ah yes, well, she mentioned working here."

"Really? That's crazy. What did she say?"

"Well, she said that we made her feel like a person—that she had purpose. And she mentioned you by name, Daniel. She appreciated that you listened when she called in drunk that one night. Sorry if that's too heavy, friend. I just needed to tell people. I need a drink. Wait . . . yeah, no, I definitely need a drink. I didn't know you talked to her on the phone."

"It only happened once. She was very drunk, and I tried to call her back after she just hung up. I was going to try to get her some help."

"Ah, well, that was nice of you. Apparently, she didn't forget."

She sat by the phone—watching the light turn on with the zzz . . . zzz . . . several times—thinking how lovely it was that I wanted to help, but she didn't ultimately think she was worth it.

"Can I sit out here for a while?" I asked Abby.

"Of course you can. You ready to go in, Tony?"

"Yeah, I'm good."

I don't think I moved an inch for the next fifteen or twenty minutes as my soul anchored my limbs to the bench. Cars whizzed past. Lives—from the fantastic to the mundane—were passing, and almost none of them would ever know who Janice was. They didn't need that. They probably didn't care. How was I supposed to feel about someone complimenting me as they faded away from the shallow banks of the unknown?

XV

Suicide was common by this time in the pandemic. The economic impact of the choices made was starting to hit the poor and forgotten. It always hit those considered lower in the caste and rarely the upper echelons of society. Elites made decisions that crushed the others. Autonomy—bodily or otherwise—was only abstract when you had the full weight of the government bearing down and offering those government checks. That free money allowed so many to turn to comforts like drugs and alcohol. I was no stranger or saint to leaning on the bottle. I drank at work most days. But I was glad I had something to do in a grocery store to keep me from going all the way down.

Maybe Janice could've been saved. If she had just talked to someone instead of diving into the bottle, maybe she would have been able to see her first grandchild born. I stood up, thinking about hope and how to foster it. I didn't believe in closure, but I did think we could accept the burdens and own them. The best I could hope for was peace—peace of heart and mind and a relinquishing of that savage pain we all carried inside. I still had a job to do. Work needed to be done. I opened the door, let the air out of my lungs, inhaled the grease-filled draft, embraced what little direction I had, and walked inside.

* * *

"You ready to go, bud?" Tony asked.

"Yeah, just have to finish up this dumbass paperwork. Did you take our nightly pictures?"

"Nah. I just used some old ones from a few weeks back. No one looks at that shit. But I sent them to you to attach to your email."

"Thanks. And good thinking. Wish I could do that with this shit."

"Shit, dude. Why do you care? You are down to your last few days. It's over. Fuck them and this stupid shit."

I was listening to him, but the fatigue in my fingers and in my eyes barricaded a good answer to his question, and I said, "I guess I just want to do a good job."

He burst out laughing. "A good job?! Dude, you've done a great job the whole time. No one is watching."

"I know, but I am."

"That's fair, but I'm fucking thirsty. I wanna get whiskey drunk. I need to run downstairs, but I expect you to be done when I come back up."

"What do you need to do downstairs? Sneak a drink?"

"Exactly."

"Why go downstairs? There aren't any cameras around, and I need a pull too."

He smirked and said, "Here." He handed me a bottle of Evan Williams.

I crouched over as if someone might see me and took a moderate sip of room-temperature whiskey, and a calibrated, quenching burn filled my throat, lungs, and face as I handed the bottle back to him and wiped leftovers from my mouth. For the moment, my life filled with brightness. But it faded fast as I composed an email summing up our day's wins and losses, callouts and accomplishments. I always tried to say nice things about the people who worked for me. I knew that whoever might replace me could very well not give a shit about them.

And they worked hard. It was a busy store, and we were perpetually understaffed. We all were overworked. Well, some were; others got away with fucking around or causing trouble and received no true backlash.

And then I noticed I was transcribing these thoughts into the email. I deleted the partial rant, attached the photos, and sent the fucking thing out. I grabbed my shit, and we both headed out the door.

We decided to go to Cheesman Park for a couple of drinks, but it was about a mile away, and we needed to choose our path. "Do you want to walk through the fancy neighborhood or go the short route?" Tony asked.

"Anytime you can walk through Country Club Historic Neighborhood, you should. It reminds me of my place in the world."

"It reminds me of *your* place in the world too," he responded.

I couldn't help but laugh.

At the entrance to the neighborhood were brick columns towering up at least twenty feet with lamps at the top. We walked in the street because the neighborhood didn't have sidewalks. It gave you a powerful feeling to walk in the middle of the street lined on each side by ancient, established luxury and wealth. Plush lawns with carved hedges and freshly planted tulips and rosebushes peppered the sprawling domestic landscapes. These houses were almost exclusively made of veneer brick. Some had gates keeping the rest of us out.

"How many of these people do you think come into our store?" I asked.

"Well, we don't see these people at all. We see their housekeeper. Most of them don't have time for the plebs."

"That's a good point. Hand me the whiskey while you wax poetic."

I tipped the smooth plastic bottle back for a long hearty sip of whiskey. My lips were starting to go numb.

"Well, aren't you going to say anything?" I asked.

"Eh, I got nothing. There is too much emptiness here to talk about at length. Everything has a pretense to it that doesn't sit well with me, ya know? Ostentatious for no reason whatsoever. Like, see those lights in the tree— those orbs randomly placed amongst trees that are two hundred years old? How much do you think those cost to be put up?"

"I have no idea," I said, smiling in my soul and kissing a bottle of transcendence.

"They cost probably as much as what we get paid in a week. It's disgusting."

"Hold on. Is that what you're *actually* mad about? The lights in the tree? Or is it the fact that you didn't think to rent a truck and rob these rich fuckers like the guy who put those lights up? Is this rant out of jealousy?"

"Well, maybe a little. Give me the bottle. But my point still stands. And I'm a little drunk now."

We walked for a while longer and talked about random things. As we sauntered through this neighborhood, I liked to imagine people suspiciously looking out their venetian blinds at poor people walking by with backpacks on while sharing whiskey and talking far too loudly for eleven o'clock at night in a dead, quiet, wealthy neighborhood.

"Dude, do you hear that?" I asked.

"Hear what?"

XV

"Exactly. It's so fucking quiet around here. I know it's kind of late at night, but my apartment complex is way louder right now."

"All their money keeps the noise away," Tony replied.

"Like what, they stuff their backyard walls with hundred-dollar bills or something?" I asked.

"Well, yeah, but they also design the city around these people. Just look how they eliminated sidewalks. When we get to the poorer part of the neighborhood, you see sidewalks again."

"All good points."

"Is that enough poetry for you?"

"Right up there with John Keats or Bukowski."

"Who?"

"Never mind. Drink more."

We arrived at the park.

Tony and I were sitting at a concrete picnic table with six half-quart cans of Old Milwaukee apiece, a pint of whiskey, and a vape pen. He had more gray hair in his goatee than I had noticed during our time working together. His knuckles were covered in hieroglyphic tattoos. He lit a cigarette. "So you wanna hear about my past, huh?"

"Yes. Please."

"Not that I won't tell you about it, because I promised, but why do you want to know?"

"You look like a sinner. All sinners have a good story."

He exhaled, then shrugged. "Shit. That's a pretty good reason. What do you want to know?"

"Whatever you want to tell me. You went to prison, right?"

"Yeah."

"Okay. What for? What was it like? Did you kill someone? Why—so many questions . . . let's start with those for now?"

"Jesus. You're like a child."

"A curious child."

"Fair enough."

The air around us was soaked and cold, and the idea that snow might fall held us in limbo. Soon, or not, the sky would open up, and the snow would build on the streets, where people walked dogs and the homeless asked for a taste of fine liquid insulation. I wasn't worried about either of us. We were prepared and half-lit when we finally got into the conversation.

He continued, "When I was young and trying to make my way through culinary school, I got into a burning-hot, stupid lifestyle. I liked living fast and dangerous. Food was a passion but didn't pay the bills. Dad left when I was young. Mom was never home. You know, the typical bullshit. Anyway, I started dealing weed. That went so well that I started peddling other stuff. I climbed the ladder. And did I ever climb. Up and up. I didn't want to distribute, so I set up labs—meth labs, everywhere. It was *Breaking Bad*, but I didn't have to cook, and this was before the cartels were in complete control."

My jaw was wide open. He looked at me for a moment, took a sip of his beer and a swig of the whiskey, and passed the bottle to me. I had a taste and set it down between us.

"You okay?" he asked.

XV

"Of course; please continue."

"Alright. Well, I did that for a couple of years. High-risk, major-reward-type shit, at least monetarily. I practically burned money in the streets. I gave zero fucks. It was fucking great."

A warming blanket of alcohol massaged my back and shoulders and temples. "But you got too arrogant and had a shoot-out with the cops, right?"

"What? No. I rarely had violent interactions. I had a gun or two pointed in my face."

"No shit?!"

"It comes with the territory. But I never got in any shoot-outs. It was actually pretty anticlimactic, and I got jammed after one of my cooks got pinched and ratted me out."

"Snitches get stitches," I replied.

"Yeah. I suppose they do. But if I'm real honest with myself, I had it coming. It was bound to happen. I got out easy. Only had to serve three out of the fifteen-year sentence. It's not fun on the inside."

"Did you have to shank anyone?"

"Do you learn everything from movies?"

"Yes. I mean, kinda. Sorry, I'm curious and drunk."

"It's all good, man. I did not shank anyone."

I peppered Tony with questions about prison life and dealing drugs. He warmed up eventually as the alcohol hit our bloodstreams. He'd seen some shit. Like wild, broken lives. Dream Grocers was his redemption story and his chance to rekindle with food and rebuild a life he deemed worth living.

We talked for hours in this manner. The sun was gone, and the snow started to fall. "It's getting cold as fuck out here. You wanna go to the bar?" Tony asked.

"I'm down," I said as I stood up and nearly fell over.
"You good?" he asked.
"I'm fine. Just getting my bearings."
"We will see about that."
"Huh?"
"Nothing. Let's go to Park Tavern."
"Sounds good."

Tony exemplified what I enjoyed in people. He was a straight shooter with a good soul who had been sipping on whiskey and slipping into oblivion for as long as he deemed worth remembering. He was a saint in my eyes. Everyone liked a good redemption story. I only hoped I could have something similar after I'd imprisoned myself all those years. We stared at TV screens as the ground turned progressively into a winter wonderland and talked late into the night until the neon gods were full.

* * *

My day-to-day tasks were coming to an end as I handed off little things and mentally checked out. In my new Zen-like state, patience for the petty bullshit that was commonplace among the disgruntled staff began to dwindle. If arguments broke out, I did nothing to help the situation. I simply let it be. I knew nothing I did could change my life or any of my employees' lives. I would simply give the customer what they wanted and move on; then I would explain to the employee what was up. It wasn't personal. I just didn't care about Dream Grocers in that way anymore.

Everyone was overworked and underpaid and short staffed. Now that the world was starting to open up again, people were finding new jobs. People were leaving in droves. There was a more rebellious spirit within the store during my last two weeks. More smiles, less festering rage.

Rumblings of unionization had been growing for a couple of months. Ozzy and Jake were spearheading the effort, and they were getting damn close. I admired their resolve. They were convinced that things could change, and I had all the reasons to think otherwise, but I'd once heard a rap song that said, "If you don't like your life, change it, then." And that was the truth. So I told the boys if they could get a meeting together before I left, I would vote yes. But time was running out.

"Why only because you are leaving?" Ozzy asked.

"I'm just not invested in this anymore. If y'all think that a union will help the employees here, then I'll trust you."

"Aren't the reasons obvious?" replied Jake.

"Well, like I said many times, they consist of trade-offs. I'm just making the trade-off to leave and try my own thing. I hope it works for y'all. Like, sincerely, we have been through some shit together. I hope you win this war, because it is so rare to win anything."

Ozzy slapped my shoulder. "Thanks, brother. We are going to miss you."

"Gonna miss both of you sweet bastards."

Jake smiled. "Aww . . . thanks, dude. Well, you'll be happy to know that we have a meeting set for tomorrow night. It's not an official vote. We think we can get that done by next week. But we would love for you to come by tomorrow night. And, honestly, it's more of a party than anything," he said, then laughed. "I even have some deeelish Special K that we should dabble with."

"Hell yeah! I am always down to hang out with you guys."

"We can make it your going-away party too. How's that sound?"

"Perfect. Alright, fellas. I better get going. If I leave Pedro alone much longer, the man or boy—whatever he is—will blow a gasket."

My life had been filled with disagreeable people, but Pedro might have been the worst. He had such a punchable face. His attitude brought everyone down. But it was no longer my problem. I tried not to give a shit. Not completely, however. My parents had instilled a work ethic that seemed compulsory, to the point where it made me hate it. A sense of duty was good, but when it was driven by history instead of reality, I think I had the right to second-guess it. And when I walked out to the front end to find the line in complete disarray, nothing restocked, and Pedro staring deep into his phone while two people waited patiently, any sense of loyalty to my role as a manager went into the air like a mortar and exploded—raw, unfiltered, and disgusted.

A new employee was cleaning up something that had been spilled, and the customers sat there waiting, some patiently, others . . . not so much. That was how Lindas and Daves were formed—in a hot oven of incompetence. But then I remembered that it was probably more of a combined effort between bad service, a troublesome lack of morals and ethics, the beauty of unearned generational affluence gone unchecked, and the loneliness of modernity that allowed Lindas and Daves to turn against the plebs of the service industry.

Watching Pedro's disrespect for the customers, the new guy, and everyone who worked with him pushed me to the point of no return. For the first time in my life, I was completely free to embrace my rage. I walked up to him, grabbed his phone, threw it in the sandwich toaster oven, and closed the door. He popped back, as I had caught him off guard. But he looked hazy and startled and clearly stoned, like he had no idea what was happening. I pressed the start button, and the instant heater fired up at 350 degrees.

He lunged out. "What the fuck, man?!" I pinned him by the neck up against the wall. He whimpered.

"Fucking pussy," I replied. "For all your shit-talking and arrogance, you sure whimper a lot." He fidgeted against the wall, but I was adrenaline-fueled lower management, and I was not going to be moved. I continued. "Fucking burnt-out parasite. What did your parents do to you that you fully embraced and turned you into what you are today? Fuckin' loser." I had, like, fifty pounds on him. I pulled his head down to look inside the oven. "You need to watch this," I said with a clenched jaw.

"Man, I didn't mean to," he pleaded as he tried to look away.

"Oh, no, no, no . . . you are not getting out of this one. That's all you've done since you have worked here. It's probably your whole life." I peeled back his eyelids and shoved his face to the window of the toaster. The plastic on the phone was buckling and peeling back. The slave-produced metals burned bright. Pedro began to cry. I let him go, and he dropped to the floor and wept.

My lens on the situation zoomed back out. Oddly, no one had noticed our interaction. The line grew as

Pedro cried on the floor. I stepped over him and did my job. "Hi! Sorry about the wait. How can I help you?"

When I had finally cleared what felt like an endless line of needy customers, I looked back, and Pedro was gone. The reality of what I'd done hit me, and I knew I was probably finished at the store for good—ahead of schedule. I could be in serious trouble. Assault charges, prison, knife fights in the yard, and a horrid life I'd seen only on TV or heard about from Tony. A loud *"Ruff, ruff!"* broke me out of my stupor. I looked over to find the barking man walking up to the Chef's Case. I loathed that fool normally, but I was glad to change the subject.

"I need a pound of your tuna salad. *Ruff, ruff!*"

"Sure thing."

"Where is that other dude that usually stands up here? Paco? Paulo?"

"Pedro. Pedro is his name, and he is on break right now."

"Good. *Ruff, ruff!* He is rude."

"I know."

"Huh?" he replied.

"Nothing. Was there anything else you need?"

"Ruff, ruff!"

As usual, he walked away without saying anything else. I thought for a moment I was going to miss that asshole. But that was a short-lived fantasy, and I turned my attention back to the possibility of prison time.

But nothing happened. No one even mentioned anything to me. In fact, when I walked into the back, Pedro was leaving the cooler after putting away the remaining meats and cheese from the sandwich station. "Can I go on my last break?" he asked.

XV

A little perturbed by how polite he was, I responded, "Yeah, dude. Go for it. I'll keep an eye on the front."

When he returned, I looked at the clock, and to the best of my knowledge, it was fifteen minutes later. I was dumbfounded. Now that I didn't give a shit, was he caring? Had our interaction scared him straight? Or was he fucking with me? Needless to say, the night went off without a hitch. I expected to walk in the next day and be escorted out within minutes of arriving.

XVI

Abby greeted me as I walked through the door. "Hey, short-timer! How are you today?"

"Uh, I'm allllright. How are *you*?"

"You know . . . I'm surprisingly great."

"Why is that?"

"I honestly don't know. I just have a good feeling about today."

"I'll cheers to that," I said as I lifted a fresh-squeezed organic limeade that I'd spiked with vodka to my lips.

"Well, thank you for the support, Daniel. I forgot to ask you. I know you are only here for a week or so, but can you work the inventory 'overnight' shift tonight?"

"I'm sorry; I was invited to a party yesterday."

She looked at me like she was surprised I was acting like I had a choice.

"Seriously, though," I said, "I have previous commitments, and you asked me last minute."

"Are you talking about Jake and Oz's party?"

"Yeah."

"Well, they have to be here too. It won't run that late. So y'all can party after. Speaking of which . . . you are too old to party, Daniel. It's unbecoming to not act your age."

"I am quitting this job to become a full-time online influencer. My age is irrelevant. Everyone should embrace that fact. That way they don't end up being middle management at a grocery store."

"Hey! That's not fair. We are pretty much the same age, and I'm technically middle management."

"My point stands."

She punched my arm and said, "I'm gonna pretend I don't know what you're talking about so I avoid a panic attack, but I'm *your* manager, and you should listen to my wisdom."

"Of course," I replied.

"I worry about you, Daniel."

"Jesus, Abby. Settle down. It's gonna be fine. It's just a party."

"It all starts with 'just a party'; then you spend the next years of your life not finding something meaningful to do."

"Abby, I appreciate your concern, but don't worry about me. You should be concerned about those new duties you have to do because they failed us on purpose."

"I think if we nail down all of these new tasks, they will leave us alone."

"What gave you that idea?" I responded.

"Honey, they don't like you." Achilles was finally here and chimed in, and I began to laugh.

Abby was pseudo offended, with her mouth agape. "Fine, you can stay for inventory too, Achilles."

"Don't try and throw some magical weight around here. That shit was on my schedule for weeks. Yours too, Daniel. Dumbass."

"But I wanna partay!" I protested.

"Poor Daniel," Achilles said and rested his hand on my shoulder. "Have you learned nothing?"

"There was something to learn?"

* * *

"Everyone gather around. We need to go over tonight's agenda," Richard announced.

There was a collective groan as the group of maybe twenty people gathered around.

"Goddamnit, I hate these shifts," Achilles said before taking a gulp of an organic energy drink.

"Me too," I replied.

"I think it's a power play. Todd has taught Richard to be an asshole. And this is Richard's masterpiece."

"Is this Richard's *Starry Night*?"

"What is that?"

"It's a painting by van Gogh."

"Never heard of it."

"Really? I mean, it's right up there with the *Mona Lisa*."

"Is that the picture of some bitch smirking?"

"You could say that."

"Yeah, I'm not interested."

"Wow, umm . . . Achilles. I feel a little sad that a friend of mine has no interest in art."

"Sorry. Here . . . show me *Starry Night*?"

I did a quick Google search and showed him my phone.

"Oh, wow! That's pretty. Thanks for sharing."

"I'm glad that I can help culture you."

"Me too. Let me ask you . . . was that what it looked like when Lila gave you that blowjob in the park?"

On impulse I grabbed his shoulder and asked, "How did you know about that?"

"I have my sources, Daniel."

"Who?"

"Don't worry about it. But you enjoyed the stars while she did it, right?"

"Goddamnit, Achilles. Who told you?"

"If you give me more details, I will tell you who it was."

"It wasn't the stars, per se. More like the city lights."

"Go on."

"It was a great night. Cheap wine and fooling around. There really isn't much to say beyond that."

"Are you sure?"

"Yes. Now tell me how you found out."

Achilles began to laugh. "I found out from you, sweetie."

"What? I never said anything to you—or anyone, for that matter."

"You didn't need to. I can just tell. I've received and given enough oral sex in my life to know when a man is satisfied, and you weren't able to wipe that smile off your face for weeks."

"Shit. Wait . . . you need to keep that to yourself, okay? I don't want to get mixed up in the store drama."

"Why not, honey? It's fun. Everyone here is fucking somebody. Everyone fucks, Daniel. Even your parents."

"That may be, but I don't need to hear about it."

"Well, I will keep my lips closed, but I'm not guaranteeing that other people won't find out."

"How would they find out?"

"Have you heard of the grapevine, Daniel? Jesus. It's like I have to explain everything to you."

"Well, whatever. You promise not to say anything, right?"

"Pinky swear. Jesus, Daniel! Stop looking at me like I already told everyone." He put up a peace sign casually and lowered his voice and said, "I am not a crook!" Followed by a giggle. "I'm just happy my boy is getting some play. Now . . . more deets . . ."

"Fuck off!"

"Daniel, don't be like—"

"Attention, everyone!" Richard said. "Here are your section assignments for inventory tonight."

I looked over the paper. There were about one hundred sections that all needed to be counted. "Goddamnit. This is going to take forever," I whined.

"Oh, we will probably be here for four or five hours. Then it's time for draaanks." Achilles replied in an attempt to cheer me up.

My phone said it was eight o'clock. "My god."

"Yeah, shit sucks. Wanna grab some people and smoke the vape, then come back?"

"Is that even a question? Yes, of course."

* * *

Maybe five minutes later, Achilles, Jake, Sunshine, and I were gathered around the side entrance that faced a busy street.

"Do you think we should be smoking right here?" I asked.

"We are not smoking, Daniel," Achilles said. "We're *vaping*. Big difference."

"If you say so," I replied. "I am just worried about the cops driving by."

"The cops? How long have you lived in Denver? They give zero fucks."

"Ah, I guess you're right. Hell, I've admitted to being high around Rory the Entrance Cop."

"God. You white people get away with murder."

"Achilles. Like you said . . . no one cares."

"For y'all white folks . . ."

"Achilles, you're smoking—excuse me . . . *vaping*—right now in public. If you meant what you just said, you would not be doing that," I replied.

"Whatever . . . I love giving you gringos shit."

"Oh, I know."

"Technically there's a huge difference," Jake chimed in. "And it's much better for your lungs."

"Huh?" I replied, a bit confused. Then it hit me. "Oh, yeah . . . that's what we were talking about."

"Yeah, dude. Let's stay focused on getting high and complaining about work. You can debate the finer points about getting high around the cops and race relations another day."

"He has a point," I replied.

"I agree," Achilles said. "Thanks, Jake. Love you, Daniel."

"Real talk," Jake said, followed by a long drag.

"How's the Sunshine doing over here?" Achilles asked.

"I'm good. Maybe a bit too stoned. So maybe *reasonable* is a better response. Yup. I'm reasonable."

We all snickered at her reasoning. My thoughts began to float away. I swam out to them. "So is this a standard protocol for work?"

They all stared at me in silence until finally Jake said, "What?"

Confused, I asked, "Huh? What did you think I said?"

"You just said the word *protocol*, then stared off into the distance."

"No shit? Well, ain't that something."

An earthquake of laughter rang out into the night.

"I think some of us better lay off the vape. How long have we been out here?" Achilles asked.

"Time is an illusion," proclaimed Jake.

"Right . . . but we do need to go back to work," Sunshine replied.

"Fair point. We better wrap this up," I said as I stepped out of yet another fog of THC.

"He speaks," Sunshine announced.

"Speaking is an illusion."

Achilles put the vape away, and we headed inside.

* * *

"Man, I'm gonna be so glad when I don't have to do these night shifts anymore," I said as I scanned the manuka honey and counted backward. Looked like we had never sold a single one of the hundred-dollar little jars. The only one not completely covered in dust was the front one, which had probably been cleaned off by the person who'd counted them last time. "Huh. I guess everything isn't as it seems."

"What? Honey? Oh no . . . it is. People literally die to make that shit," Jake replied.

"Really?"

"Yeah, dude. It's a modern-day gold rush. That's what capitalism does, man; it pits us against each other in competition. It makes us fight for no reason."

"But there must be a reason. Manuka honey is delicious and has medical benefits. We shouldn't just 'blame capitalism' like it's some monolith. There are dark parts to every story. There is good and evil in this world, my dear friend. Any route you choose is going to have a mix of both," I replied.

That was when Jake asked a weird question. "Do you think people are good or evil, Daniel?"

I looked at him for a moment. His eyes were glossier than normal. He was in my presence but not completely directed at me in actions. "You alright, Jakey?" I asked.

He squinted. "Yeah, dude. Just got the party started a little early. I have the next few days off. And it seems I may have mixed up the bag of blow with Special K, but I'm just going to go with it. And see how far down the rabbit hole I can go. But that doesn't change my question. I know it's something that you probably asked yourself when you were much younger, and it's

XVI

surprising to hear it come from my mouth, but I'd like
to know if you think we are inherently good or evil."

"I think we are selfish. How we utilize that feature
of our DNA is how we get to evil or good. We are sup-
posedly intelligent beasts. If we accept that we are selfish
and govern our lives individually, I think that we end up
living on the 'good' end more because we know that we
need each other in our selfish pursuits. I'm not the first
to say this, by the way. I'm regurgitating what many
people smarter than me have known."

"Eww, Daniel. Don't you think we should live to
higher ideals than just being selfish?"

"That's what I'm talking about. I believe you can
only live to a higher ideal when you first understand
that the reason you do anything is grounded in your
self-preservation and your own happiness. I'm happier
with other people in this world, and I want us to thrive
as a species. Everyone else is concerned about themselves
first too. I want our individual lives to be tantamount in
this life. We—individually—are what's most important.
Jesus, I feel like I'm on Special K, too, talking to you."

"Want to be? Here . . . follow me."

I followed Jake to the back, where he opened up a
tiny bag, and I took a bump of K. What did I care? I was
about to be a free man.

"Ah, so *this* is why you don't like unions," Jake said.

"Collectives can help bring forth change. They have
a purpose. Problem is that individuals still hold the
power within groups, and, like I said, they are selfish
like the plebs. Except now they have power over others,
and corruption happens when you have a very uneven
scale of power. But like I said, I support you guys doing

309

it. I'll vote for it if it happens in time." We walked back to the sales floor.

"You are making some salient points. I just think it's the only way to make change at scale in a corporation like Dream Grocers."

"I see where you're coming from, my friend. Hey, watch out there, buddy. You nearly stepped off the ladder onto the shelf."

"Wooo . . . thanks, man. Are we almost done here?"

"I think we are on the last aisle," I replied.

"Good. You gonna come party with us?"

"I'll sit and have a beer in the parking lot with y'all. Not sure about a crazy late night. I have a midshift tomorrow, and honestly, I can't hang like I used to."

"Eh, no judgment here, homie. Just glad I had the opportunity to work with you."

A voice came from the other aisle. "Same here!" It was Ozzy.

"Aww . . . well, aren't you guys the sweetest. Oh, looks like I'm done with my section."

"Me too," Jake replied.

"Achilles. Oz. Sunshine. How's everyone looking?" I asked loud enough to hopefully bring everyone into my range.

"Done."

"Done."

"Aaand done."

***

XVI

They convinced me to stick around for more than
a beer. Jake and Ozzy's house was about a mile from
my place, and I had on a warm coat to walk home in.
I left my bike locked up inside the store and asked if I
could get a ride from Lila, who'd shown up with Neal
and some others. She didn't hesitate and said yes, and
I thought this might be my last opportunity to try to
make things right.

She stopped outside the car with her hand grazing
the door handle. "One thing, though. I don't want to
talk about us. I'm dating someone we will be hanging
out with tonight, and I don't want it to be awkward.
Besides, you apologized, I have forgiven you, and I just
want to be friends."

"Oh . . . well, alright. That works."

"You sure?"

"Yeah. I'm fine."

"Sweet. Now let's have some fun."

We pulled up to the house. Neal got out right away.
"Wooo! Party time," he said as the car door shut behind
him. I looked at Lila. She was going through her bag for
something. I put my hand on the door handle. "We're all
good, right?" she asked.

"Of course," I replied.

"That's good. I liked you. I mean, you're sweet,
smart, and you fuck well, but I don't like insecurity.
Lying to others means you are willing to lie to yourself. That's not something I can be involved with. You
know?"

"Yeah, I get it. I just wish I could go back in time and
make things right."

"You don't have to go back in time. Just go in there,
hug your friends, meet my boyfriend tonight, be nice to

him, take shots with the crew, and have fun. We have history. I think that's great."

"I can get used to that," I said, knowing it might not be true. I had a feeling this was all going to be a fond memory quickly.

"Wanna see what I brought for the party?" I asked.

"As long as it's not your dick or something."

I laughed. "It's not. Here, look."

"Oh, you brought Frankie along? Hell yeah!"

"And the fixin's for espresso martinis."

"You're so weird, Daniel. I like it," Lila said, then leaned in and gave me a kiss on the cheek. "Now, let's send you off in a proper way."

* * *

Their two-bedroom apartment was the corner unit on the third story of an old walk-up. Several neighbors' doors were open, and people were moving from spot to spot. Some folks were smoking cigarettes on the patio. I walked around the building, threw on the panda costume, and walked up the stairs.

When I opened the door, Ozzy jumped into the air. "My god! Frankie is here!" he exclaimed. "Look everyone! Frankie has *arrived*!"

A thunderous cheer broke out from the crowded room. Ozzy handed me a bottle of bourbon. "Here, Frankie—you need this."

"I agree," I said as I took a healthy swig. "Where can I go to make some espresso martinis?"

"The kitchen is over there. Jake should be there too," Ozzy said and blew a kiss.

I maneuvered my way through the sea of people. In the kitchen, I found Jake, Lila, a guy I hadn't met, Neal, and Sunshine. "Frankie!" they all screamed in unison.

Jake looked a little faded behind the eyes as he sauntered over to me. "He's arrived. He has arrived. How are you, my friend?"

"I'm good. How are *you?*" I replied.

"I'm grade A right now. You want some?"

I looked at the mirror covered in white dust. "Sure," I responded. "Let's get weird."

"That's the right attitude, there, short-timer."

I inhaled what I could. Fire ants crawled up my nose. I felt a tap on my shoulder.

It was Lila. "Hey, Daniel . . . this is Teddy. Teddy, meet Daniel—or when he is in this form, he is Frankie."

"Nice to meet you, man," Teddy said.

I nodded. "Yeah, dude, good to meet you. So what's your story?"

"Well, Lila helped me get a job at Dream Grocers. This will be my first weekend."

"Oh, what are you going to do?"

"I'm going to work in the prepared-foods department as a supervisor."

"Wait a second. Are you going to be working nights and writing production?"

"Yes sir."

"Ha. I'll be training you."

"No shit. Well, I hope I learn fast," Teddy replied.

"Me too, Teddy. Me too."

Teddy touched the outside of his pockets. "Shit, I'd love to smoke with you as a celebration, but I forgot my weed in the car. I'll be right back."

I looked at Lila. She smiled and said, "That wasn't so bad, was it?"

"If you say so."

"Oh, come on, Frankie. Don't be a sad panda."

"Okay. Fine, fine. Here, do you want an espresso martini?"

"Sure thing."

Jake walked over and put his arm around me as I made the drinks. "Thisss is much better than a union vote, huh?"

"It's more fun, for sure. When is that happening?"

"Very soon. But for real . . . fuck that place. Wan' anotha bump?" he replied with glossed eyes.

"Sure."

He handed me the mirror and wandered away without saying another word.

Someone turned on a disco ball during the night. The bass thumped away as I smoked a joint with Teddy and Lila and talked about our respective futures. The kitchen was spacious in comparison to most of the apartment, but I needed some air. "I'll be back in a bit. This panda needs a breather."

This was the first time I had moved more than a few feet since Jake had given me the bump of Special K. I floated through the crowd. I discovered Neal talking to Sunshine. They were in a serious, drunken conversation about important things. I waved. They didn't notice, and I moved out to the patio.

"Jesus, dude. You scared me," Ozzy said after I put my hand on his shoulder.

"What are ya looking at?" I asked.

He pointed out to the park that lined the back of the complex. "Jake has been dancing out there for a while. Shirtless, not giving a fuck."

"Oh, shit! Should we go get him?"

"I tried. But he told me that he was trying to find the happy planet. I figured that I'll keep an eye on him, and if he gets too squirrely, I'll bring him in."

"Sounds reasonable. Hey, can I have one of your cigarettes?"

"You smoke?"

"No, but I'm in the market for a new vice."

"Sure. Here you go."

I lit the cigarette, took a deep inhale, and coughed. I hadn't smoked tobacco in fifteen years. Everyone started laughing as I wheezed and heaved. I looked at my reflection in the glass door. I loved who and what I saw. But why? Well, I was breaking the rules and going back to square one. Then it dawned on me . . . I needed to film this for my YouTube and other social media channels. I opened the sliding door, pulled out my phone, and began to record. The crowd shivered and flexed. People danced and burned bright in that apartment. They were young and happy and open to possibilities. I was *trying* my best. The night carried on. I interviewed some women in their early twenties and showed them Frankie's social media. One with blonde hair and fantastic green eyes kept rubbing my shoulder; then she grazed the front of my pants and looked me in the eye. More drugs and espresso martinis were consumed. The swirl of reality and fantasy—combined into the spiral down, down, down the psychological rabbit hole. I hugged so many people. I cried with Sunshine. She was going to miss me.

I looked in the mirror, and I liked the man I had become. I found Green Eyes again. We talked for a while on the patio and watched Jake twirl round and round in the park. We kissed. I melted.

She was rubbing my stomach when I opened my eyes to let in the unforgiving midmorning light.

"That was too much fun," she said.

"Those are my people."

"I can tell. So am I your people too?"

"I think so. Do you want to be?"

"Yeah. I'd be okay with that. I wonder what happened to your friend, Jake, last night. He looked pretty wild there at the end when he was talking on his phone."

"Yeah. I'm not sure. I'll give him a call."

"Wanna get some breakfast?" she asked.

"Lord knows."

XVII

The sun toggled in a half-cocked perch over the eastern sky as I walked down to the communal patio of my apartment complex. It was morning but not too early. Work started at ten o'clock. Abby had been kind enough to give me my last couple of evenings off. Lila's new beau—the young and ambitious Teddy—had taken over the closing shift, and Abby wanted him to jump right in. Sink or swim. Do more with less. A garden hose for a forest fire.

On my phone, a message from Neal read, *Dude Jake is going to get fired.*

Me: What?!? How? When?

Neal: I guess at the party he called up the store and left a message on the machine saying how Todd was a giant insecure asshole. He told him that he was pathetic and that he could go fuck himself.

Neal: Richard told me and he said that Jake is no longer working with the company.

Me: No shit. Damn. I should've brought him inside when he was twirling around.

Neal: We all could've done that.

Me: I guess but I feel responsible and devastated.

Neal: Me too, man. But we will all still hang out.

Me: I sure hope so.

Neal: You in today?

Me: Yeah

Neal: Good. See you then

Jason was smoking his first cigarette of the day. His nocturnal ways usually led to late mornings, but he always got a smoke in earlier in the day right before probably going back to bed until one o'clock.

"It's a godsend of a day. This weather, my lord," I said.

"Are you happy that the grocery life is over?"

"I feel fucking incredible, man, like a giant weight has been lifted." My eyes began to water, but I refrained from letting the tears drop.

"I'm happy for you, dude. What are you going to do next?"

"Well, the beauty of my next gig is that I'll be making my own schedule, and I started stockpiling videos and editing them. I think I've set the narrative for my content to last for at least a month. But I'm also going to take my time and explore other journeys. I have some ideas. Maybe that novel is on the docket after all."

"No shit? You're finally going to sit down and take the time to put it out in the universe?"

"Yeah. I've been jotting down some notes, and I've got a flow to it."

"Just remember that it might not end up being what you planned."

"What do you mean?"

"Well, did you plan on working in a grocery store?"

"No."

"Did you expect a pandemic to keep you there?"

"God no."

"But here you are," Jason said with a blank stare.

"Here I am," I replied. On a long road that I started only god knows when. With uncertainty everywhere and hope in my heart, I press on. It may have been the drugs talking, but suddenly I was reminded of the pervy old man who had either wanted to fuck me or help me or both, and how I had known then that I would carve my own path and define my future in writing.

After a long drag of a cigarette and a quick exhale, Jason said, "Right. Plans and expectations are silly if you let them blind you to the possibilities. Structure and purpose are great, but at some point you have to just flow with it and understand that you will never be in complete control. Otherwise you will drive yourself into a maddening downward spiral. You must rid yourself of that burden your parents passed on to you. It's the same one they received from their upbringing. If we are to do anything meaningful with our lives, at some point, we all must let someone else carry that cross. Some people give it to Jesus, others to drugs or the government, but what we really should do is just leave all that bullshit where we stand, in the dirt below our feet that is made from the same carbon from which we evolved—so when you think about it that way, you can leave all the pain and anguish behind you right here, right now. That doesn't mean we shouldn't take responsibility for our lives. I'd say the opposite. Letting go of perceived control is taking the ultimate responsibility."

"But don't you think that we should remember the hard parts? I heard once that we should cherish sadness."

"I've heard the same thing. And they aren't wrong. In fact, they are so right that it influenced what I'm about to say. Holding on to pain like a talisman will never benefit you. In the last year, there has been an incredible amount of suffering, but that's our constant reality, and we must make do with what we got. Struggle is as much a part of the human spirit as anything. All there is left to do is know that the hurt is real and it will pass—bask in that moment, knowing the feeling is unique, universal, and unexceptional in the same breath, and finally, know you are human and fallible, and move on."

"Is that true?"

"Shit, I don't know, man. I'm still high from the marijuana edible I ate last night."

"Jesus, really?"

"Which part? The edible or the still being high?"

"The part where you tell me that all of your solid advice spun out of your brain because you're stoned."

"What's the difference if I am or not? Would it make it any more legitimate if I was a straightedge kid rather than chain-smoking cigarettes and listening to hardcore?"

"Probably a little."

"That's a shame. I disagree."

"Why so?"

"Let's talk over it tonight. Wanna grill out to celebrate you putting your cross down?"

"Yeah, dude. That sounds good."

* * *

I ripped down Corona Street, through Cheesman Park, and across Sixth Avenue; hit an empty street with a strong downhill; and then coasted almost the entire way to work. I thought about Janice on the way to the store. Everything happened so fast at Dream Grocers that I rarely thought about her death. Years later I would probably have to come to grips with her passing, but I appreciated the time we had. I didn't want that day to be sad, so I focused on the Mile High sun cracking through the trees, making the street look like the back of a tiger. There was a subtle air of peace to my ride as I remained sanguine heading into my last day at Dream Grocers. With the cool wind at my back, it was as if the world wanted me to be there early and take it all in. I thought, *Goddamnit, I love this city.*

* * *

On my final morning at Dream Grocers, there wasn't a line to get into the store. Neal was sitting on a chair at the front, talking to Rory. It looked like a serious conversation. I assumed Neal was telling Rory about Jake, so I decided to stop and try to lighten the mood. "You boys gonna miss me?" I asked.

"Not even a little bit," Neal responded.

"Wait, you're leaving? How come no one told me?" Rory asked.

"Because snitches get stitches, Rory," Neal fired back.

Rory looked at Neal for a short moment and, with a deadpan face and serious tone, said, "Not for something like this, Neal. First Jake, now Daniel. Damn this day is rough."

With a laugh, Neal said, "I know, buddy, the Jake thing is rough, but as far as Daniel goes . . . you are literally a *narc*, and you're going to get mad at me for keeping a secret?"

I laughed. "It wasn't exactly a secret. I have been yelling it from the rooftops for two weeks. I guess I just don't work with you enough, Rory. Sorry."

"It's all good, man. I'm happy for you. What are you going to do next?"

"My next career will be as an online influencer."

"Jesus Chaa-rist," Rory proclaimed. "Kids these days."

"I am pretty sure we are the same age, Rory."

"Well, whatever. I'm a baby boomer at heart."

"The one involving Frankie or something else?" Neal asked.

"That's the one. I mean, I already started making money off him, so I might as well keep going."

"Wait . . . you made money dressing up like a panda?" Rory asked.

"Yes, Rory," I said. "Welcome to the modern world."

"I'm so lost," he responded.

"Well, I, for one, think that's fucking awesome, dude. We are proud of you," Neal said.

"Aww, thanks, bro," I said.

My eyes watered a little bit. I felt a twinge of sadness knowing that this could be the last time I saw so many of these folks. Life was getting back to normal, and with every passing day, I accepted my journey as a rolling stone a little more. Of course, we would still have social media connections and texting, but I had learned enough in my thirty-some years to know that you could have only so many really close friendships. We had only so much bandwidth. That didn't mean I wouldn't give all these wonderful people hugs if I saw them some years from now, but the reality was that most of our lives were meant only for a temporary and random dance, and like high school friends or ex-lovers, things faded or changed just like they were supposed to.

Even as I write this ending, memories of my life on the grocery line are fading from my view like childhood fantasies of being a Hall of Fame baseball player. I have a hard time remembering what my world was like in that store. Maybe I blocked it out, or maybe I'm just getting old. I guess that's why I quit but rekindled the romantic air of it all with the written word. I needed to write this book as an homage to those aisles filled with the almighty food—the tragedy and triumph contained in those walls, the soft-skinned Lila with her beautiful eyes, the monstrous Todd and his triumphant path, the laughter, the pain, and the moments of exposed soft tissue under the weight of a global pandemic. I worked there to pay my bills, sure, but I wanted to live, too, and I realized I didn't need to be married to an unfaithful job. Opportunity was everywhere. I would no longer allow myself to commit to anything but my own creations from there on out. I was heading out to face the strange land that is the internet.

"Well, fellas, I better go clock in," I said.

"Why? You can be late. Honestly, I'm shocked you showed up for your last day. Most people bail."

"I don't know; I guess I just wanted to see it through."

"That's honorable," Rory said.

"Sounds dumb to me," Neal rebutted, followed by his distinct laugh I will never forget.

"I hope I see you before you leave for the day," I said.

Neal nodded. "You probably will."

As I walked into the building, I could almost hear the bellows of laughter from some inappropriate joke echoing off the walls of the narrow hallways. In some remote corner of the building, a manager was walking the store with an employee behind them, pointing to this corner or that shelf, showing what areas needed to be cleaned, and the poor sap nodded along as their soul slowly died with every step.

The front end was jamming along while Mary and Lila occupied the first two registers. Both waved at me. Mary did so with overt enthusiasm. Lila gave a small obligated gesture. I knew, in part, where we had gone wrong, but any and all analysis would be done at a different time; I chose not to worry and left the burden in front of register two. I have yet to pick it up again for evaluation, because maybe there isn't anything to say or do as the big world turns, with me helplessly on it.

Christian and Sunshine waved at me. Everyone was so happy for me. The sadness was a bit too much. I said, "Heyo!" but moved on quickly.

Everyone was lined up in neat little rows at the checkout on a savage Sunday that I knew would remind me both of why I wanted to leave and of why I would never forget. Broken window shades rained down stark sunlight onto the registers, roasting the cashiers trapped in plexiglass cages, still muzzled by masks that the customers no longer had to wear. Never in my life had I experienced such an obvious distinction between the hierarchy of our society. Of course, I hadn't lived that long, and many far worse crimes had been perpetrated against the people of the United States and around the world, but here it was in front of me, plain as day—indiscriminate rules that only some people had to follow. Not those people but *my* people. And it was reinforced by the company and government. I'd been aware of the gulf between the groups from the get-go, but it was at that moment the bleak and unabashed reality of the grocery-store workers' plight came to fruition.

I thought back to all the conversations with Jake and Ozzy about unionizing, about uniting in the struggle. And I concluded that I was fine with private collective bargaining. Whatever you could do to leverage your human capital in this life was important. Make the most of what you got. Evaluate the problems and the solutions and assess the risks and rewards. There wasn't a one-size-fits-all solution to problems. And this book isn't political. That is for a different space. But whether it's taking classes to learn something new or unionizing, everyone should scrutinize their path and seek the proper reward for their contribution.

All that shit weighed on my mind as I walked past the registers and headed up the stairs to clock in for the final time. At the last register before the stairs, a

Norman flailed his arms and demanded to talk to a manager about the price of the focaccia bread he'd just purchased. I slowed down for a moment to hear. "This pesto should not be so expensive. That paired with the bread makes my favorite meal outrageously expensive. I need . . . no, I demand a discount."

He demanded a discount. *Demanded.* That fuckin' ego really was something grand. I should have tapped him on the shoulder and reminded him that it's important to remember that when you look out into the sky, you have no choice but to be nearsighted. If you use your imagination, paired with basic facts, you will realize that the sky goes on forever and ever. You are looking into infinity. And when you *demand* things of your fellow man that you can't produce yourself, you have lost the plot, and your nearsightedness has taken control. Lift people up. Don't tear them down. Or kindly fuck off.

I glanced at my phone. It was 10:10 a.m. I was late. I looked around for Richard or Todd, but neither were in the area. But I *finally* didn't care anymore. I was looking for acknowledgment or for management or a customer to come out and congratulate me. *You made it, Daniel. You survived!* But the reality of the situation was my last day was only for me.

When I reached the top of the stairs, I came upon a group of employees facing the time clock, crowded in neat little rows that swayed ever so gently in front of me. A few moments passed where no one moved before I realized none of them were actually trying to punch in for their shift. They were just standing in the way.

"Hey, can I get through to clock in?" I asked. There was no response. I looked around to see if I recognized anyone, but their faces were Ken and Barbie types, indiscriminate, and they didn't hear or see me. But just as I was about to push my way to the front of whatever was happening, they all started to shuffle toward the clock, *and* they began to say things like, "Happy Sunday!", "Ha. What up, brotha?", "Welcome to the Thunderdome", "How are you doing today?", and "My god, I hate this shit." They said these phrases out loud, not to anyone but kinda like a script. And the people packed into a tight group—more and more folks came, surrounding Daniel. I mean, surrounding me. I looked around—still didn't find anyone I recognized. I became uncomfortable as they pressed into me from all sides like a crowd rushing a concert stage. I was surrounded on all sides and as far as I could see in the room.

Finally, the clock came into view. I readied my badge in case my pass code didn't work for some reason. My turn came. Some indiscriminate asshole tried to jump in front of me, but I jammed my arm in front of him and boxed him out from the clock.

"Hey, man. No need for that. I'm in no rush," he replied.

I looked back and snarled at him. He was a faceless man. Utterly corporate and plastic. They weren't what I'd experienced but definitely what I might become. I punched in my employee ID for the last time and found the first hole in the crowd and leaped down the stairs to my right.

The kitchen was bustling with life from the properly staffed morning crew as they built our in-house garden or tuna salads and packed out chicken wings and rolled lettuce wraps.

"Hi, everyone!" I said. They all looked and waved, then went right back to work.

Achilles was at the computer. "Hey, asshole. You're leaving me."

I was relieved to see people I knew.

"Hey, asshole. We can still hang out, right?" I replied.

"Only if you go check the temperatures on the floor."

"Promise?"

Without looking at me, he replied, "Promise."

His face was stern and controlled, but I saw a slight smile from the side. My guess was that whatever email he was writing was upsetting, but maybe he was bummed I wasn't going to work with him anymore.

"What's going on, Achilles? You alright?" I asked.

"Yeah, I'll be fine. We just have those extra corporate visits, and now we will be extra short staffed. Can't they ever leave well enough alone? I hate being under all this pressure."

"Pressure is privilege, Achilles. You should know this," I said with a smile.

"Fuck off. Pressure is insecurity attempting to be leadership . . . at least from Todd."

"They are worried because you are losing the cornerstone of the department."

"More like a cornerstone made of salt being dissolved by the rising waters in the department. You were bound to fall apart anyway."

"Damn, dude. Are you sure I'm the one that's salty, with Mr. Cranky Pants over here? If we could please change the metaphor to that of a cornerstone made of sugar, pure sugar, I would appreciate it since it's still water-soluble and tastier."

"You're delicious, Daniel. I know."

"What the hell are you two talking about?" Tony said as he walked through the door.

"We are talking about how scrumptious I am," I replied.

"Well, that's my cue to get out of here. Oh, you up for more whiskey drinkin'?" Tony asked.

"I can't tonight."

"Heard that," Tony said.

"He is probably avoiding you because of shame. Everyone knows about his torrid love affair with Miss Lila," Achilles said.

"I have no idea what you two are talking about," Tony replied.

Dripping with sarcasm, I turned to Achilles. "I wonder how they would know that."

Tony looked at us both and said, "I'm gonna leave now," then walked out of the room.

"Well, everyone knows just by watching you two. It's obvious," Achilles said.

"Jesus Christ," I said. "That's one of the reasons I am glad to be leaving. The drama."

"You love it, Daniel."

"No. You love it, Achilles, and by proxy, I am involved in it. Was it you that told everyone me and Lila were a thing?"

"No. Like I said, it was obvious and cute, and you two weren't really a thing in a serious way, right? Like, just fooling around? Oh, and by the way, it's all good, dude. It happens. We are getting old. Beautiful younger women are scary," he said and laughed.

"Goddamnit. I gotta go. I'm gonna go check the temperatures."

"Oh, maybe a heat pack will get blood down to get that thing up!"

"Asshole."

"You mean, sasshole."

"That's fair."

The temperature-gun reading was erratic at each station, and the process took longer than expected. That piece of shit hadn't worked for as long as I had been in the department. Sure, I could have grabbed the meat thermometer and been more thorough, but I was in no mood on that busy late morning. And I was consumed as I waited for the lady in blue yoga pants to stroll by one last time.

Jeanie walked by. "Hey, Daniel." She continued for a moment, then stopped and turned around. She stared at me.

"What's up, Jeanie?" I asked.

"You still chasing that blue bird, ain'tcha."

"Jeanie, I have no idea what you're talking about."

"Bullshit. Look at your lonely ass not doing work, hoping to see that blue-pants beauty walk through. Shit, if you don't ask her out, I'm gonna get her number today."

"Now that's some bullshit, Jeanie. You don't know if she's interested in you."

"*You* don't know if she's interested in *you*. But *you'll* never find out unless *you* try. Me? I don't give a good rat's ass if she is interested in me like *that*, but I bet she would be down to have a workout buddy. Maybe sparks will fly. But if nothing else, I make a friend."

"Ahhh, the long game," I said with a smile.

"No, no. It's not a game; it's called being an adult."

"Ohh, okay." I winked at her.

"Fuck off. You're just scared."

"Of her? No. But you scare me."

"Well, good. Now, when you see her, you better be asking her out."

"Fine, fine. If I see her."

"You will. She's here. Now get back to work, ya fuckin' slacker."

"Jeanie?"

"What's up, hun?"

"Did I ever tell you how endearing your accent is?"

"Fuck off, Daniel. Get to work. Goddamn slacker." A smile crawled across her face as she turned to walk away.

When I was done with the temperature readings, I grabbed my checklist for the wall and headed back out to the floor to write production. Achilles was still in the middle of something, and no one else was around, so I *had* to work and not bullshit around. Honor required this of me. Realistically, since the sun had melted the snow, I wanted to just walk out, go to Cheesman Park, and drink beer, but I wasn't going to leave my coworkers hanging.

The wall of food towered over the people milling about while they decided what their hearts of hearts desired. They walked in front and behind where I stood, pinning me in with their indecisions and capitulations. I wished they would clear out to let me be alone with my idealism.

I loved and hated my wall. I had responsibility. My task was important. And I did it every night.

The wall was my life's work; at the time, I acted as if I was going to pass it to my children one day, and they would gift it on to their kids. Our legacy and tragedy wrapped all in one single stupid palisade of prepackaged, overpriced food. I didn't know why I put such a stake in the godforsaken thing. I loathed the way it looked with massive sections of product missing. I saw failure when I should have seen success. I couldn't let go of strings better left to fray.

This place was where lazy people went in search of nutrition. Everything was made for them. Their decisions were minimal. It was luxurious and expensive. Only the top 1 percent of the world shopped at such a place in such a store.

Despite all my contradicting attitudes, the food needed to be made, and someone needed to plan it . . . one last time. And since Dream Grocers let me, I was the one who decided what we made. It was one of the bigger roles in the department, but it was stressful and ridiculous—overreaching in scope with a background of labor shortage and overabundance of recipes. So. Much. Shit was crammed onto the wall. But usually I had no one to make it.

Many a night, I had contemplated walking out of that godforsaken place or sticking my head inside our pizza oven until the gas filled my lungs and I succumbed to the long dark night. Or maybe I would use the baler wire and jump from the rafters above the meat department. I could see it even now: hanging above all the other mammals brought to slaughter—pale, eyes bulging out hollow but full of the devil's sympathy.

People picked up items, read the ingredients, and set them down indiscriminately. Dave grabbed a triangle sandwich and looked at it for a moment, walked a few feet, and then set it back on a different shelf, in a completely foreign spot. Bullshit like that happened more times than I could count just in my store. I couldn't imagine the collective disregard shown to grocery-store employees nationwide and even worldwide. The weight of that disrespect could drive a man insane with anger. In my early years, I'd trembled in bright rage at people doing whatever they damn well pleased without regard for their fellow man. But I learned to forgive or forget, depending on how you looked at it. But with enough time, I began to understand that the erratic and narcissistic behavior wasn't something that would ever truly go away. We were a selfish species for good and ill. People were just dumb animals. Plain and simple. And most of us only pretended to have a fucking clue what was going on in the world, and if you were one of those self-aware rarities, then you probably chose to ignore it in many instances.

I wanted to finish the production list earlier than normal since it was my last shift, and Teddy might be slow. I needed to get it out of the way so that I could relax for the rest of my shift and maybe see the woman in blue yoga pants. The closing manager, Teddy, would have less to worry about too. All he would have to do was make sure everyone cleaned and got out of there on time. And there I was standing tall, thinking of myself as quite grand.

Two Lindas walked by with a three-year-old girl sitting in their cart. I knew they were Lindas because they had name tags stating they were proud members of the Birch Society, like they had just come from a conference or something. Or maybe I didn't, but I wanted to be judgy in that moment. And I'd said before that it was my right as someone in the service of these people to say they were guilty until proven innocent.

They stopped at the salad section, their cart carrying two large begonias, a cutting board with a set of Pampered Chef knives, and a few papayas. The younger one noticed me, pointed at the salads, and asked where these were made. With a twinge of pride, I told her that they were made in-house, by hand. The older woman, who was playing with the child in the cart, said, without looking up, "Do you use proper sanitation when you assemble them? I have seen one of you people eat a slice of pastrami with a bare hand while working."

The child chewed on an organic fruit wrap, and the old woman paused for me to answer. Her vague accusation of disregard for health and safety irked me. "Of course we use proper sanitation. Everything is cleaned before making the salads, and everyone wears gloves," I said.

"And how would you know that with absolute certainty?" she sneered. The baby girl held the food up to her grandma, but Linda the elder motioned for her to eat the candy, and she went back to what she was doing.

"Well, I am the supervisor for the department, and all of our team members are trained and retrained regularly to make sure there aren't any slipups."

"If that is true, what happened to the person who ate the pastrami?"

"I am not sure what happened there, but if something like that is seen, it's addressed right away."

The younger one chimed in with a southern accent, "I gotta be honest. I don't believe y'all. This place is disgusting. It's the worst Dream Grocers I have ever shopped at."

"Well, I am sorry to hear that, ma'am. If you would like, I can call an assistant store manager over to talk with you."

"That won't be necessary," the older Linda said. "However, I would like to sample this walnut cranberry salad."

"You would like to sample the salad?" I asked.

"Yes, the last time I got one, it was trash. I don't want that to happen again. Make sure it is the newest-dated salad too."

"I monitor the sell-by dating on all of our items, and these were made last night."

"Oh, that's nice. Please double-check anyway."

The portly, younger Linda said, "Mom . . . make sure to chew. We know you tend to get carried away when you eat."

"Shut up, child. I will donate your inheritance as fast as your father left me if you tell me how to live my life one more time."

With that scolding, young Linda recoiled and moved the cart down the aisle and around the corner.

One by one I pulled each salad off the wall and placed them in a cart. Linda, or whatever her name was, watched in satisfaction. "As I mentioned before, all of the salads were made last night. What one do you want?" I asked.

"I'm glad you looked at each one, considering the unsanitary conditions I have seen here in the past. I'll take that one towards the bottom. It had plenty of walnuts. I love walnuts."

I handed her the salad, and she stared at me. "I need a fork."

I returned with some plastic utensils. She looked at me with revulsion again. "Do you not have metal cutlery?" she asked.

"Sorry, ma'am. We do not."

"Fine," she said, then dropped the packaged utensils on the floor.

Her overmoisturized hands with gnarled knuckles dug into the salad like a bulldozer. She opened her mouth and shoved a fistful of salad into her face. I watched in horror as she followed up again with another handful of cranberries and walnuts. For someone so entitled, her savagery was unparalleled. She paused for a moment in an attempt to chew. A quarter of the salad was already gone as she tried to chew. A few chomps in, she stopped and looked at me with wide eyes, dropped the salad onto the floor, and motioned to me that she was choking.

Panic came over me. I looked around for help from another employee, but only customers were around us, and they were starting to notice what was happening.

"Somebody help her!" a man yelled as Linda reached out like a zombie with one arm and held her throat with the other.

"Does anyone know the Heimlich maneuver?" I yelled. No one responded.

I decided to take charge. "Here, let me try." I reached around her waist and pulled back to the centerline. Nothing came out. Not even a cough. I tried again with more upward force. She squealed. I might have broken her rib.

"Does anyone know the Heimlich? Am I doing this right?"

I wasn't sure if I had been trained on the Heimlich maneuver. Either way, I couldn't remember if I was doing it right.

I pulled in again. I heard a pop, and she yelped in pain.

"Anyone?"

Finally, other employees arrived. Mary and Neal popped out from around the corner.

"Mike is calling an ambulance," Neal said.

"Good. Do either of you know what to do? I'm trying the Heimlich, and nothing is happening."

Mary and Neal looked horrified. I looked at Linda. She was turning blue and leaning on the shelf. The younger Linda arrived. "Oh my god! Mom! Quick, somebody do something."

"Here, I'll try," Mary said.

Still, nothing came out. The salad was stuffed in there too tight. Her daughter screamed, "Help! Somebody *help*!" We all tried to excavate the walnuts and cranberries a few more times, but again, nothing changed. Then came attempts at CPR, but she had no airway to push air through. For some reason, everything became quiet. A group of maybe thirty people stood around Linda's lifeless body as it lay flattened out, her warmth receding and veins popping out of her face and neck.

The former middle, now eldest Linda stared off into space. The little girl in the cart—the future Linda—cried for a short while as she sat in her basket and watched Grandma die, but no one seemed to mind. A husband finally showed up holding a bag of non-GMO, grain-free, organic tortilla chips; let's call him Dave. Dave didn't say anything for a while as the EMTs tried to revive the now-deceased Linda until he finally asked,

"What happened?" No one had a proper response, so we all just stared at the body in silence. The paramedics tried every trick they could to bring her back, but it was too late. I'd like to think that their failure to revive her let us all off the hook. We all had given it our best shot. We *really* had tried to help Linda.

The police eventually showed up and asked me questions. I told them exactly what had happened. Witnesses vouched for me, and they let me go.

Everything blurred together at that point. Dave stood there with a puzzled look on his face as he held his Lindas. The crowd eventually dispersed. I helped one of the EMTs hoist Linda up onto a gurney and cover her in a sheet. The woman looked surprised that I was helping, but I thought I owed dead Linda one last lift.

A motley crew of Dream Grocers employees assembled around the fallen Linda: Mike, Mary, Neal, Lila—Todd had been called in and would be there soon—Pedro, Jamie, Achilles . . . even Jeanie was close by, distracted, talking about the blue bird. It was amazing they all worked that day.

We talked for a short while about random things: weird moments from the party, the demise of Jake and his message, and what Frankie's next video should be about. The spirit of Jake sat quietly. I gave imagined dabs to him and a real one to Ozzy. I knew everyone would be fine.

Ozzy told me that Jake had decided to just deal shrooms and K for a while. I'd agreed to buy some. Lila touched my shoulder, and we exchanged smiles. She gave me a hug, and the scent of her organic raspberry lip balm drove me wild. Mary, oh sweet Mary, was horrified at the scene she had just witnessed. Neal consoled her with sarcasm and levity. Mike asked me if I was going to be alright. I told him that I'd be fine. Chase and Tony were bringing out some U-boats of product, and Abby was in tow. They had missed the whole thing. There would be much explaining to do. The ghost of Janice watched over us. Achilles grabbed my cheeks like he was going to kiss me or have a serious talk, but instead he screamed, "It's about goddamn time you checked out of this place! I'm gonna miss you, my friend." A tiny smirk crawled across my face, and he gave me the biggest hug.

Jeanie waved at me to come over. "Just a second!" I yelled like a fool.

Before I could leave, and after everyone walked away, I had to take a moment alone with Linda. I leaned over and told her that was a hell of a way to go out—on that cold linoleum floor, choking on her demands. I was proud of her, in a way—die how you live, ya know? It's rare for a person to follow through and see something to the very end. I also mentioned, in passing, that I hoped she was somewhere warm—like really, really warm— and that maybe in a different life, I could have better served her needs.

About the Author

Adam lives in Denver, Colorado. He has worked in customer service since he started working at age fifteen. He is the author of *Life on the Grocery Line: A Frontline Experience in a Global Pandemic*. This novel is his second book.

Special Thanks

Tiann Roberts
Jackie Walker
Elizabeth Schick
Aaron Kaat
Sam Shaughnessy
Regyna Carbone
Jeffrey Grier
Kylee Linn
Billy Deal
John Turton
Lexi Kemp
Mary Monroe
Sam Layle
Aaron Schneider
Tiffany Trinco
Jeremy Holt
Carol Rautmann
Kelli Bastien
Jennifer Merck

Nicholas Bennett
Chris McAdams
Joseph Petrovich
Kayla Mattson
Zachary McClain
Michael Walker
Kelli Aimar
Saul Garza
Luke Hipsher
Lee Dananay